Rising Empire
Part 1

The Chronicles of Celadmore

by c. s. woolley

A Mightier Than the Sword UK Publication

©2013

Rising Empire

The Chronicles of Celadmore

By c. s. woolley

A Mightier Than the Sword Publication

Createspace Edition

Copyright © c. s. woolley 2013

Front cover design created using weavesilk.com and licensed under Creative Commons

All rights reserved. No part of this publication may be reproduced, stored in a retrieval system, or transmitted in any form or by any means, electronic, mechanical, photocopying, recording or otherwise, without prior permission of the publishers.

For Benjy

Also by the same author

Chronicles of Celadmore
Shroud of Darkness
Lady of Fire

Nicolette Mace: The Raven Siren
Filling the Afterlife from the Underworld: Volume 1
The Kevin Metis Saga
The Derek Long Saga

Poetry
Standing by the Watchtower: Volume 1

Further information on these titles can be found at
www.mightierthanthesworduk.com

Lord, who may dwell in your sanctuary? Who may live on your holy hill? He whose walk is blameless and who does what is righteous, who speaks the truth from his heart and has no slander on his tongue, who does his neighbour no wrong and casts no slur on his fellow-man, who despises a vile man but honours those who fear the Lord, who keeps his oath even when it hurts, who lends money without usury and does not accept a bribe against the innocent. He who does these things will never be shaken.

Psalm 15

Author's note

What follows is the account of the fall of Her Royal Highness, Queen Kasnata, Anaguran & Queterian Queen and Queen of the united peoples of Celadmore. The language of the Order is highlighted by the use of a different font in the paperback copies and in bold in the electronic format. The difference in font style between **Rising Empire** and **Shroud of Darkness** is due to **Rising Empire** containing an older dialect of the language of the Order to that in **Shroud of Darkness**. The language of Roenca is also displayed in a different font in the paperback copies and is underlined in the digital copies.

The Characters

Queen Kasnata –	Queen of the Order & Nosfa kingdom. Wife of Mercia
King Mercia Nosfa VI –	King of Nosfa kingdom. Husband of Kasnata
General Lord Rathe Bird –	General of Nosfa
Phoenix General Marissa –	General of Kasnata's Phoenix division
Kestrel General Amalia –	General of Kasnata's Kestrel division
Hawk General Kia –	General of Kasnata's Hawk division
Eagle General Hesla –	General of Kasnata's Eagle division
Condor General Renta –	General of Kasnata's Condor division
Vulture General Quisla –	General of Kasnata's Vulture division
Raven General Misna –	General of Kasnata's Infiltration division
Horsemistress Cara -	Horse mistress of the Order
Swordmistress Anna -	Sword mistress of the Order
Bowmistress Serra -	Bow mistress of the Order
Horsemaster Horace -	Horse master of the Order
Swordmaster Oswin -	Sword master of the Order
Bowmaster Wist -	Bow master of the Order
Cassandra –	Warrior, mercenary, pirate and spy. Guardian of the Wilds
The Abbott -	Warrior, mercenary, priest and spy. Guardian of the Spire
Hermia Nosfa -	Former Queen of Nosfa
Tola, hero of the war of the east	Rathe's second in command
Lord Haston Bird	Lord of Mercia Nosfa's court
Shaul	A Queterian
Methanlan	A Queterian

Rosla Nosfa	Former King of Nosfa
Lady Marcia Bird	A lady, deceased
Lady Mia Bird	Forced consort to King Mercia Nosfa.
Jephthah	Shield of Hermia. A bodyguard
Haman	Leader of the Gibborim
Mathias	Assassin
Neesa	Assassin, Bodyguard of Mercia. A Valian
Ariella	A Valian
General Avner	General of Kasnata's Order of the Hound
General Shamgar	General of Kasnata's Order of the Bear
General Yoav	General of Kasnata's Order of the Wolf
The Baron of Fintry	Mercia's steward and dogsbody
Jack	A soldier of Nosfa
Harry	A soldier of Nosfa
Benaiah	Queterian Forge Master
Duke Kelmar DeLacey	Regent of Delma, a nobleman
Joab	Shadow of Hermia. A bodyguard
Layla	Shadow of Hermia. A bodyguard
Prince Jayden Delich	Prince of Delma
King Baruch Delich	King of Delma
Queen Adina Delich	Queen of Delma
Helez	Shield of the Gibborim
Asahel	Shield of the Gibborim
Ilana	Sister of Helez
Leinad	Prince of Nosfa & the Order
Kasna	Princess of Nosfa & the Order
Kia	Princess of Nosfa & the Order

She was born to a line of great warriors. Her mother and father were King and Queen of the warrior tribes known as the Order. In her infancy she killed her first moorin, so the legends say. In truth she was four, barely able to raise her spear and the creature was no more than a pup. But these things are often exaggerated.

She was marked for greatness by all around her and by the age of twelve could best any with a sword. Her training was intense. She was pushed harder than any of the other warriors upon her parents' orders. She spent hours on horseback until she would be so tired that she had to be tied to the horse to keep her in the saddle.

She had to fight with broken swords and spears until she could grasp them no longer. By the age of fourteen she was scarred on her arms, legs and body so badly that healers were called from outside of the Order to repair what damage they could.

At sixteen her mother was taken from this world by a sickness of the lungs and her father followed out of grief mere weeks later. She was raised to the throne of her people before she had been prepared to rule. The leaders of the nine kingdoms saw a moment of weakness; saw their chance to grasp power.

War came to the lands of Celadmore; neighbour fought against neighbour, old alliances were forsaken as men and women desired power and destruction.

Kingdoms splintered, rose and fell, of the nine great kingdoms of Celadmore, only four survived the first ten years of war, two were burnt to ash and plundered and the other three splintered into twelve.

She saw a chance to save her people from destruction in an alliance through marriage to a king who showed mercy to those that he ruled and those that he fought, King Mercia Nosfa VI.

But in this she was deceived. More than any of the other Kings and Queens, he desired an empire that spanned the width and breadth of the realm. He used her and her people as pawns in his great scheme. Their training in battle exploited to bring nations under his command.

When she tried to resist, he took her children from her and threatened to have them murdered if she did not do all that he desired. An army of women were brought to him so that he could sire children that did not share her blood and prayed that she would be killed in battle.

So she fought and thought. Fought to survive the war and power struggle that consumed the world and thought of how she could end this war and rescue her children from their father.

Her abilities and those of her warriors gave rise to the Order being named for the first of their people, the Queterians and the Anaguras. Her name was Kasnata.

She began her reign by forming six regiments within the Anaguran army. It had never been done before and has remained in place since.
Hawk, Kestrel, Vulture, Phoenix, Condor, Eagle.

All were created to serve different functions within Kasnata's army. Hawk were the scouts, Kestrel were the intelligence and communication division, Condor were her cavalry, Eagle were the fliers, Vulture were the main force and Phoenix were her elites and Royal Guard.

Her actions caused murmurs amongst the Queterians that she was warmongering and would bring ruin to the Order, but her mind was looking beyond the Anaguran Empire, but amongst the Anaguras she was untouchable, unequalled and worshipped.

The greatest of the Anaguran Queens, my Lady Kasnata, married a warlord to bring peace, she brought civility to the tribes with compassion for those who were born unable to fight and expanded the cities creating an Empire that all of the Order could be proud of. However my Lady, Queen Kasnata of Anamoore shone most when on the battlefield. Her brilliance and radiance blinded those that dared to step to close, her fire and sword cut down all enemies that stood before her. She was unequalled and adored by all and deserved the happiness she found; especially when she could not escape her fate.

Kestrel General Amalia
Aide to Queen Kasnata

Chapter 1
2430GL 34ᵗʰ Spregan

"The battlefield; a place where heroes are made, legends thrive, myths enthral and lives are broken."

    A sword slashed through the dark and pierced the cushions that lay in its path. Feathers and torn rags of silks plumed into the air. The night was still in the Castle of Anamoore, nothing was out of place in the darkness. The patrols of men and women moved without seeing any enemies moving to strike against them.

    All things belonged to Kasnata, only daughter of Tsmara & Jadow, Queen of fire and destruction, bringer of death, dark angel, scourge of the wicked, wife of King Mercia Nosfa VI and Sovereign of the people of the Order. She had been woken by turbulent dreams of the war that had endured for so long in these lands.

    "Such needless destruction." She muttered to herself. Her brow was beaded with sweat as she sat amongst the feathers settling on the furs around her. Her sword, the Ralenetia Estral, was clasped tightly in her right hand, the blade embedded in the cushions she had slaughtered in her dreams.

    She shook her head and freed her weapon from the upholstery. Her dark dreams cursed her nights. She had sought the wisdom of many different people in an effort to end them, but none had been able to rid the queen of the nightmares.

    She looked around her bedchamber, assessing the damage that had been done by her nocturnal turbulence. It was not as bad as it had been on previous occasions. The furniture was still intact. She had not been sleep slaying the bed, tables and benches this time. Besides the shredded cushions and abundance of loose feathers, there did not seem to be any damage.

She rubbed her hand over her stomach and letting go of her Ralenetia Estral rose carefully to stare out of her widow at the night sky. Her room looked out over the plains as well as the city of Anamoore. In the distance she could see the twinkling lights of the watch that walked the battlements of the city of Queteria.

She smiled in memory of her first love. He had been a man of the city watch in Queteria. There had been many nights when she had stolen away from the palace in the city to spend the dark hours talking with him as he walked his patrol.

He had been a kind boy, quick to laugh and clumsy in affairs of the heart but it had endeared him to her. He had dreamed of being a warrior of legend, one to charge across a battlefield to fight beside the woman he loved, but fate had taken him before he had the opportunity.

An infection in the lungs had slowly drawn the breath from his body, a painful end for both him and his love affair with the now Queen. She closed her eyes and smiled sadly at the memory, wondering, as always on nights like these, what might have been had he not died.

Below her in the city, all was still except for the town watch that strode between the buildings, searching for spies in these days of war as well as those who committed crimes. There were extensive building projects taking place in the city below her. A new market district was growing to the west of the castle and the castle itself was being extended.

New stables were being built at the request of her horsemistress, Cara, who had insisted that battle mounts must be trained in greater numbers given their current diminishing stock due to the continuing hostilities on the mainland. Kasnata looked out and marvelled at how skilled her people were to create such things.

She knew, as she gazed, that this was the last time she would look out at her beloved homeland for some time. She had been summoned to the battlefield once more by her husband, King Mercia Nosfa VI.

The land of Celadmore had been plunged into war by the death of her parents. Her family had held the military forces of the nine kingdoms in check for the last four generations, none of the kingdoms dared to move or declare war whilst Queen Tsmara and King Jadow were alive.

When the nine kingdoms were established, it had been the suggestion of both the Guardian of the Wilds and the Guardian of the Spire that a council should be formed to mediate disputes and prevent war from breaking out on a large scale. The Order, renowned for its wisdom and battle prowess, had been appointed head of the council.

With the death of her parents, Kasnata was not only made ruler of the Order but head of the council. At sixteen, she was not prepared for the chaos that erupted and could not prevents the council from dissolving as war between all nine kingdoms broke out. Not even the words of the Guardian of the Wilds could stem the dissolution.

The Order did not abandon its duties to protect the freedom of the nations and moved to defend the borders of those kingdoms that counted them as friends and allies. They watched as the plains of Celadmore were washed red with the blood of its people. It had hurt Kasnata to watch all that happened. She blamed herself for not being strong enough to keep the lands from war and vowed that she would bring an end to it, no matter what it took.

There had been days when Kasnata would cry herself to sleep over the mistakes she had made, but those days had been short lived. She regretted marrying Mercia, marrying outside of her people, even though her intentions had been good.

It had been her desire to end the terrible war that had led her to marrying King Mercia Nosfa VI; he had seemed to be the key to bringing an end to all the conflict, but in this Kasnata had been deceived.

When she had first met him he had presented a gentle nature, one that detested conflict and wished only for peace and a time to rebuild what had been destroyed. He had told her that he wanted to lift his people out of the mud and create better lives for the children born into the time of unrest.

In truth Mercia was nothing more than a warmonger, looking to expand his kingdom and influence as a side to increasing his wealth. He ruled with a fist of iron and rode over those that stood to oppose him. There were rumours that even those closest to him were not safe from his wrath.

His mother had died and been taken from his castle one night after she had demanded that food be sent from the castle kitchens to the poorest quarter of his capital, Grashindorph, where people were dying from starvation in large numbers. No investigation was launched to try and explain her death and no questions were asked as to where her body was taken.

He ruled through fear and malice. Kasnata was a prize to him, a creature that was beautiful and should be his to adorn his arm, her lands and people to come under his rule. He had courted her, hiding his true nature until they were wed.

When Kasnata discovered his true nature she had strived to change it. She had refused to bow to his will and so Mercia had waited. He refused to divorce her and instead pressed her for an heir. When she gave birth to their first child, a son, Leinad, she had become trapped.

He was taken from her as he drew his first breath and held hostage. Mercia threatened to kill him if Kasnata did not do what he wanted. Her forces became his to command through her and as she gave birth to two more children, both daughters, his hold over her grew tighter.

She had tried to resist, but her love for her children was so great that she would risk no harm to them. She was allowed to see them only under guard and when the King was present. It broke her heart that they could not see the land she loved so dearly, nor be raised in the culture of her people as well as that of their father.

Mercia knew that as long as Leinad was his only heir there was only so much control he could exert over his wife, his daughters were expendable to him, but his son was the survival of his line. He sent his wife away from his court, expelled her to her homeland and decreed that she may only return to his presence and lands at his request.

His wife gone, he ordered his steward to find him young women that were strong and unmarried nobles in his kingdom that might bear him a son. They were brought to him in droves, a harem of concubines so that he might sire another heir.

The fathers of the women that protested were cut down and their homes burnt with their households locked inside. When word spread of this, no further resistance could be found.

Kasnata was not ignorant of her husband's actions and had endeavoured to rescue her children from his clutches. Should Mercia march his army against hers it would be broken on the walls of her cities and she would free herself of his hold. Many had tried to infiltrate the palace in which the children were held but none had succeeded. The Queen of the Order had been trapped for so long now she had forgotten what it was like to make her own decisions in war.

She was not without enemies amongst her own people either, namely the Valians. The Valians were people descended from the same line as Kasnata, but they did not recognise Kasnata's right to rule. Instead they believed that the descendants of Queen Valia should be seated upon the throne of the Order.

Valia had been branded a traitor after she had murdered her younger sisters and caused the only civil war that had ever been fought in the history of the Order. Queteria himself had decreed that she was not fit to rule and removed her line from the right of succession.

Her descendants and those warriors loyal to her had chosen exile from the Order and had plotted for generations to overthrow those that they believed had usurped power. In the last eight years Kasnata had seen the number of Valians grow, the men and women unhappy with the connection to the mainland kingdom of Nosfa and their military action being dictated by Mercia and his desires had left to join their brothers and sisters in exile.

She did not blame them for their actions but she found herself in an unenviable situation seemingly without solution. Those that remained loyal to her also provided constant petitions, discussion and opposition to her husband's whims.

For the last twelve years Kasnata had been living in a nightmare. Yet every attack and attempt the Valians made to seize power, she repelled. Every assassin sent was thwarted. She took every day as it came and by some miracle and the will of Arala, she held the Order together. Her strength throughout all this won her the respect of her people. Those that had doubted her now believed in her and Mercia became ever more uncomfortable and troubled by the thought that she would move against him.

She planned and schemed every day to try and break the hold that her husband had over her, to bring her children home and restore the balance of power in Celadmore. Mercia's spies kept him well informed of her plans, and vexation started to curse his waking hours. So he conceived a plan to dispose of her completely and place one of his daughters on the throne of the Order whom he could control.

Under the law of Nosfa, a married woman found to be an adulteress, even a Queen, could be divorced, forfeiting all rights to her husband's money and their children and even be executed. He dare not risk the people of the Order raising arms against him for executing their Queen so ordered his wife to the worst of the fighting, hoping that she would be killed in battle.

Yet she survived, but this did not deter Mercia, he kept sending her to battle and sent his own men with her, men he felt could seduce her and become close enough to her to assassinate her, discretely, so the enemy would be blamed.

Her latest orders saw her being sent to the northern lands of Celadmore, to the lands where bandits had control of the highways and three kingdoms fought for the land which had become so polluted with blood that it would be generations before anything could grow there.

She had been told a new general would be joining her forces there, a Lord; reported to be the last son of the oldest noble family in Nosfa. Her spies had informed her that he was seen as an honourable man, but Kasnata did not want any of her husband's retainers within her camp, no matter how honourable they might appear.

Most of her army had already departed for the mainland and would be setting up the camp and her forward command before she arrived.

"You still aren't sleeping well?" A familiar and friendly voice asked from behind her.

"No, not for two years now." The Queen of the Order sighed and turned from the window to face the source of the voice.

"Understandable really, it's been that long since you saw your children last. Given their incarceration, your lack of rest is what any might expect." The visitor to the Queen was a woman dressed in tight hessian trousers and a brown leather cuirass. At her waist hung two daggers and a claymore, her auburn hair was held back from her face by a strip of fur and she had war paint streaked across her nose and cheeks.

"Your blunt assessment of situations is always welcome, Cassandra." Kasnata replied with a raised eyebrow.

The Guardian of the Wilds smiled and shrugged in response. She had been as she appeared now for as long as Kasnata could remember and for as long as her mother could remember. She was a fearsome woman, wild and free as the animals that roamed her domain, but she counted those amongst the Order as her friends. Kasnata could remember her grandmother telling her that Cassandra had known Anagura and Queterian; that they and the Guardian of the Spire had many adventures in their youth.

From what Kasnata could see Cassandra was still in her youth. She had not believed her grandmother as a child, but as she grew and Cassandra did not age, credence was leant to these tales. The Guardian of the Wilds had her own people that followed her, a small army of barbaric warriors, warriors that had tried to rescue Kasnata's children from their father. None returned from their attempts, but it did not stop more from trying.

"Stating facts without embellishment saves one from pointless conversations with simpletons. Of course you do not fall into that category, but when you form habits over hundreds of years, they are difficult to break." Cassandra said with a smile. Kasnata laughed at Cassandra's words.

"I'm glad that I do not fall into the category of dim-witted individuals that have led to such habits forming. As for behaviours being difficult to break, I am not sure I can hold with your excuse." The Queen said with a frown.

"Oh?" Cassandra asked with surprise. "Why is that?"

"It's the same excuse that people use to allow them to fight wars against each other, that allow feuds to fester and spread like poison, that cause prejudice to form in rational minds. No, I cannot hold with it at all." She said decisively and stepped away from the window. The Guardian of the Wilds did not reply immediately but instead she moved across the room to where the Queen stood. Facing her, Cassandra placed her hands on the Queen's shoulders and kissed Kasnata on both cheeks.

"Your mother would have been so proud to hear you say that." Cassandra said quietly, betraying her tenderness in a rare moment of affection. "Still." She said releasing Kasnata's shoulders and turning away to move and lean against the window ledge. "I find that directness avoids confusion, though it is often unwelcome as it seems to strike at sore points. I apologise for any pain my words caused, highness, it was not intentional." The Guardian of the Wilds said with an apologetic smile.

"No, I should apologise, I fear I have become overly sensitive in recent years." Kasnata said shaking her head. "With your lack of tact none could tell by speaking to you that you are an excellent spy." The Queen said playfully.

"It has always been a superb way to avoid arousing suspicion. It also helps in obtaining detailed accounts from gossips. For people who acquire useful information, they seem to have a preference for spouting the most awful nonsense if you let them." The Guardian of the Wilds said scornfully.

"Did you manage to discover anything of interest about my husband's latest enemy?" The Queen asked as she walked back and sat on her bed.

"The toad seems to have set his sights on securing not only the lands on the coast that belong to Delma, but also the lands to the north that the kingdom of Vasknar holds." Cassandra said with disdain. Kasnata smirked at hearing the Guardian of the Wilds describing her husband as 'the toad'. Cassandra had never liked the King of Nosfa, even before Kasnata had married him.

"Has he moved against Tulna at all?"

"No, he still seems oblivious to the significance of the village to the

Order. I'm sure that if he did know he would have tried to take the place long ago." Cassandra smiled to herself at the thought. Tulna was a small village of free people that lay within the borders of the kingdom of Nosfa. As king of Nosfa, Mercia only ruled the cities and villages that swore allegiance to his throne, those that did not were free villages, towns and cities. It was the same across the nine kingdoms. Free cities avoided living under the rule of a central hub but they had no Lord to appeal to in times of crisis, no central army to march to their aid if they were attacked.

Tulna was the oldest of the free cities on Celadmore, so old that it had been there before Anagura and Queteria had been born. It was led by Kania and Nodarto and had been since it had been founded. The two had been great friends to Anagura and Queteria and to those that were descended from their line. Tulna was also the place that Cassandra had been born and raised alongside her brother. The idea that anyone would be able to attack the village and survive to tell of it was laughable to the Guardian.

"His desire for domination over the other nations dwarfs his desire to weaken my stronghold of power." Kasnata said sadly shaking her head.

"That may be so, but I doubt that he will always be so blinkered in his vision." Cassandra said seriously. "You depart in the morning, you should be sleeping." The leader of the barbarians of the wilds soothed.

"What is it that you came here for?" Kasnata asked abruptly, realising that despite all the light conversation that they exchanged. Cassandra had not revealed her purpose.

"My bandits of the wilds are all engaged in subterfuge and intrigue on your part, I am somewhat bored without their daily antics to entertain me." The bandit warrior shrugged.

"That I do not believe." The Queen said flatly.

"No? Well then. I met with the Abbott; he sought me out in fact."

Cassandra began thoughtfully.

"That is unusual." Kasnata observed.

"Indeed. The last time he did so was to inform me of Valia's descent into madness. He came to me bearing the news that your children are being moved. Only your son will remain with his father. Your daughters are being taken elsewhere." The Guardian of the Wilds said as gently as she could.

Kasnata felt her body react before her mind did. She began to choke on her breath, her eyes grow wide and she staggered backwards seeking support from her furnishings.

"Where?" She asked in a weak voice.

"I do not know." Cassandra said softly. She had moved quickly and had taken the dark angel into her arms. She held the Queen of the Order as Kasnata began to shake in shock. "Not yet." The Guardian of the Wilds whispered into her hair. "But I swear to you, Venia, I will find out." There was sincerity in the bandit warrior's voice that Kasnata had not heard before. The sound of her childhood nickname, Venia, was oddly comforting and brought a certain amount of peace to her heart.

Chapter 2

The palace of King Mercia Nosfa VI was one of foul ostentation. Comfort was not considered a priority in its design, more a passing nuisance. White marble inlaid with gold, silver and more precious gems than most could recite were the chief building materials used in the construction of the great monstrosity that lay outside the walls of the city of Grashindorph.

The city had a castle that was perfectly suitable for any monarch save for Mercia. Upon his ascension to the throne, he had his palace built away from what he considered the mundane drudgery of his subjects and had his own mount Olympus created. None were allowed within its walls without his expressed invitation.

He held court for two hours for two mornings a week when his landowners were permitted to come before him with petitions and when new women were presented to him for inspection. The rest of the time was spent indulging himself in pleasure.

Amongst his court there were unsettled grumblings at his behaviour, but none would move against him whilst he commanded not only his army, but could bring his barbarian child bride to bear against them. There were none in the court who were as disconcerted as Lord and General Bird.

Lord Haston Bird had been a close friend of Mercia's father, King Rosla Nosfa VIII. The two had been almost inseparable as boys, riding across the country of Nosfa; wenching and fighting bandit raiding parties. It had been Haston that had introduced Rosla to Lady Hermia and had watched as their relationship had developed to love and eventually marriage. A year or so after, Rosla had introduced Haston to Marcia, his second cousin and had enjoyed watching the two court and marry.

They had been golden days of youth that were now immortal in their rose-tinted film of memory. Times of stress of the kingdom had caused Rosla to fall into ill health not long after the birth of his son. Three summers passed and Rosla's health failed. He called for Haston to be at his bedside in his last hours. The two spent time reminiscing together of the glory days, laughing and remembering the friends they had lost. Haston watched with a breaking heart as the last flickers of life faded from his dearest friend's eyes. And he wept.

Rosla's final instruction to his court had been that Haston should rule as steward until Mercia was old enough to assume the throne. Mercia was three at the time of his father's death and Rathe had been born a year before the death of the king. Haston had moved to the castle of Grashindorph with his family to oversee the day-to-day running of the kingdom and left the care of the young prince Mercia in the hands of Queen Hermia and the castle household.

Haston hoped that the prince would grow into as good a leader as his father had been, but sadly it was not to be. By the time Mercia was seven his mother fell gravely ill. The onset of her illness was so sudden that there was rumour within the court that there was foul play afoot and amidst the intrigue, Mercia was left to grow by his own design. No one had realised just how selfish and wild the young prince had become until he reached the age of twelve.

Mercia demanded that the throne be given over to him and that Haston and his family be removed from the castle. With the intrigue surrounding the continuing illness of Queen Hermia still circulating throughout the noble families of Nosfa, Haston could not refuse. His son was second-in-line to the throne and any declination on Haston's part would be seen as coup to seize power.

Rathe was ten and had Mia, a younger sister of seven years when

Haston took them and his wife, Marcia, from the city of Grashindorph and returned to their own lands and the city of Afdanic.

Twenty years had passed since that day and much had changed in the nation of Nosfa. They had been embroiled in war with the other nations of Celadmore for the past fourteen years. Queen Mother Hermia had worked for the good of her people amongst her son's court, but had mysterious died fifteen years ago, despite her illness there was no reason that the royal physician could find for her death.

Haston suspected that her son had become sick of her meddling and had her infuriating influence removed from around him. Rathe hoped that she had been taken in by the resistance that was growing against King Mercia and was working to end his reign of terror.

Marcia had died trying to give birth to Haston's second son. Rathe had stood beside his father as he watched his father mourn as he cradled his wife's lifeless body and was brought the news that the baby had also passed. Mia had been spared the sight of her father's grief, she had wept at her mother's graveside and been comforted by her brother.

It was not long after that Mia was summoned to the court of Mercia. Haston had received a letter two weeks later to inform him that his daughter would not be returning home as Mia had been taken into his household to act as a lady-in-waiting to the Queen. A queen that lived in a different nation and was rumoured to be a fierce warrior that was in no need of handmaidens.

Rathe had never met the queen. He had seen her on the day of her wedding to Mercia, but that had been from a distance and all he could remember of her was the colour of her hair. Haston had been introduced to her twice but had no real claim of acquaintanceship with the Queen of the Order. She showed no interest in life in Grashindorph and seemed quite content to wage war and rule her people apart from Mercia.

Neither Haston nor Rathe had seen or heard from Mia since the day she was taken. It was the same for all those of the noble houses of Nosfa who had daughters of childbearing age. Some of the Lords had been driven to grief, others to aggression, but both had led men to desperate action that had led to their imprisonment for treason.

These were dark days for the aristocracy of Nosfa as well as those of lower station. Brides had been taken from their grooms on the day of their weddings; no daughter was safe from being swept from her home. Some Lords had prayed that their daughters would grow as plain so as not to attract the desire of the king, but appearances mattered not.

No resistance could be offered against the might of the king for all those that opposed him there were an equal number that supported him. The threat of being imprisoned for saying the wrong thing to the wrong person held many tongues in check. Those that were unafraid of the jail were kept under control by their daughters being held captive, the threat of the king taking their lives if they dared to move against him.

The king knew who his enemies amongst his court were and for the most part he knew how to control them, only Lord and General Bird seemed to be above his manipulations. Neither had done anything openly to move against the throne, but Mercia knew it would only be a matter of time.

His main bargaining counter for their unquestioning obedience had been having Mia as part of his household, but it had been an ineffective play. General Bird had remained vocal about matters of court and the war that was being waged and Lord Bird had refused to raise taxes on his people to pay for the continuing campaigns across Celadmore.

Mercia had threatened Mia with execution if she did not bring her father and brother under control. Mia had responded with a polite smile and asked for the execution date to be within the next few weeks.

He could not stand self-sacrificing people, especially when there was a whole family of them, they were so difficult to influence and govern, but there were other ways of dealing with them. He had laid plans to dispose of each member of the family Bird without suspicion.

Mercia had plans laid for every possible eventuality. His wife had proven the most difficult of his problems to solve, refusing to die in the heat of battle and being strong-willed in the political sphere. Holding his children hostage would only make an effective deterrent to her difficult behaviour when he had other heirs to supplant his need for them.

No matter how many women he took into his bed, no pregnancy resulted. His first physician had examined him and reported that he was infertile. He was promptly executed. His second physician had tried many different salves, herbs and cures to try and solve his inability to conceive, though none had proven affective.

He had sent many of his loyal retainers to act as Field Generals to try and find incriminating evidence of his wife's treason, aside from her refusal to bow to his every wish; but they had been unsuccessful in finding anything. Some did not return from their mission, killed on the battlefield, though Mercia suspected that Kasnata's loyal people often had a hand in the deaths of his spies.

It has taken a suggestion from Mercia's steward and most loyal subject, the Baron of Fintry, before a satisfactory solution had presented itself. None within his own court were aware of the rift between him and his wife except for those that had been sent to the front lines as assassins. Part of the fear Mercia wielded was the threat at a word from him, the armies of the Order could be brought against any enemy, even his own nobles. At the same time, his wife was ignorant of whom his enemies in his own lands were.

By sending one of his enemies as the general at the head of his forces to be commanded by his wife, her people would assume him another assassin and work to have him disposed of like so many before him and the general would assume that at the first hint of treason, he would be killed. He could keep them both as enemies and distract the energies of those that would otherwise work against him; earning a reprieve in which he could plan and act to remove those that threatened his position more permanently.

He had sent for Lord and General Bird and made sure that Mia was amongst those assembled on the upper balcony, reserved for members of the royal household. The boring daily business had been conducted with the usual tedium that King Mercia expected. There were the usual complaints about taxation, families starving, moorin attacks becoming more aggressive, bandits raiding farms and outlying villages; nothing that was terribly important in Mercia's eyes.

He sat and listened with a bored look on his face until the petitioners had finished. The Baron of Fintry then cleared the floor and called for General Bird to step forward.

"Rathe, son of Haston, you are hereby promoted to the position of Commander of his royal majesty, King Mercia Nosfa VI's free company. You are to report to their forward camp on the shores of Marsden Lake in no less than a week from this date." The Baron read from the proclamation he held.

Mercia casually studied the faces of Haston, Rathe and Mia as the edict was read. The girl nearly fainted in shock. All colour had drained from her face and her white knuckles gripped the balcony rail to keep her on her feet.

Lord Haston had looked confused as the steward had begun, but the realisation of what such news truly meant had quickly permeated his thick skull and though the horror he felt at such news could not be read on his face, but for those who knew him well, the pain he felt could be clearly read in his eyes.

Glee flooded through the king's veins at such manipulation. He loved to watch his enemies squirm and seeing the desired effect so readily apparent on those who would remain in his kingdom was like a drug to him. So happy was Mercia with his own accomplishment that he almost failed to observe General Rathe.

Such an odious man. The king thought. Rathe had been sworn to the king's service at the request of his father as an attempt to crush rumours that Haston desired the throne for his own. He had come into service as soon as he was old enough and worked hard to rise through the ranks to that of a general. He had seen service in minor skirmishes, the king wanting to keep him from the bigger battles to stop him from making his name one surrounded by glory and gaining renown.

A military hero to the people is the last thing that Mercia could want. The king let his eyes fall onto the form of Rathe Bird as the general stood in the centre of the hall. Not a flicker of emotion showed anywhere on his face. Not in his eyes, not in his stance, to look at him you would think him completely unphased.

"From there you are to lead your forces to the east and rendezvous with her royal majesty, Queen Kasnata of Nosfa and of the Order. You will lead the forces of Nosfa according to her wishes. Her location will be provided to you when you have joined with the free company at their camp on the shores of Marsden Lake. Your second-in-command awaits your orders." The Baron continued droning on.

Haston wanted to call out and demand that Mercia stop and spare his son. Mia was close to tears as she stood on the balcony and looked down on her brother, wanting to comfort him, feeling that this might be the last time she would ever see him.

Rathe listened to everything that the Baron had to say, waited until he had finished speaking, saluted in response to show he had received his orders and with a sharp turn, marched from the hall.

His heart pounded in his chest, his ears were flooded with the sound of his blood pulsing in them. He could feel himself begin to shake as he negotiated his way to one of the small reception rooms that lay off the main corridor of the palace. He felt his chest tighten and his breathing shorten as he paced about the reception room he had found vacant. Beyond it lay one of the many small private gardens that belonged to each reception room that Rathe burst out into gasping for air.

There was no one in the garden, the court was still in session and would be for another hour yet. No one would be leaving the king's presence until then, which meant that no one would see him now.

He collapsed to his knees and began to weep. Fighting a war alongside a hostile, battle-hardened, warrior queen was very different to the skirmishes with bandits that he had fought in before. The king wanted him dead with as little effort at possible, removed from the kingdom that he adored and would happily give his life to defend, but now all he saw was his death in foreign lands whilst the king destroyed the country of his birth.

He had not wanted a life in the army, he had wanted a quiet life ruling the city of Afdanic beside his father, to marry a sensible woman who would raise strong children and that the problems of the kingdom would be resolved by the king coming to his senses.

Life, as far as Rathe was concerned, had not turned out as he had imagined at all. He had listened to stories of his father's childhood and younger years with great interest. Learning of the man his father was and who the king had been before Mercia. He felt jealous of his father growing up in such carefree times when there was such suffering now.

"Why are you crying?" A boy's voice asked from behind the general. Rathe turned sharply and stared at a young boy, no older than twelve, who was stood looking at him with curiosity. He had striking dark hair and stunning clear blue eyes. He was not short or tall for his age and was dressed in a purple tabard over pale rough-spun trousers. There was nothing about him to indicate who he was or why he was roaming the gardens.

"There are times when life can bring you to tears." Rathe replied to the question as he regained his composure and rose back to his feet. "Do you never feel like crying?" The general asked.

"I'm not allowed to cry. My father has me beaten if I cry until I stop." The boy said with a shrug.

"What about your mother? Does she not let you cry?" Rathe had been slightly taken aback by the boy's response.

"I'm not allowed to see her." He said sadly. "My father doesn't like her."

"I'm sorry to hear that." Rather said awkwardly.

"You don't need to be sorry. I'll see her soon. She doesn't listen to what my father has to say." The boy had a grin on his face as he jumped around until he could grab the low hanging branch of a tree to swing on. "But you didn't say why you were crying."

"I have to go away from my family to fight." Rathe said sadly.

"That makes you sad?" The young boy asked as he sat down on the grass.

"It does. I may not come home again and I like my home." The general felt rather foolish and childish as he spoke to the child before him, it was clear that the boy did not have a happy life and yet seemed to be unphased by the pain he suffered. In comparison to his own problems, the boy had far bigger concerns.

"I would like to go on adventures away from here one day, you are lucky to get to go to other places."

There was a lull in the conversation as Rathe considered his own predicaments in a positive light.

"I should be getting back to my room. I snuck out and will be in trouble if they find out I am not there. I hope you get to go home again when you have finished fighting." The boy said with a smile and disappeared over one of the garden walls.

Chapter 3
2430GL 45th Sagma/Sumar

Kasna and Kia missed their mother. They hated their father and the way he acted towards them, to him they were merely commodities that could be disposed of if they caused him any trouble. It had been two years since they had last seen their mother. She had been defiant in the face of their father, which had encouraged not only Kasna and Kia to defiance, but their brother, Leinad as well.

It had been this rebellion that had caused their father to send them away from his palace to be held captive in the provinces. Neither girl knew where they were in the kingdom. They had been taken from their beds in the night by the elite palace guards, thrown into a carriage and driven until well after midday before they were dragged out of the carriage.

Kasna and Kia had found themselves in the grounds of a rundown castle. A housekeeper and a detachment of guards were the only social interaction they were permitted and though they were free to wander the castle and grounds, they were forbidden to go beyond them.

It had been the same in the palace before they had been taken in the night. They had spent days starring at the city walls of Grashindorph, wishing they could be out exploring the city. Neither of the girls was even allowed to attend and audiences with king or the court. Both know that to their father were insignificant, they were not heirs to his throne, nothing more than bargaining chips against any action their mother might take or in forging alliances through marriage with kingdoms that were beyond his ability to control otherwise.

Most of their time was passed running around the castle grounds, hiding from the housekeeper in all manner of exciting hiding places. On their first time exploring the grounds, they had discovered that there were several hollow trees that they could squeeze inside, small hill rises that could be used as a maze to crawl through when the palace guards were called out to find them. The days that had followed had led to more discoveries; more places to hide that didn't involve climbing onto rooftops.

Hiding always led to scolding, but neither of the princesses cared. They instead focused on practising the skills their mother had bought them in secret, learning to use swords, staves, shields and bows, waiting for the day that their mother would appear and take them home to her castle and their people.

Neither Kasna nor Kia considered themselves to be part of their father's kingdom, having been so rejected by him and kept apart from those that lived in the capital; they did not share the identity of his nation's subjects. Instead they were proud of their warrior blood, the blood of Anagura and Queteria that flowed in their veins.

Kasna sighed as she lowered herself down into one of the hollowed out trees and took hold of one of the many swords the two princesses stored there.

"She will come for us." Kia said positively, her descent into the weapon store not far behind her sister.

"I know, but I am so tired of this waiting." Kasna replied sadly as she began to run a whetstone across the edge of the blade.

The weapons had all been stolen from the palace guard over the weeks that had seen them arrive. They had, at one point, owned an entire compliment of Anaguran armour and weaponry; gifts from their mother, gifts that their father had destroyed when he found them under the floorboards of his daughter's rooms.

The whetstones they both owned were the only things that still remained from those gifts as they could be more easily concealed than any item their mother had given them.

"There is nothing else we can do." Kia shrugged as she sat beside her sister and watched her progress with the blade.

"We could run away, escape and try and make our way to her." Kasna said defiantly. Kia shook her head and looked at her sister with a look of despair.

"And either be caught in a few hours and beaten as a punishment? Or get lost in the wilds and be eaten by moorin, or bears, or lions? Or find ourselves captured by bandits?"

"You don't know that any of that will happen!" Kasna said with fire in her eyes as she threw down the stone. Kia stared at her for a moment, she wanted to leave as much as Kasna did, but all her instincts told her it was a foolhardy errand.

"Kasna, we don't know where we are. We don't know where mother is, let alone hot to get there. Trying to find her without any ideas, information, resources or allies just won't happen. We'll end up dead or worse." Kia said gently.

Kasna sighed and leant her sword against the trunk.

"But we can't just stay here and do nothing."

"You are impetuous." A new voice joined the conversation. Neither girl had heard anyone approaching and froze where they sat. Fear crept up their spines and stole the warmth from their blood. The voice was not one that either Kasna or Kia recognised.

"I'm not entirely sure where you have gotten that from as your mother certainly isn't impetuous and your father is far too calculating to rush into any form of action." The voice belonged to a man. He seemed to be talking to himself rather than either of the princesses.

"Who, who are you?" Kia stammered in a broken voice that betrayed her fear.

"Me?" The voice sounded surprised at the question. "I would have thought you would have recognised my voice, but no, maybe not, you would have been too small I think." The fear was slowly ebbing from both girls as he continued to ramble to himself.

"That being the case, then knowing my name would serve little purpose as it would mean nothing to you." He finished his thinking.

"The purpose of a name is not to find meaning in it." Kasna said frowning as she stood and started to negotiate her way back up the trunk.

"On the contrary, to assign a name is to find an identity to give to something. For the reason I am here, my name is not a necessity." The mysterious man said casually.

Kasna paused at the top of the trunk, reaching her arm down to take hold of her sword that Kia was holding up to her. She grasped the hilt and jumped from the trunk. Kasna could hear Kia clambering up inside the trunk as she landed and cast her eyes on the owner of the voice.

He was unassuming in status, barely a head and shoulders taller than Kasna. He wore a long brown robe that pooled on the floor at his feet. His head wasn't covered, so the princess could see his shock of dark hair that made him look as though he were a ranger, despite his lacking in weapons. His eyes were dark and framed with long dark lashes that betrayed little emotion.

Kasna heard the sound of a bowstring being drawn back that heralded Kia's arrival at the top of the hollowed out trunk.

"There is no need for that." He said with a slight sigh. "If I had meant you harm, you would not have heard my voice, you would have simply been killed." The underlying note of menace in his voice caused Kasna to shiver slightly.

Kia begrudgingly lowered her bow and dropped from the tree to stand beside her sister.

"If you do not mean us harm, then what do you want?" Kia asked.

"Ah! Well what I want is not why I am here either; it is what your mother wants that brings me here." He said with a slight smile and touch of glee.

"What do you know of our mother?" Kasna asked narrowing her eyes and flexing her fingers around the hilt.

"Much. I have known her every day of her life. I was there at her birth, at her parents' deaths. I was there the day she married your father and I was there the day that each of you were born." He said with a smile.

"Then what is it our mother wants?" Kia asked, gently placing her hand on Kasna's arm to make sure her sister did not do anything rash.

"To know where you are." He shrugged simply.

"Is that it?" Kasna snorted.

"Well I am sure that there is much that her heart desires, but what she has asked me to do is to discover where you are. Now, having done so, I can inform her of your whereabouts."

"You are not here to help us then?" Kasna asked with irritation.

"To what end would you need help? You are safe here, no war threatens to overwhelm you all the way out here; you have plenty of places to hide if you are chased. You are fed and watered. I fail to see how you are in need." The man raised an eyebrow as he spoke. He voice did not betray humour or sarcasm as he steadily met the gaze of the two princesses.

"We are not ignorant of our situation." Kia replied harshly. "We know that as soon as our usefulness expires, our father will have us killed." She spat on the ground as she finished speaking, trying to rid herself of the bad taste talk of her father left in her mouth.

"Ah, so it is the threat of death that you fear. I would have thought that your blood was void of that fear, ferocious warriors that you are." The dry tone he spoke with was not lost on either of Kasnata's daughters.

"We want to be with our mother, to escape from this place." Kasna growled.

"And there is why you are impetuous." He said with a wry grin. "Have you thought of the implications of your actions, not only to yourselves but those around you?"

"What implications?" Kasna demanded.

"What will happen to your brother? Those that guard you here? What will your mother think when she finds out? What will your father do? Do you even know where you are? Will the guards pursue you to the ends of the earth to bring you both back again? All of these things should have been considered before you take even the smallest action." He said in the most serious tone he had used in their conversation so far.

Kia and Kasna looked at each other and wondered who on earth the man stood before them was.

"If however you have considered all those implications and are certain that your escape is the wisest course then I will do what I can."

*****

The Guardian of the Wilds stared up at the sky and sighed. It still caught her off guard as to how unfamiliar the stars could be. It was not the same sky she had seen in her childhood, many of the stars had long been extinguished and replaced with new tiny beacons. She could still remember watching her favourite moon being destroyed by a passing asteroid shower.

Once there had been seven moons that hung in the night sky of the Wentrus days, but now there were four at most and that was only every ten years or so.

The new stars were as alien to her as many of the people who now dwelt on Celadmore. She had once had those she could call friend amongst every group of people, but now she was outcast by most of them, left to unite and lead those that were abandoned by others, not even staying with those of her own blood for too long.

Even the land seemed different under her feet, not solid or unflinching but shifting like sand being constantly displaced by the desert wind. There was a call on the air, beckoning her to sail the oceans, to embrace the constant changing nature of the world and live as part of it, not as separate, but it was not yet time for that.

There was a power balance that needed to be corrected.

Her people were moving through the wilds at her order, looking for information as to troop movements in the area. Some had been born into this time of war and has known nothing but this life of spying, but there were some who remembered the days before the war. It had been those days that had seen the people of the wilds travelling between the major cities, trading meats, furs and crafts at markets and living as one with the wilds when there were no markets.

It was those days that Cassandra yearned would return, but she knew it was a hope in vain. The people of the wilds would soon have no place on Celadmore as the new age began.

It would take weeks for her to reach her next destination, her call of service to her bloodline was one she could not ignore, but it would take a great deal of skill to infiltrate enemy lands without being discovered or her presence even being suspected.

Chapter 4

Kasnata stood tall despite her exhaustion. Her journey to the forward camp of her people had not been a pleasant one. Storms had raged across the Silver Ocean, causing rough seas that had afforded her little sleep. When they had reached the shore, bandits had attacked the villages that lay not far from the Port, so now the streets were clogged with refugees trying to escape the destruction.

The Governor of the Port had refused to send troops out to drive off the bandits under the pretence that the Port would need them to defend it if an attack from enemy forces or other bandits should happen.

The truth of it was that the Governor was a greedy woman, for years she had been slowly siphoning funds out of the taxes that the king called for to line her own pockets. Her wealth had reached substantial levels and now required half the Port's guard to protect it.

Kasnata was aware of the Governor's activities but could do nothing about it directly. If she reported it, she would be helping a man she despised to gain more money that should have belonged to the people.

So instead she had arranged for some friends of Cassandra's from the underbelly of the Port to break in and slowly take back what had been stolen in the first place. The Queen knew that if the Governor ever came to count the funds she believed she had accumulated, then she would discover the theft; but equally be unable to report it as she could not account to the king as to why she should have such funds in the first place.

The dark angel was quite satisfied with her solution to the problem, but she could not release the Port guards to remove the bandits.

She had sent all but a small detachment of her forces on to meet with the rest of the army and led some of her finest warriors to remove the bandits. She received no thanks for doing so, nor were the people grateful that the bodies of the dead had been buried. Yet the Queen acted without regret.

For four days she rode her elite warriors hard, with rest only allowed to keep the horses from expiring beneath them in order to rejoin the army that she had sent ahead.

Valian forces were spotted following their progress to the south and each morning a handful of men and women were brought before Kasnata as traitors having tried to desert or had been found to be spies for the Valian forces. The law of the Order did not allow for mercy in the case of treason against the crown, and every day Kasnata had to order the execution of those she had trusted and known for years without a moment's hesitation or showing any sign of weakness.

Relief had flooded her when an attack had been launched by the Valian forces. They had come in the dead of night and been caught in an ambush that had been set by the nightwatch. As dawn had broken, the last of the Valians had died. The bodies of Kasnata's warriors were buried and honoured whilst the corpses of the traitors were left for the scavengers to pick clean.

By the time Kasnata's forces joined with the rest of her army, a tenth of the number had dwindled away. Relatives of traitors were informed of the executions; some protested the innocence of their brothers, sisters, mothers, fathers and cousins; whilst others were so shamed they forbid the names of those now dead from being spoken.

Despite all this, the Queen of the Order and Nosfa stood tall and received all complaints and reports from the camp. She listened attentively and spoke calmly to all, no matter how they raged at her. She walked with poise and dignity at the end of the council to her quarters that had been prepared.

She was led through the camp by Amalia, General of Kasnata's

Kestrel forces and childhood friend to the Queen. She was shown no favouritism, no special boons were granted to her. When she had been given the position of General, many had feared that she would receive preferential treatment due to her close acquaintance with the Queen.

Amalia did not crow of her friendship with Kasnata either; none could fault the General for her tact and discretion, though many had tried to pry secrets from her in relation to the dark angel, they had all been unsuccessful.

It was Amalia, however, who was trusted above all others by the Queen. When in need of counsel, it was the Kestrel General that Kasnata turned to.

"That was not an easy journey." Kasnata sighed as Amalia followed her into her tent.

"Long journeys from home to war are never easy, your majesty." Amalia replied as she took the thick cloak from her queen's shoulders.

"True." Kasnata said pursing her lips as she weighed her next words carefully. "Made all the harder for seeing good people suffer for the arrogance of those that lead and rule them." She shook her head as she spoke.

"Something our people have always been blessed in not having to suffer from." Amalia offered her queen a comforting smile.

"That is not true; Valia was just as corrupt and oppressive as any ruler that has ever sat on the throne in any kingdom of Celadmore." Kasnata sighed.

Her quarters were by far the largest in the camp and were almost the same size as the war tent. It was split into three sections. One was filled with cushions, silks and furs for her to sleep in, another was where her clothes, weapons and armour were stored and allowed her to dress in privacy. The third contained a table that had been built from timber found around the camp, four chairs, two small round tables and a large pile of cushions.

From Kasnata's point of view, all the cushions, silks and furniture were unnecessary in a war camp. She would have been far happier with a pile of furs and space to store her weapons and armour, but there was a tradition within the Order to have such decoration within the ruler's quarters.

"When you have rested, a camp inspection is expected and the commanders of King Mercia Nosfa VI's forces wish to have an audience with you." The Kestrel General poured a glass of water for the queen from a silver jug that stood on one of the small round tables.

"Has the general arrived yet?"

"No, majesty. His arrival is expected shortly, but we have heard nothing since we received word that a new commander was being sent." Amalia said handing the water to the dark angel.

"I see. What else has been happening here?" The queen asked as she gratefully sipped the water.

"There are the usual tensions in the camp between the two armies, but there have been no altercations as of yet. The scouting party went out this morning and should be back in three days with information on the enemy numbers, formation and movements." The Kestrel General said as she watched the queen stare off into space.

"Very well. Tell the commanders I will receive them in the central tent. Don't call it the war tent for the moment, I want to gauge the commanders' responses and their suggestions for action in a, what they would consider, a more civil arena." Kasnata said placing the goblet onto the table and drumming her fingers on the wood.

"I will inform you the moment we hear anything on the general's whereabouts. Rest well, majesty." Amalia bowed and retreated from her queen's quarters.

"I will do my best, Amalia."

*****

Lord Rathe Bird shook his head to try and keep his eyes open. Since leaving the court of Nosfa VI, he had not slept for more than two hours a night.

He did not trust the men that he was travelling with. Each one of them had been handpicked by the king to accompany him. He had several weeks of travelling on his own amongst men he was certain were under orders to dispose of him if the opportunity arose.

The journey from Grashindorph to Lake Marsden was uneventful; no signs of bandits could be seen, even when travelling through the dark parts of the forests of Nosfa. The camp commander met Rathe at the edge of the camp.

"My Lord, it is good to see that you have all arrived with us safely." The commander saluted as Rathe reined to a halt and dismounted. His mare, Ebony, had been skittish since they had departed from the capital and was not any calmer for having reached their destination. Rathe wondered if it was because she also sensed the danger that surrounded him.

"Thank you, you are?"

"My name is Tola, my Lord. I am your second in command." The man said with a smile. Rathe studied his subordinate. He had many questions for the man but some were more dangerous to ask than others.

Tola was not particularly old, in fact he was only just in his early thirties, but his skin had weathered under the sun whilst marching to war for his king and his black hair, which hung down to his waist, had already begun turning grey. His eyes were dark and sharp; they held warmth and humour, something the young Lord Bird had not expected.

The commander of the camp was dressed in simple leather armour that bore the scars of many battles that it had seen and a short sword hung at his waist. Neither seemed particularly practical for fighting an enemy on the battlefield given their apparent age and condition, but Rathe did not think that they were worn for practicalities sake.

"Tola, the hero of the war of the east." Rathe said offering his hand to his second.

"It seems to be the name that follows me, my lord." Tola grinned as he accepted the offered hand.

"Well then, I am honoured to meet you. How long before we break camp?"

"A few hours, sir." Tola indicated that Rathe should follow him. "I need to discuss our destination and our enemy with you before we can leave, but we need to have cleared the south-eastern corner of the forest before we make camp this evening."

"Then let us make haste."

*****

Lord Haston Bird did not stay at the palace after he watched his son depart. He paid his respects to the king and the lords of the court and left, cursing under his breath.

He had not expected to make the journey home alone and now he did not expect to see his son alive again. He rode without an escort, not believing that a lord should need a household guard to protect him whilst travelling. If a man could not fight and defend himself, then he did not deserve his title.

He was aware that the king had tried to take advantage of his mind-set by paying bandits to attack him as he journey between his lands and the palace, but none had even come close to unhorsing him, let alone killing him.

"All alone on a dangerous road, my lord." A voice called out sweetly to him. It was a female voice, not young though. The notes of her words carried the weight of wisdom and an edge of bitterness that came only from surviving the harsher storms of life.

His eyes fell upon the owner of the voice, a cloaked figure sat beside the road slightly ahead of him. He reined in his horse to slow the geldings gait as he drew closer to the woman.

"I would return the comment, dear lady, but you do appear to have at least four men accompanying you from the shadows." Haston said with a dry tone.

"A woman, unlike a man such as yourself; can never be too careful whilst travelling." She said rising to her feet and moving towards Haston.

"What is it you want?" Lord Bird asked, his legs firmly keeping his horse moving forward and its head out of the reach of the woman.

"I am not here to rob you, have no fear of that." She said with a tired tone.

"With four men that keep to the shadows, it is not an unfair conclusion to arrive at." Haston replied quickly.

"They are there to ensure that we are not disturbed." The woman sounded almost cross as she spoke.

"Who are you?" Haston asked. He had watched her walk and concluded from her bearing that she was not a peasant, bandit or thief. A warrior perhaps, one of the barbarians that belong to the wife of the king or a spy from an enemy nation, all of these possibilities passed through his mind as he asked for her identity.

"Who I am is not important, but you will be accompanying me without protest." She smiled as she laid a hand on the reins of his horse.

"And if I do protest?" Haston asked eyeing the men that were now stepping from the undergrowth.

"An unconscious man does not protest." A gruff voice sounded from behind Lord Bird.

"Lead on then, my lady." Haston sighed with resignation. With a sinking feeling in his chest, he allowed his horse to be led from the road.

*****

"Your majesty?" Kasnata's Condor General, Renta was knelt beside her queen and was gently shaking her to wake her.

"What is it?" Kasnata asked as she yawned and tried to gather her thoughts.

"They have arrived. Do you wish to see the general now?" Renta asked as she stood and collected one of Kasnata's thicker cloaks.

The Queen of the Order allowed herself a few moments to clear her mind of the shackles of sleep before replying.

"What time is it?"

"The third flight of owls has just passed." Renta replied offering the cloak to her queen.

"Then most of the camp is asleep?" She asked as she took the cloak and wrapped it about her shoulders.

"Three hours into the new day, only the watch is currently awake. The soldiers that he has brought with him are already bedding down for what remains of the night." The Condor General said with a smile as the Queen rose from her bed and moved to sit at her table.

"Is Tola with him?" Kasnata asked drinking from a goblet of wine that had remained from dinner.

"He is." Renta suppressed a slight giggle and Kasnata smiled.

"Well that is something at least. I will receive them in the central tent in four hours. Awake the rest of my generals and ask them to attend as decoration. I wish him to see the strength of our people. I would prefer Tola not to be in attendance, if you could distract him, I would be grateful, Renta."

"Thank you, your highness." Renta saluted and went to carry out her queen's instructions.

"Wake Shaul and Methanlan too, I want them to observe the troops that have just arrived and they can pass almost completely unnoticed, as though they were men of Nosfa, not of the Order." Kasnata added almost as an afterthought.

"I will see that it is done, your majesty."

*****

Tola sat beside the fire and watched as the troops around him settled into the encampment. He smiled as he listened to the men swapping stories of the men and women of the Order they had seen as they had explored.

Tola liked life as a soldier. His family had come from a small village in the wastelands of Nosfa, a village that had been constantly raided by desert bandits. When he had very young bandit slavers had tried to take his mother and he away from the village. It had been then that Tola had first encounter the men and women of the Order.

King Jadow had been journeying to visit with Kania and Nodarto of Tulna when he had come across the commotion in the village. His guard had consisted of four warrior; two men, two women. The bandits had numbered close to fifty.

Tola had watched in amazement as Jadow and his warriors intervened. Jadow was a giant of a man, he looked more like a bear than a man in size, and the claymore he wielded was as likely to crush a man as it was to cut him.

The battle was brief, but in truth it was more like a massacre. The bandits were no match for the highly trained warriors. They had rushed enthusiastically towards the village's newly arrived defenders and fell before any blood of the Order could be spilt.

When the bandits lay dead, the warriors had carried the bodies from the village and buried them in the forest that surrounded the settlement. The village leader had offered gifts and money to Jadow for saving his people, but the king had refused them gently.

Tola had never seen such men and women before, honourable killers his mother had called them, but the young child disagreed. To him they were the heroes of legend born into the darkness of the world around him.

Jadow and his guard had returned to the village months later and continued to visit every year. On his third visit to the village, King Jadow had brought Queen Tsmara and the young Princess Kasnata. Tola had been presented to the members of the Order as a promising young soldier that they expected to do well.

He smiled at the memory of his home, of the village known as Roenca. He missed the simplicity of life there. It had been many years since he had seen his home and his mother.

"Your mind is busy tonight, I see." The warm voice of Renta greeted him as she approached his fire. Tola looked up and smiled at her.

"Reminiscing, that is mere preoccupation whilst waiting for my men to settle in for the night." It had been seven months since he had last seen the general and he was glad that it was she that had sought him out.

"Do you need to watch over them or are you able to come and tour the encampment with me?" The warrior woman gave the Roencian a wry smile. She was not attractive, not to the minds of most men. She was tall and muscular. Her face was sharp, its features proud and severe even when she smiled. Her eyes were hawkish but they held humour that the rest of her face lacked.

Tola rose to his feet and stood at least a foot taller than Renta. He enjoyed spending time with the Anagura, she reminded him of the warriors he had first seen in Roenca and of all the women he had met in his life, she was one that he found he could talk with freely.

"I am sure they can manage without me for a while."

The two walked in silence as they negotiated their way through the chaos of Nosfa's men making camp. Many of the men stared at Renta as she passed, some whispered, others sniggered, but none of it registered on the face of the general.

"How is the queen?" Tola spoke first as the two neared the corral where the horses of the Order were being stabled.

"Tired. Her journey was not an easy one. But she will get no rest now." Renta sighed as she reached out to stroke the neck of the nearest horse.

"No, I expect there will be precious little time she will be able to call her own." He replied as he leant against the fence and watched the Anagura.

"What is the new general like?"

"From what I have seen so far, he is not all he appears to be. Whether that is for good or for evil will remain to be seen." Tola shrugged. Renta tilted her head in thought.

"Why did you stop braiding your hair?" The Roencian asked catching the general slightly off guard.

"For the same reasons I imagine that you did." She replied after a moment's consideration.

"I do not think that your commanding officer threatened to hang you from the battlements of Grashindorph castle if you did not remove them." He joked as he moved closer to her and ran his fingers through her hair.

"Please, Tola. We agreed that we would not do this again." Renta pleaded with him, yet she did not pull away.

"Is that what you truly want?" He whispered as he let her hair fall through his fingers.

"No. But..." Renta admitted begrudgingly

"Then sit with me and tell me of what has happened since last I saw you." Tola gently reached out and took Renta by the hand.

*****

The newly arrived men of Nosfa were tired after their long journey, but their exhaustion was not enough to drive them to their beds. Instead they had met with the merchant train that followed the army.

Merchant trains were not uncommon on the plains of Celadmore but not something that the men and women of the Order had any use for. They comprised of traders who offered cheap and poor quality wines, beers and spirits to the soldiers alongside a list of products that were not legally available in any kingdom.

They often caused more disruption than any leader would tolerate but they provided a lot of very useful information to the armies that they followed, which led to a great deal of allowances from those in command.

The warriors of the Order did not trade with the merchant train; however the distraction it provided was welcomed by those wanting to pass amongst the soldiers unseen. It was under the guise of browsing the merchant train that Shaul and Methanlan managed to slip unnoticed into the ranks of Nosfa's army.

"Do you think any of them will stop us?" Shaul asked as the two meander through the men looking for those suitably drunk to make conversation with without attracting too much attention.

"I doubt it. Depends on how many of them have orders not to deal with the trains and to keep their eyes open for new faces." Methanlan shrugged as he offered a cheery wave to a group laughing round a campfire. Shaul cringed at the looks his friend received from those passing by, but Methanlan was rewarded with the lifting of glasses to him and a beckoning invitation to join them.

"Sidney!" One of the drunken revellers shouted a welcome and grasped Methanlan in a bear hug as he and Shaul joined the group of seven men. "Guys, this is Sidney! Fought beside him a year ago. Thought you would have gone back to your farm and that lovely wife of yours."

"I would have, Jack, but I was made an offer I couldn't refuse." Methanlan shrugged and clapped the man on the back.

"Oh, we've all had a bit of that kind of luck. Harry here was just telling me how he was forced to stay on three years ago." The man known as Jack indicated a stout man across the fire from him.

"I hope I don't get stuck with that too." Methanlan moved to sit by the fire. "This is Tam, worked the farm next to mine until last summer when he got drafted. We grew up together, one of the best men I've ever known."

"Good to meet you, Tam. Drinks are by the fire, help yourself." Jack said slapping Shaul on the back. Shaul smiled and did as he was bid, praising the Goddess Arala for Methanlan's luck.

*****

Rathe was filled with apprehension as he followed the aide sent to collect him across the camp. The other high ranking officers had insisted on accompanying him, but Lord Bird had flatly refused to allow them to join him. He hadn't wanted his opinion of the queen to be coloured by the presence of his king's loyal retainers.

Outside the council tent there were forty men and women lined up either side of the entrance. Each was dressed in what Rathe could only consider to be full battle armour. The different commanders all wore variations of a basic breastplate, greaves, arm guards and boots decorated with the different birds of the Order emblazoned upon them.

The cavalry commanders were dressed in heavier armour than those that commanded the infantry. The full suit they wore was crafted from meran that had been heated and cooled several times to make it stronger that was underlain by shadcrag leather that had been reinforced by creating a thin woven mesh from boiled moorin bones.

Rathe had seen the war horses that they rode into battle, horses that were twice the height of the horses ridden by the soldiers of Nosfa. When they bore down on an enemy the ground shook beneath them terrifying even seasoned troops from the field. The horses wore armour that matched their riders. Neither needed weapons in order to inflict damage upon their enemies as a single blow from the arm of a rider or the hooves of the mounts could crush more bones than most knew existed.

The infantry generals all looked to be dressed in shadcrag leather that was inlaid with lighter meran that had not been heated as much as the metal used for the heavier armour, yet it was still strong enough to protect the warriors in battle but slight enough not to restrict their movement or reduce their speed.

The archery generals wore nothing more than shadcrag leather that had boiled moorin bones inlaid into it. Amalia was stood dressed not in armour but in a light breastplate of moorin fur that left her stomach exposed and her legs were wrapped in tight hessian strips. Her blade, Ashanna, hug at her side and was the only indication that she was the highest ranked amongst all the generals.

To her left stood three generals that were dressed differently to the rest. One man and two women wore a kind of leather that Rathe had never seen before. It was greyish blue in hue and looked to be much thinner than the shadcrag leather that the others wore and there were no emblems upon it. There was nothing to indicate what it was made from or what the role of the generals was.

Rathe didn't know why, but something about the three generals made him think of the ancient stories his mother had told him about the dragon rider of old that had been led in myth by a pair of immortal twins.

His escort held open the flap of the tent to allow Rathe to enter. As he stepped inside he was struck by the simplicity of the council tent. A single carpet crafted from thick grasses lay down the centre of the tent at the far end of which stood a throne that seemed to be freshly carved from the forest that stood to the east of the camp. Weapons of every conceivable variety lay in three deeps rows lining the walls of the tent. Nine rows of benches stood either side of the carpet that like the throne looked to be freshly carved.

Nothing about the council tent spoke of intimidation through grandeur as it did in Nosfa. If the reception line of generals outside of the council had unsettled Lord Bird, then stepping into the presence of Queen Kasnata of the Order was like finding himself in the company of the Goddess.

Here before the barbarian queen there was nothing but power that demanded obedience and respect. His eyes fell upon her as he approached the far end of the room where she sat. Her dark hair was held up and crowned with the wings of a raven that sat behind the circlet of silver and onyx that she wore. She wore loose fitting robes of purple and silver silk that fell over the contours of her body in the most flattering way possible.

Rather felt the colour in his cheeks rise. He had expected to see a woman dressed in armour and painted with the blood of her enemies. Instead she looked more civilised than any of the women that currently attended Nosfa's court.

"Ma'am, I am here to serve you." The general saluted as he stood before the feared warrior Queen. She was sat, straight-backed, on the makeshift throne that had been assembled in the central tent for her war councils. She seemed disinterested in the general as she sat reading reports that her aides had prepared.

"No, general, you are not." She said in an off-hand manner, not shifting her attention from the papers she held. "You are here to serve my husband and his interests. You are here to spy on me, nothing more."

"Ma'am?" He asked with slight confusion.

"My esteemed husband does not trust me to fight a war that could lead to his ultimate downfall, so he sends generals to spy on me. When they report back to him that I am merely fighting against our enemies, he assumes that I have corrupted them and sends for a new general to spy." Kasnata sighed and looked up for the first time.

The man that stood before her was very young to be a general. He was tall and muscular unlike the other generals that had been sent before him. His dark hair was short for the most part, all except for the warrior's braid that started at his right temple and reached down to his waist.

She regarded him with a cold stare that betrayed only indifference to the general that stood before her. He did not sense hatred only impatience at the inconvenience she predicted he would cause her. After a moment her eyes returned to the documents in her hand. The general stood, unsure of what to do. He was used to childish leaders demanding that he stand to attention until called upon to make some unintelligent and unnecessary comment in support of his leader's plan and against that of any out of favour advisers.

This woman however was a Queen raised to command without need of courtiers. From what he had heard of the Anaguran women and their rulers, there was no favour-mongering through chivalrous acts of little to no importance. Women and men were assigned to jobs based on their skills and abilities – their leaders were expected to outperform all on the battlefield in skill and finesse. Ergo they were trained and fought from almost infancy to be brutal and merciless with all weaponry.

The Queen that sat upon a makeshift throne was the product of the refinement of skills and the training of hundreds of thousands of warriors distilled to perfection. She brought dignity to her shabby surroundings making the draughty tent into a hall of stone, centuries old that had witnessed the passing of many great dynasties.

"What are your orders, ma'am?" He blurted out, nervous by the silence and his own lack of purpose.

"Your orders, I would have thought, were self-evident." She replied with slight amusement, her eyes still skimming the papers.

"Ma'am?"

"My orders, general, are to train hard and treat those beneath you as you would expect to be treated by comrades-in-arms. Maintain discipline through fair judgements and punishments that befit the severity of crimes committed. Though, I am sure, these will be secondary to anything King Mercia Nosfa VI has ordered." There was no malice in her voice, but a tinge of weariness laced each word.

"Ma'am, I feel you do King Mercia a great injustice..." The general began. Kasnata's eyes flared suddenly, the papers she held thrown down at her feet as she drew herself to her full height and addressed the general, for the first time, with her undivided attention.

"What is your name, soldier?" She demanded.

"Rathe Bird, your highness." He replied.

"General Bird, my husband arranged to marry me to ally himself with the only nation that threatened his military capabilities. He keeps my children away from me and our people in a hope that it will control me. He sends me to fight his wars and spies to accompany the troops because he fears that I will turn against him. He writes to warn me of how fragile young lives are when he thinks I am being particularly unruly and fills his own castle with whores from his court to pleasure him as I refuse to. So please enlighten me, General, as to where the injustice in all this lies." Her voice was not raised, but low and threatening in its calmness. The air around them seemed to bristle with her rage and the ground quaked slightly as her anger rose.

Rathe was stunned into silence. He stood gaping as Kasnata re-seated herself, picked up her reports and began to read again.

The air behind him moved as the tent flap was lifted and closed as one of Kasnata's aides entered. She stood beside the general but showed no indication that she had noticed him.

"Highness?" She asked softly.

"It is all right, Marissa, have you received any further information?" She asked quite calmly.

"Yes, highness, also Cassandra sends her compliments."

"Is she moving again?" Kasnata asked as she finished reading.

"She is. She requests you meet with her, she says she has some interesting things to report."

Kasnata smiled broadly and clapped in almost glee at the news.

"Wonderful. Arrange a rendezvous point as soon as it is convenient for her. Would you also please show the General around the camp and explain how our army functions as there seem to be some gaps in his knowledge."

"Of course, Majesty." Marissa saluted and led the general from Kasnata's make-shift throne room.

Kasnata sighed as the tent flaps closed behind her two subordinates. Her heart was still pounding in her chest. She felt like a trap was being laid before her that she couldn't avoid walking into. His voice had been a warning to it; smooth and deep, enough to cause her to shiver slightly and when she had looked him in the eyes, her heart had risen in her chest, trying to burst free. It had taken all her self-control to keep her composure in his presence.

Her husband's tactics were changing subtly but still were obvious to her observations. She tapped her fingers on the arms of her throne as she thought of what action was open to her. Sending him back would produce outrage and endanger her children, that much was clear, however keeping him within her camp was a danger to her position and her children.

"Definitely a trap." She murmured to herself.

"Well, it was only a matter of time before he tried something like this." A familiar voice drifted from her right.

"This is true, I had expected it after the birth of our son, but he seems to have waited or been far less intelligent than I deemed him capable of being. I am glad you are here though, Cassandra, it has been too long."

Cassandra smiled and moved to sit at the feet of the Queen.

"For you it has been, for me it has been a mere flutter of moments. It still seems like yesterday since Anagura's funeral."

Kasnata slipped from her throne to sit beside the bandit warrior.

"It must be hard to watch your daughter die and then each of her descendants. Still yearning for a life at sea?" The Queen asked.

"Yes, I think that it is almost the right time for me to leave and embrace the wild oceans as my brothers." She grinned and gently placed her hand on the Anagura's forearm. "You need to be very careful, my dear friend. We may treat King Mercia with scorn, but he is very dangerous and his advisers are not only cunning but filled with hate for you. They want nothing more than to tear you down." Cassandra spoke in low tones in case any undetected spies might be close by.

"I know you are right. This General Rathe Bird seems to affirm that." Kasnata sighed.

"Though there is no intent within him to harm you. That much is clear. He may not be aware of his purpose beyond that of commanding your husband's forces." Cassandra said thoughtfully.

"Telling him would only serve to jeopardise the scheme. Any suspicion would lead to his torture and relating the plans in full. It still doesn't decrease the threat he poses."

"True, but it also means he could easily be turned to an ally." Cassandra mused.

"You clearly have been spending too much time with your brother. Our other plans – are you sure that you can do what is necessary for all this to happen?" Kasnata asked with concern.

"With absolute certainty. I know it is important to you and it is equally close to my heart. I will do all that is possible to accomplish it." Cassandra assured the Queen. "Will you be able to reach the rendezvous point in three weeks?"

"That shouldn't be a problem. I will also be able to have uncovered all I can from this new General." Kasnata mused.

"Be careful." Cassandra warned. "I will have the Abbott report anything he can to you as soon as he is able."

"Where is he? I have not seen him in months." Kasnata stood and moved across the tent to where her battle armour was displayed.

"He is busy." Cassandra said in off-hand manner and smiled. "The Guardians also wish to meet with you, the Oracles are coming too. This could be more important than you realise."

"Significance of the action, in this case, does not change the course of action. Are Kania and Nodarto coming too?"

"Yes, my mother and father are most anxious to be there. This is the changing of our times, none of them wishes to miss this." Cassandra said gently.

"The changing of our times...to be done by so few..." Kasnata shook her head. "Was I wrong in marrying Mercia?" She asked sighing.

"There is never anything you have done that has not been right when you have decided to do it. You are sovereign; whatever you decide is for the best." Cassandra shrugged. Kasnata turned and scowled at the would-be pirate.

"Of all people, that is not what I would expect you to say. You are not one of my subjects. You are my great grandmother to some degree, you speak to me honestly, do not presume to speak to me like I am a simpleton." Kasnata snarled slightly. Cassandra raised an eyebrow as she stood and walked to stand opposite Kasnata looking her straight in the eye.

"I am your great grandmother. I am stronger, older and wiser than any of you, any of this line that has ever lived. I have watched empires rise and fall around me. I am a granddaughter of Arala. I have seen my children, lovers; grandchildren all wither and die around me. I have known pain that you can only imagine. Do not think for one moment that you can threaten or intimidate me, Kasnata. You ask for knowledge of a path you chose not to walk, knowledge that no mortal has the right to know. Whatever you choose to do, you live with the consequences, but do not look to me to absolve you of your decisions."

The tension that filled the tent sparked around the two women. Anger flared inside Kasnata at being addressed as a child, anger flared inside Cassandra at a child attempting to manipulate her.

"You have a good heart, young one. Any mistakes you may have made you can correct. The good choices you have made will prove themselves to be good in time. Trust your judgement." Cassandra soothed after a few minutes of silence and leant her forehead against Kasnata's.

"Would you answer me one question?" Kasnata asked closing her eyes.

"I may." Cassandra answered.

"Was I always to be the one to change these times?" There was tiredness and weariness in her voice as she spoke. Cassandra wrapped her arms about her granddaughter's shoulders.

"You have been given no more or less than you are able to bear. No other has been born that can do all that you can. You were asked when you were a child by the Goddess herself and you accepted. No other can do this, and you have not been asked to do this alone." The immortal smiled and kissed the Queen's forehead. "You are strong, little girl, but you are not an island."

"I am tired of this already, tired of fighting. I want to go home, to the place my ancestors have gone to." Kasnata sighed.

"You will when the time is right, even I will meet you there one day. But the time has not yet come for this. You have much work to do here and little time to do it in. It will not be this hard forever, but for now you must endure. I will see you in three weeks. If you need me before then, you know how to find me." Cassandra said stepping back from Kasnata.

"Thank you. Be well." Kasnata offered Cassandra a warrior's salute and turned back to her armour. The flap to her tent was opened and General Amalia stepped in.

"My lady, the General Bird wishes to speak with you again. He seems displeased with something." Amalia saluted as she entered.

"Indeed? What could it be that could distress him so when he has been in the camp less than an hour?" Kasnata muttered sarcastically as she turned to return Amalia's salute. Cassandra had gone, as suddenly and silently as she had arrived. Amalia had not seen her go, nor was she aware that the bandit warrior had been in the tent moments earlier.

"I know not, my lady. Will you receive him in here?" Her aide asked with a wry smile at the thought.

"I will meet him at the training grounds. I wish to stretch my legs." Kasnata replied tapping her fingers on the hilt of her sword.

"Very good, highness." Amalia saluted and left. Kasnata smiled to herself and shook her head. Politics was a dangerous game to play, more dangerous for her husband than he realised and it was time his general was shown just how hazardous it could be to play with fire. She took hold of her staff and walked out into the sunlight that bathed her encampment.

Sounds of daily life were rich in the air. Metal on stone sounded from her right where the smiths had set up their tents. Fire's crackled as food was cooked and water boiled. Horses snorted and whinnied in the corral, voices called to each other in different languages and the sound of sword on shield echoed from the training ground. Of all the sounds that living in encampments brought, the sound of battle was her favourite. It was a sound that every Anaguran and Queterian was raised to and there was nothing more comforting for her to hear than this.

Chapter 5

Lord Haston Bird sat in the dark. He didn't know how long he had been sat there, only that it was the most unpleasant place he had ever been.

Since he had met the woman on the road he had not slept. He had been dragged from his horse when he was far enough not to be seen from the road. Beaten unconscious, bound and gagged, Haston had awoken to the smell of wet fire, fungus and acrid smoke. He could hear people moving about overhead, but he had no way of knowing just how many there were or how far above it was.

It had taken less than a day of careful exploring to discover some sharp, broken brickwork that allowed him to free his hands and feet as well as the bloated corpses of several rodents and reptiles. There was a stream of water that he was sat in, almost stagnant, that suggested to the Lord he was incarcerated in one of them old sewers of Grashindorph.

When he had fought in the frontier wars as a boy of 16, he and Rosla had led a small detachment of men through the sewer system to launch a surprise assault on the bandit men of the desert that were laying siege to the city. Since then much of the sewer network had been blocked off and a new smaller, more extensive system of pipes and drains had replaced them.

He passed the hours and judged the time of day based on the snippets of conversation he could hear. He had not yet been fed or brought clean water; his stomach could bear the deprivation of food without too much discomfort, but his parched throat was making the foul smelling water around him seem increasingly inviting.

He cupped his hands and dipped them into the water, then thought better of it several times before someone finally came to see him.

Loud sounds of stone dragging against stone and creaking rusted metal heralded the arrival of his captors. The end of the tunnel he was held in slowly edged open allowing a flood of light into the gloom.

Haston clutched his eyes and collapsed to his knees, the stinging light burning more than he imagined light could. A man stepped over to him and hauled him to his feet.

"He's gotten loose." The man growled as he wrapped giant fingers around Haston's throat.

"That was expected. Let him go." A female voice replied. It sounded familiar to Haston, thinner, reedier than it should have been. He opened his eyes gingerly and beheld a proud woman dressed richly in furs that lay over finery that Lord Bird had not expected to see in this disgusting place.

The fingers around his neck loosened, letting Haston fall to his knees in the filth around him. His hand went to his throat automatically to check the damage that the vicelike grip of the giant man had caused.

"The years have been kind to you, old friend." The woman said as she approached. Haston raised his eyes, a ready defiance already mustering itself.

"Old friend?" Haston growled as he rose back to his feet.

"I know living outside of the elegance of court has been wearing but surely you haven't forgotten me." She said playfully as she stepped past her bodyguard. Haston shook his head and blinked several times trying to clear his vision.

"Hermia?" Haston couldn't believe his eyes as he stood and beheld the former Queen of Nosfa.

"You'll find that rumours of my death have been greatly exaggerated." Hermia said dryly. Haston laughed in spite of himself. It was hollow in his throat and cracked as he croaked. Hermia nodded to the giant man that had held Lord Bird by the throat. The man reached down to his belt and brought forth a water skin that he handed to Haston.

The Lord of Nosfa's court gulped down the water with gratitude, pausing every few seconds for breath.

"Jephthah." Hermia spoke to the giant man.

"Majesty?" He grunted.

"Fetch Haman. Have him meet us in the lower tunnels." She said as she knelt down beside Haston.

"Aye, majesty." Jephthah bowed slightly before he strode into the darkness of the sewer beyond the ring of light cast by the torch.

Haston watched the man leaving and his eyes fell on the smaller man that remained, holding the torch. He was almost invisible, even stood beneath the glowing light of the torch.

"You still keep one close at hand then?" Haston chuckled. Hermia followed the line of Haston's eyes to where her second man stood.

"Joab." She smiled and motioned for the silent man to approach.

"Ma'am?" Joab's voice was much deep than Haston had imagined, almost comical combined with his slight frame.

"Would you be so kind as to help Lord Bird? He may find walking somewhat difficult." The former queen took the water skin from Haston and stepped back to allow Joab to help Haston to his feet.

The contrast between Jephthah and Joab was striking up close. Jephthah was almost three times the size across the chest as Joab and at least two feet taller. Joab was young, barely halfway through his teens and still void facial hair, whereas Jephthah was almost fifty if the colouring in his long plaited hair and bushy beard were any indication.

Haston thought it was likely that Joab had been trained from birth to act as Hermia's shadow under the orders of King Rosla. Her previous shadow had been a woman, Layla, Haston knew little about the woman's past save for she had been brought to Rosla by the Abbott. What her connection had been with the wandering monk, he had little idea, but felt it was something he did not want to explore to deeply.

He suspected that Joab was also an associate of the strange man of the cloth, but knowing too much of a shadow's business and history was often hazardous to one's health.

The three walked in silence through the maze of dark sewer tunnels. Joab supported the weight of Haston with ease and without complaint as they moved. The ground was slippery underfoot and although Hermia and Joab had no trouble with their footing, Haston did not possess the same. Every corner they turned or intersection they crossed saw Haston sliding into the fetid water that sat about their ankles.

The lack of sound unnerved the Lord, every so often he would hear a shuffle, scuttle or the noise of a stone clattering against the tunnel walls that would almost stop his heart.

"There is little to fear down here. The biggest creature that you will find, besides our men, are the rats." Hermia soothed after Haston had reached for his sword times only to find that it was not there.

"Nosfa doesn't send men searching for his enemies in these tunnels?" Haston frowned as he fell once more into the sewage.

"We are all dead men as far as the king is concerned." Joab said shortly. Haston waited for an explanation, but the party lapsed back into silence as they continued through the maze of sewers.

After half an hour of walking, they reached a metal ladder that rose through the ceiling to the tunnels above. Joab left Haston's side and moved quickly up it without a sound and disappeared into the darkness above.

"He has gone to make sure the way is clear." Hermia explained as she placed her hand on Haston's arm to keep him from climbing up after her shadow. "He will be back shortly to let us know if we can continue up or not."

"I thought you said there was nothing other than rats living down here." Lord Bird replied with no small amount of confusion.

"No." I said the largest creatures down here were the rats. The reason he is checking is not quite you might think. There are many other dangerous to living in the sewers besides the wildlife." Hermia said with a wry smile as she dropped her arm.

"I'd forgotten how vague you could be." Haston sighed and leant against the ladder. Hermia smiled and shrugged.

"There are many advantages to vague speech and instruction"

"A lack of accountability being chief among those." Haston but back more forcefully than he intended. "I'm sorry. That was uncalled for."

"Your temper has not improved then? I am glad; it always was one of your more endearing flaws." She replied with amusement. "Joab has gone ahead to see if the floodgates have been opened in the newer sections of the tunnels, the ones that are still in frequent use."

"What if they are open?" Haston asked.

"Then our planned and preferred route will be impassable and we shall have to make a detour." Hermia shrugged as though the answer were obvious.

"A detour?" His scepticism plain in his voice.

"Yes, it is something we try and avoid as much as possible as it requires going up into the city itself and having to evade encounters with the city watch and most of the populous – as Joab said, we are all believed dead." Hermia tried to sound as off-hand as possible as she spoke.

"Except for me." Haston corrected her. Hermia looked away from her old friend and nodded. "Hermia?"

"Yes, Haston?"

"I am not believed to be dead, am I?" He asked urgently.

"We did not have a choice." Hermia admitted. Haston rounded on the former queen with rage flaring in his eyes.

"What do you mean; we did not have a choice?" He roared.

"Nosfa had issued orders for your execution. There was a group of mercenaries waiting to ambush you further down the road. We decided that you were more valuable to our cause alive than dead, so we dispatched our own forces to intercept you before you could be ambushed and killed. Your household will have contacted Nosfa by now asking why you have not returned and he will have sent word that you are dead." Hermia explained calmly.

"Won't the mercenaries tell him they never came across me, that there was no ambush?" Haston growled, his anger getting the better of him.

"The mercenaries won't tell him they did not kill you if the king says they have; no mercenary I have ever come across valued the truth higher than gold." Hermia was unmoved by his rage.

"What of my children? They will think I am dead and Rathe's life is already in danger from that barbarous queen Nosfa married. My poor Mia will think herself alone in the world, what if she goes mad with grief?" Haston ranted.

"Peace, my friend, peace. Your son is in no danger from Kasnata. She is far more civilised than Nosfa, let alone how he portrays her. No matter what her reputation, she will not bring intentional harm to Rathe unless he first tries to harm her. She values good warriors and strong allies as much as she despises my son." Hermia soothed.

"She despises the king?" Haston's rage was culled by curiosity at Hermia's words.

"She does. Of all his enemies, he has made his worst and strongest in her, but we shall talk more on that later." Hermia assured him.

"What happened to you?" Haston changed the subject to a question that had been burning in his brain since he had discovered his old friend was alive.

"Nosfa was poisoning me. I knew he was and it broke my heart. Layla and I decided that it would be best to allow him to think that he was succeeding in his place to remove me and set about making plans to leave. Layla went in search of help in our friends outside of Nesca and she returned with a woman named Kania." Hermia related the secret about her past that none save Layla, Kania, Haman and Joab knew.

"Kania?"

"Yes, she is the leader of the village of Tulna. She introduced me to Haman and arranged for me to disappear. Between Layla and Kania they managed to create a corpse that convinced my son he had been successful and was now free of me."

"What happened to Layla?" Haston asked as sounds from above heralded Joab's return. Hermia chuckled.

"She will be pleased to know that you did not recognise her at the roadside." Hermia smiled. "As far as my son knows, she took her own life due to grief at my passing."

"Then why is she not your shadow?" Haston furrowed his brow in confusion.

"She is."

Haston spun round to see the silhouette of Layla leaning against the tunnel wall.

"Did you think that we would leave anyone as important and precious as my queen alone with a stranger?" Layla asked as she knelt down beside her mistress.

"I am no stranger." Haston protested.

"No shadow would leave their mistress without protection." Joab said gruffly as he knelt down at Hermia's other side.

"Are the floodgates open?" She asked as she signalled that her shadows should rise.

"They are. There is no way through, not for at least two days. If we are quick we will not cross any patrol in the west quarter of the city." Joab reported.

"Then we will not delay. Lord Haston's strength has somewhat returned to his limbs so we should move with all haste." Hermia set off through the tunnels once more at a pace just shy of running, Haston, Joab and Layla not far behind.

"Why do you need two shadows?" Haston asked as the brisk pace changed from walking to running.

"I do not. Layla is as good as three shadows, if not four. Joab has been in training for a far more dangerous role that he is now ready for." Hermia replied slightly breathless. Layla glowed and blushed slightly at the high praise her mistress bestowed.

"A more important role?" Haston slipped as he ran and fell face first into the ankle deep water. Layla stopped and hauled him back to his feet before continuing.

"Yes, I shall explain when we reach Haman."

*****

The streets of the west quarter of Grashindorph were all but deserted. Joab led the small party out of a sewer entrance at the bottom of one of the brothels' gardens.

Haston followed Hermia and Joab as the three negotiated their way soundlessly through the night. Layla had disappeared almost the instant that they had emerged from the dank underbelly of the city. Neither Hermia nor Joab seemed disturbed by her disappearance or even acknowledged it.

No lights glowed on the streets; the torches that Hermia and her company had carried had been extinguished before they had exited the tunnels. The light cast by the moon and stars was enough to light their way through the night without drawing attention to their presence.

Hermia had told Haston that they could not speak until they were safely across the city and underground once more. He obeyed her command despite all the burning questions he had.

Every so often Joab would signal that they should hide. Footsteps echoing off the walls around them soon after could be heard and occasionally they would be accompanied by light cast by a torch being carried; the flickering orange light skirting around the edges of whatever Haston had chosen to hide behind.

Joab would sound an owl's call to say that it was time to move again once the danger had passed and the party would once more move on.

Haston found it strange that every alley and street they hurried down was vacant of beggars and vagrants, no trace of them could be seen, no evidence of them even existing in the city let alone having slept a night or two in the gloom and the garbage of the gutter.

Joab stopped suddenly as they moved into one of the narrower alleyways. Haston was so consumed by thoughts of beggars and vagrants he didn't notice. It took Hermia grabbing him by the hand to shake him back to the world around him. Before the three of them stood twelve heavily armoured and armed guards.

"I thought it had been too quiet." Joab growled.

"You will surrender your weapons and come quietly." The sergeant demanded as his men drew their swords.

"What is the charge?" Haston replied drawing himself to his full height. The guards broke into laughter around him.

"It is a simple enough question." A new voice entered the conversation. Hermia smiled at the sound, Haston turned to see Layla stood with two men; one stood in shadow to obscure his face, the other in a full cassock.

"This does not concern you, Abbott." The sergeant growled.

"All matters of injustice concern me, sergeant." The Abbott replied with a smile.

"My lady." The man in the shadows whispered. Hermia moved towards him, dragging Haston with her.

Layla and the Abbott stepped forward to stand beside Joab.

"Stand aside monk, my quarrel is not with you." The sergeant warned.

"We must go." The man in the shadows instructed urgently.

"But what about them?" Haston asked gesturing towards where Layla, the Abbott and Joab stood.

"They'll be just fine." Jephthah announced his arrival, flanked by two other men that looked just as terrifying as he was to look at. "My lady, go, it would not do to find yourself at the scene of such a fray."

Hermia nodded.

"Haston, we must go. They are more than capable of dispatching the guards."

Lord Bird begrudgingly agreed and allowed himself to be led through the night.

"Is there nothing I can say to dissuade you from this course of action?" The Abbott asked with a sigh.

"We are under orders to arrest that woman." The sergeant replied.

"I see. Well I am afraid that we cannot allow that to happen." The Abbott shrugged. "I am sorry; I did not want it to come to this."

"Helez, keep the Abbott safe." Jephthah snarled at the younger of the men he had brought with him.

"That won't be necessary, Jephthah." Layla said with a smile.

"Layla, you have far too much faith in my abilities." The Abbott smiled with affection at the shadow of Hermia.

"Jephthah? Layla? Helez?" The sergeant faltered slightly at the sound of familiar names.

"Ah, fame at last." Helez grinned maliciously.

"Then the others, they're..." The sergeant gulped and stepped back a touch.

"Just as famous." Joab growled as he pulled his twin daggers from their scabbards at the base of his spine.

"We only have orders to take the lady." The sergeant stuttered as he edged backwards away from the small band.

"Do you know who she is?" Layla asked circling to the left of the sergeant.

"No, I only have orders to bring her in alive." The sergeant said, his eyes following Layla's movements carefully.

"Then there is something that you should know." Jephthah smiled, almost a grimace.

"Yes?" The sergeant said with expectation.

"I will have been cold and buried more times than years I have lived before I will allow that to happen." The man mountain ran his finger across the edge of his blade very slowly and his companions attacked.

The sound of the fracas echoed down the side streets. Haston glanced back as he heard cries and the ringing of sword on stone and steel. Haston glanced back as he head cries and the ringing of sword on stone and steel.

"Where are we going?" He asked between gulps of air.

"Haman is taking us to where we should have met him." Hermia replied over her shoulder.

"Haman?" Haston asked with a frown.

"Pleased to meet you, your lordship." Haman threw him a brief smile before they darted down another, darker street.

Haston couldn't quite believe that the city streets could be so dark and yet Haman seemed to be able to see through it as though it were lit by the midday sun. Obstacles that Haston collided with such as low walks, deep gutters, low hanging roofs and even the market stalls, Haman and Hermia avoided with ease.

As the sound of violence faded from their ears, their pace slowed. The three stood to catch their breath and listened as silence once again descended on the streets.

"You came in search of us." Hermia was the first to speak when she was sure they were not being pursued.

"Yes, Jephthah heard the floodgates being opened on his way to meet with me; he decided that it was best to make sure you were not in danger." Haman explained. Hermia chuckled to herself.

"Dear Jephthah, he never was able to trust Layla or Joab." She shook her head and sighed at the actions of her shield.

"His worries were not wholly unfounded." Haman pointed out.

"They never are."

Haston jumped at the sound of Jephthah's voice as the giant loomed over him.

"Every rule has both shadow and shield for a reason." The Abbott agreed. Haston looked about him to see that all those they had left behind had joined them. A vague scent of iron filled his nostrils, the putrid smell of death absent.

"You made short work of them." Hermia observed.

"If we had stayed too long, reinforcements would have come. Better to silence them and be gone." Joab said firmly.

"The opinion of a shadow." Helez tutted.

"A shadow moves with the grace and tact that a shield lacks." Layla said lightly, playing with her knives. Haston could hear their blades cutting through the air as she tossed them around.

"A shadow does all the dirty jobs a shield cannot do in the light." The other man Jephthah had brought with him, Asahel, growled.

"And if your eye sight were not failing, you would know that it is night." Joab shot back.

"Peace, all of you. I will not have you fighting each other now. Haman, we have many things to discuss and the reasons for my having both shadow and shield is not among them." Hermia spoke firmly, her loyal retainers muted to silence by her words.

"We're not far from safety, follow me." Haman led the party onward at a slow pace to avoid further altercations. The Abbott fell in beside Haston, every so often pulling the battered and bruised Lord out of the path of the unseen obstacles of the night.

Chapter 6

Haman knocked three times on the door of a very run down building in the slums of the city. The building had once stood at three storeys if the buildings around it were anything to go by, but now it was barely one with a roof that was caving in.

Jephthah, Helez and Asahel were stood in a triangle around Hermia looking menacing with their weapons drawn. Haston thought to himself that they were far more likely to attract unwanted attention by standing in such a fashion, but he was not going to tell that to the three.

Joab and Layla had once again vanished, but Haston had a feeling they were close by. The Abbott was stood humming to himself, his hands clasped in front of him, twiddling his thumbs as he waited. There was a smile on his face that betrayed amusement and contentment.

They waited in complete silence on the dark street until they could hear the sound of bolts being drawn back from the door. It opened onto a more intense darkness than existed out on the street. Without speaking, Hermia, Helez, Jephthah, Asahel and Haman all disappeared through the door. The Abbott motioned that Haston should follow.

Inside the run down building there was nothing but rubble.

"Take three steps forward and crouch. " Layla hissed in Haston's ear causing him to jump and cry out. "Keep your voice down."

Haston did as he was instructed and found Jephthah's hands gripping him round the waist, dragging him down into a narrow corridor. The sound of water flowing nearby could be heard as Haston was herded down the corridor. Haman was waiting at the far end by another door that he knocked on three times again.

More bolts were drawn back from the door and light spread through the cracks around the door as it was heaved open. Hermia strode inside, he shields following her. The Abbott bowed as he entered and Haston was followed by Layla into the chamber.

It was a cavernous room carved into the stone below the city. The light that was cast by the torches that were held on the walls were not enough to expel the darkness that hugged the far reaches of the room and obscured the roof from view.

The door shut behind Layla causing Haston to jump.

"Welcome." Hermia beamed at Lord Bird. "To our safe haven from the rule of Nosfa."

Haman clapped his hands three times and from out of the darkness there stepped men, women and children.

"Who are all these people?" Haston asked.

"The Gibborim. Hermia's sworn forces to fight against the man that has destroyed the throne." Jephthah grunted.

"The people that worked to save your life." The Abbott said quietly.

"You brought me here to join you?" Haston asked as he looked over the faces of all those that stood in the damp underground room.

"We brought you here to keep you safe from Mercia's assassins. If you choose to join the Gibborim, it will be because you are invited to after you have proven yourself." Helez grunted in slight disgust.

"We should discuss what happened on your journey here." Haman said, sensing tension growing between Helez and Haston.

"The confrontation with the city watch?" Asahel asked as the Gibborim faded back into the shadows.

"It wasn't an accident." Layla said firmly. The Abbott nodded slowly and motioned that the party should move further into the cavern. Helez and Asahel bowed to Hermia as the party began to move off.

"We should speak to the others." Helez said as the two shields took their leave.

"Very well." Hermia nodded. The remaining six walked into the darker corners of the cavern where Jephthah heaved open a heavy metal door that the party moved through into a smaller room that contained what appeared to be buildings and market stalls.

"The sergeant said they were sent for you, ma'am." Haman agreed.

"And the floodgates were opened at just the right time to force you to move across the city above ground." Jephthah agreed as he pulled back a curtain that acted as a door to one of the buildings.

Hermia led the way inside to a room that was not all that dissimilar to the meeting rooms that Haston had in his holdings for the people's representatives to meet with him in.

"The floodgates being open and forcing us to move across the city couldn't possibly be a trap unless there is a mole." Haman said with a frown.

"It is not above the realms of possibility." Layla shrugged. "Mercia will have his own shadows and given are current plans; it would not be a wholly unsurprising event."

"I would have thought you would be more concerned by that form of prospect." Jephthah growled.

"Assassins and moles are easy to find when you know they exist." Layla shot back with a raised eyebrow.

"Before or after they have murdered our leader?" The man mountain glared at the shadow.

"Enough, both of you." Hermia ordered. "It may be time for us to send Joab. If there is a mole or assassin then the sooner we send him, the less likely it is for Mercia to discover what is going on."

"You think he truly knows you are alive?" Haman asked with

concern.

"No, if he did, then he would not have sent a sergeant. I think he knows of the resistance to him but not who the people are. But with a mole then it will not be long before he does discover." The Abbott mused stroking his chin.

"I agree." Layla jumped to her feet and made for the door of the building.

"Unsurprising." Jephthah said under his breath.

"Jephthah, you will help Layla to discover whether there is a mole and who they are Do what you both must." Hermia said firmly not wishing to listen to her shadow and shield fighting again.

"As you say." Jephthah accepted her orders begrudgingly.

"We start now." Layla said shortly as she darted through the curtain, Jephthah following with a scowl set firmly on his face.

"Haman, prepare Joab. He is to depart at once so he can arrive by the time the sun is up." Hermia sat with a frown on her face as she thought through the events of the night.

"I will help him." The Abbott smiled. "By your leave."

Hermia nodded, Haman and the Abbott leaving Haston alone in the building with the former Queen.

"I will show you to your quarters. It has been a long night. You should get some rest." Hermia sighed as she rose and showed Haston out of the meeting room.

*****

In the days that followed the Abbott's visit, Kasna and Kia began planning their escape in earnest. They had never attempted escape before with such hope of success or a need to be rescued.

None of the guards at the palace, or their wardens had noticed the presence of the monk, which to the two young princess proved that escape was not only possible, but their only hope of reuniting them with their mother.

They worked in secret, talking only when they were alone and in the tongue of their mother. When they were sure of success did they decide they were ready. It took four weeks to smuggle the weapons and armour that they needed into their room and to steal food from the kitchens in quantities that would not be missed.

Kasna woke with a start to find her sister, Kia, stood over her.

"What is it, Kit?" She asked groggily as she rolled to sit up in her bed.

"Nini, there's movement outside in the hallway." Kia said handing her sister the armour and weapons that they had hidden under the floorboards of their room.

"What do you mean there's movement outside in the hallway?" Kasna rubbed her eyes and started to change into the shadcrag leather armour.

"I mean that the palace guards are missing and someone is creeping about, trying to go unnoticed." Kia said urgently. Kasna leapt to her feet, awake at the prospect of a possible assassin lurking around the building.

"Are you sure?" Kasna asked as she grasped the badly crafted iron blade she had spent hours honing to a lethal edged sword.

"Positive." Kia replied, her voice shaking slightly. Kasna looked at her sister, Kia was dressed in the same armour that her sister wore and in her hand was her own sword that she had polished and worked on for twice the length of time that Kasna had spent honing her own blade.

The two girls breathed slowly, trying to still the panic that they felt rising inside their chests. Kia moved towards the door of the room slowly avoiding the floorboards that creaked under foot. Kasna picked up the food supplies they had stored and strapped them across her back in a large sling she tied from their bed sheets.

The door was pushed open as Kia crouched behind it. A dark figure slipped into the room, armed with two curved knives. Kasna held her sword steady as the figure noticed the princess.

Kasna was sure that if she could have seen the infiltrators face, they would have a cruel smile spread across their lips. They stalked towards her watching every slight movement Kasna made, from the repositioning of her fingers on the hilt of her sword to the shifting of her weight between her feet.

The princess slashed forward with her sword and missed. The figure launched forward seeing the opening in Kasna's guard. It took Kia two steps to slash her blade across the back of the would-be assassin and a single backslash of Kasna's sword to take the head from the assassin's shoulders.

The two girls stood for a moment listening for any sound that would indicate the intruder was not alone. When they were sure there was no one following the figure the two girls slipped out of their room into the dark corridors of the palace.

As they crept through the hallways, the bodies of guards were strewn across the rugs and stone, blood staining the floor beneath them. Neither of the princesses had liked the people that held them prisoner, but seeing their bodies lying lifeless on the stone made the two girls feel sick to their stomachs.

It was clear from the number of dead that the figure that had attacked the girls was not alone. As they reached the top of the stairs, they could see light being cast from torches on the floors below. Kia looked at her sister, the two silently debating whether they should investigate further. A scream from below was all the incentive that Kasna needed to start darting down the staircase. Kia reached out to try and stop her sister and missed. She sighed and shook her head as she followed quietly behind.

As the two girls approached the ring of light being cast by the torches, they could see one of the castle maids being held by two men clad in dark leather armour. A third man stood holding the torch, dressed in the rich silks and furs of the noble men of court. He seemed indifferent to the screams of the girl before him and more concerned with the reports being brought to him by men in heavy armour.

Blood was streaked across the floor where bodies had been dragged through it and thrown against the wall beyond the light cast by the torches.

"Where are the princesses?" The nobleman asked lazily as he turned from the men in heavy armour.

"I don't know." The maid snivelled.

"I don't believe you. You've seen what I do to people that lie to me. However you are young enough to provide some entertainment before I kill you. If you wish to avoid that, I suggest that you tell me what I wish to know. Then I will let you go." The noble sounded almost bored at the prospect of having to wait for the information he needed.

Neither Kasna nor Kia particularly liked the maid that was being held captive. She was a rude creature that had been responsible for rooting through their belongings looking for items their father did not want them to have. She had taken and destroyed precious heirlooms that could not be replaced and crowed over her discoveries, the princesses helpless to do anything about it.

The two girls had no reason to interfere with her interrogation. There was no bond between them that should move the girls to action and their intervention would almost certainly lead to them being captured. Kia slinked backwards away from the men and crouched in the shadows under the stairs. Kasna, on the other hand, stepped forward into the light.

"He won't let you live." Kasna said firmly, glaring at the nobleman.

"At least one of my men is dead then? What a pity." The way he spoke suggested that he meant the exact opposite.

"Let her go." Kasna ordered with as much authority as she could muster. She was calm, didn't stutter, her voice didn't crack and her hands were still as they held her sword.

"I see. As foolhardy as your mother." The nobleman yawned and waved a hand lazily towards his guards. One of the two men holding the maid drew his sword and forced it between the screaming girl's ribs. Kasna and Kia controlled their outward emotions well. Neither princess flinched or squirmed as the blood filled the maid's lungs and choked her screams.

The other guard let go of her arm and let the maid's body fall to the floor as she drown in the blood that filled her lungs.

"Now then, where is your sister?"

"Are you here on behalf of our father?" Kasna asked trying hard to sound aloof.

The nobleman laughed with genuine amusement.

"I must thank you; it has been many years since I have laughed. What a refreshing and unexpected delight."

"Answer me." Kasna growled. The confidence of the nobleman was not that of a spoilt man that had others to do his dirty work for him. His cool demeanour, the power he exuded indicated that though he chose to use his guards, he was more than capable of assaulting and capturing the castle by himself.

"Your father? No child. Your father is not affiliated with me, nor is he of any concern." The nobleman stepped toward Kasna, careful to avoid the pool of blood that was forming on the cold stone floor.

"Who are you?" She frowned, not moving away from the advancing man. In the shadows under the staircase Kia silently took her bow from her back and drew an arrow from her quiver.

"I'm not sure knowing my name will benefit you." He said dismissively.

"You're the second person to tell me that in the last few weeks. If it was my mother you spoke to, she'd make you speak your name." Kasna fought the instinct that told her to retreat towards where her sister hid.

"If it was your mother that I faced, she would already know who I am. Where is your sister?" The nobleman's voice betrayed his growing impatience.

"I'm not sure that should be your greatest concern, Kelmar." The gravelly tone of an unknown woman caused the nobleman to pause mid-step.

Kasna watched as the two guards that had held the maid fell to the floor, blood flowing from their throats to mix with that of the maid. The nobleman, identified as Kelmar, turned slowly and looked with disdain at the men that now lay dead.

"Show yourself, witch." Kelmar demanded, Kasna and Kia now forgotten.

"Name calling? What frustrations you must have faced. Using minions to seize a castle that took you months to find and then when what you sought was just within your grasp – you fail." The woman's voice was filled with condescension.

"I have not failed yet." Kelmar spat back, his ease and confidence now gone. It had been replaced with anger and all illusion of restraint seemed to have been destroyed.

"Your men are all dead." The woman said simply. Those five words seemed to have a greater impact on Kelmar than any form of threat would. He reached for the sword that hung at his waist, a decorative weapon that looked like it had never been used practically before. He drew it and brandished it at the shadows.

"You could not have killed them all."

"If you would like their heads to make sure, it can be arranged."

Kasna jumped as the woman's voice came from directly behind her. Kelmar shook with rage. He closed his eyes and sheathed his sword.

"My failure is only temporary." He said flatly. Dropping the torch he plunged the hall into darkness. By the time Kasna and Kia's eyes had adjusted to the gloom, Kelmar and the woman had gone.

"Nini, do you have any idea what happened here?" Kia asked as she slipped to stand beside her sister.

"Lots of people died for reasons that I think we are better off not knowing, Kit." Kasna said kneeling beside the bodies of the maid and the guard. She used her shaking hand to close their dead, unblinking eyes.

"We shouldn't stay here. We were going to escape." Kia said helping her sister back to her feet.

"You're right. If there was anything before, there is nothing left here for us now. We take what we can from the armour, stables and kitchens. We must be gone before the sun rises." Kasna said firmly.

"Do you think anyone survived?" Kia asked as the two girls headed towards the armoury.

"If they did, we can't leave them behind."

"We take them with us?" Kia frowned. When Kasna didn't respond, Kia prayed to Arala that she would not find out what her sister's silence meant.

Chapter 7

Lady Mia Bird should have been weeping. Her heart was breaking as she stood before the tyrant king, yet the tears did not come. She had long ago used up all her tears and even the news of the death of her father could not cause them to fall. Instead she stood calmly, her face passive and unreadable.

King Mercia Nosfa VI sat upon his throne, the castle in habitants all called to court to hear the news of Lord Haston's demise. He knew that the gossip of his servants would make sure that most of the city would know within the hour and the rest of his kingdom would know within three weeks.

There had been gasps from the ladies of his household; the visiting nobles had started to mumble to one another almost in the same moment as Haston's death was announced. Mercia knew that the death of Haston on the roads would mean an outcry for more protection from bandits and highwaymen, but the threat of Haston's claim to throne was now neutralised.

He smiled to himself as he beheld the girl whose spirit he had broken. She had been as strong and proud as her father and brother when she had first been brought to the palace. But it had not taken long for her to realise her place.

She was left in insolation for the first three weeks, the only company she had was from two mute maids that had been assigned to clean her quarters and bring her food. She was not allowed to leave the two adjoining rooms she had been allocated. Four guards were posted to ensure she did not leave. No letters she wrote were sent; the maids burnt them in the fire before her eyes when she asked them to send them. Any letters from her family and friends were also burnt as she watched.

After three weeks her pride had gone, replaced by tears. She was brought before the court where she had cried silently. Not one member of the king's household had spoken to her, or even acknowledged her existence in the hallways or dining rooms.

For two months this continued until the night she was brought to the king's bed chamber for the first time. She had screamed and cried out for help as Mercia satisfied his lustful desires, but no one came to her aid. Every night she was summoned to the king's bed, every night his twisted desires were met, every night Mia screamed less, her tears choking in her throat.

After six months of brutality she stopped crying and screaming, her body and mind numb to the abuse of the king. She has stopped believing she would be rescued, that her father or brother would challenge the king to fight for her honour.

Her father was dead and gone, her brother sent off to a war where he would die at the hands of the barbarian queen or the enemy. His most dangerous political opponents within his court removed with one fell swoop and his prize was the daughter.

In his mind he was certain that she would be a much more appropriate queen than his wife. He only had to remove her and as far as he could see, his problems were solved.

"Until your brother returns from war, your family estate and all lands will be under the stewardship of the crown." Mercia said with glee.

Mia merely nodded in response. With a small amount of disappointment Mercia waved her out of his presence. Haston and Marcia's daughter was led back to her rooms where she collapsed onto her bed and sighed. The court would be dismissed when Mercia was through tormenting his nobles.

She missed her brother and her father. She screwed up her eyes and tried to remember their faces. All she could bring to mind was when she had seen them stood in the council chamber before the king.

Her brother proud and strong, a man of courage and honour; banished from his home because of a paranoid ruler. She could remember even from a young age that there was a great sense of hopelessness in her home.

She couldn't remember much of her mother. She knew what she looked like from the portraits that hung in the hallways of the Ivory Tower of Afdanic. What she knew of who her mother was had come to her from stories told by servants, the household and her family.

Marcia had been gentle and kind. She was beloved by the people of Afdanic and had been the favourite cousin of King Rosla Nosfa. When he parents had met they had fallen in love almost instantly. So sure was her father of his love for her mother, he had begged Mia's grandfather for permission to marry the same day they met.

Whenever her father spoke of her mother, he lit up; his eyes dancing with life that had been crushed out of his soul by her death. Mia felt the stories were more like fairy tales than true accounts of what had happened, the rose tint of time removing all her flaws and increasing her more endearing qualities.

She missed the stories and there was a pang in her heart to think she would never hear her father speak about her mother again. Despite her mother's death, her childhood had still been idyllic and so far removed from her life as a prisoner in the household of Mercia.

There was much of life within the palace of Grashindorph that Mia did not understand and even less of it that she actually enjoyed. She was assigned two maids and an assistant. The assistant was a spy for Mercia masquerading, albeit very badly, as a confidant to the young noble woman.

Mia had discovered the true purpose of her confidant and dismissed him within a week of arriving at the castle. Mercia had sent others to replace him, but each had been greeted with nought but stony silence. Rumours circulated the castle claiming that the woman the king had assigned to the barbarian queen Kasnata had been killed on sight by her warriors. However Mia wasn't entirely convinced that it was true.

There were few people within the household that spoke well of the queen. Yet amongst the servants there seemed to be few that would speak against her. The king's servants were the people from the city that were paid to do the menial tasks and could be dismissed at any moment for no reason. His household comprised of the lesser sons and daughters of nobles of his kingdom, those who were too plain or stupid to be married or served Mercia in other capacities as members of his household.

His family were apart from both the household and servants. His son was not allowed to mingle with the rest of the castles occupants unless he was under heavy guard and accompanied by two tutors. His daughters, Mia had never seen and didn't even think were in the castle.

The guards, as far as the king was concerned, were lower than servants in the hierarchy of the palace and far more expendable. They were forbidden to speak to one another or anyone else in the palace unless the king gave permission; or the queen.

Mia spent hours listening to the maids talking about the queen and her visits to the palace. Of how the guards would laugh and joke with the maids as they went about their daily tasks, of how the palace would come alive with laughter for the guards and servants but not for the household. They were a bright light of hope for her in the dark days of her captivity.

There was a light knock at the door before it opened and one of the maids entered carrying a small try of food.

"I'm sorry about your father. I thought you might be hungry." The maid said gently. Mia smiled at her.

"Thank you."

"Is there anything I can do, my lady?" The maid asked as she placed the tray next to Mia on the bed.

"Tell me about the first time you met the queen." Mia said as she picked up the silver goblet of water from the tray. The maid smiled as she started talking.

"It wasn't long after her parents had died. All the kingdoms that had held peace whilst they served on the council fell into chaos and war broke out. We were fighting against the desert folk, they had been our enemies since King Rosla Nosfa VIII was a boy and tried to take the city many times. With the fall of the council, they thought we would be unprepared for their attack, especially as King Mercia Nosfa VI was now on the throne.

"They attacked and we were losing so King Mercia Nosfa VI appealed to the Order for help. They were the strongest warriors, an unbeatable army that had retreated from the mainland and none dared to declare war on. She came herself to respond to the plea. With her came thirty men and woman as her honour guard." The main giggled slightly at her memories.

"I have never seen such men and women before. They were dressed in silks and furs that lay over the top of the most exotic armour I have ever seen. They all had braids in their hair that had feathers and bones at the end of them, covered in red stripes that looked like blood. The queen was dressed in the most extravagant colours; gold and red silks that fell over armour so dark it seemed to suck in all light from around it."

Mia picked at the food on the plate in front of her – barley and meat on the bone with green leaves from the royal gardens. They had a bitter taste that Lady Bird did not care for.

"When she walked into the council, all voices fell silent. She held everyone in complete rapture. When she spoke, it was barely above a whisper, but her voice carried to even the furthest corners of the hall. There wasn't a single person in the room that wasn't looking at her the whole time she stood in front of the king." The maid sighed.

"Was it then that the king fell in love with her?" Mia asked as she stripped meat from the bone with her fingers.

"I think that he wanted to have her as his possession after that first meeting. For him, women aren't equals; they are items to be lorded over other men. I think he though if he had her then other kings would think he was a stronger man " The maid said quietly as she glanced about to make sure that no agents of the king were hiding nearby to hear her treasonous words.

"A possession?" Mia asked with a frown, wondering how on earth the king could think a warrior queen of the greatest army nation could be kept as a possession.

"He saw her beauty, her power and her nation of warriors and he wanted to own and control it. He has spent his entire life wanting and trying to control everything around him – not caring what effect it had on his kingdom and his people. It is why we are still at war." The maid looked close to tears. Mia sensed that the maid had lost people she was close to because of the king, but she did not press her for details.

"What about the queen? Surely she wasn't so easily deceived." Mia pushed the remains of the barley, leaves and bones away.

"She was young and desperate to keep the peace her parents had presided over. The king, he showed her a man that was kind and merciful, who wanted the same peace she strove for and cared for her as an equal. She knew nothing of his true nature until it was too late." The maid moved to pick up the tray and remove it from Mia's quarters. "You should get some sleep, my lady. It has been a long day for you and tomorrow will be no easier."

"Thank you." Mia crawled under the blankets and furs that lay across her bed as the maid left, quietly shutting the door behind her. The young lady sighed as she thought of her father and mother and what she knew of their courtship. She closed her eyes as she wondered at the pain the barbarian queen must have felt in discovering Mercia's deception. Whilst she pondered this, she drifted off into a dreamless sleep.

When she opened her eyes, Mia found she was not alone in her room. She screamed and jumped out of her bed. There was a man sat motionless by the door to the sitting area of her rooms. He appeared as a shadow rather than a man. He seemed to almost merge with his surroundings.

Mia's heart was racing as she moved towards the doors to her rooms. Panic in her chest told her that no guard had reacted to her scream. *Dead.* She thought.

As she reached the doors, the shadow of a man not having moved, spoke.

"I am not here to kill you." Her voice was deep and rich. She didn't feel chill run down his spine as he spoke, but felt almost reassured. She paused, her hand resting on the door handle.

"What about the guards?" Mia asked, doing her best to keep her breathing equal.

"What would it matter? You are a woman of high birth living in the king's palace at his invitation. What do their lives matter to you?" He asked coolly. He still had not moved.

"Of course it would matter." Mia shot back, overcoming her onset of fear.

"Why? Why would it matter?" The man shadow asked standing and walking over to where Mia was holding the door. "What do they mean to you? Do you even know their names?" He challenged her with a rising note of anger.

"It would matter." Mia said firmly holding her ground. The man regarded her without humour for a moment.

"What do you know of the people you preside over?" He asked coldly.

"I preside over no one." The young lady spat and let go of the door. The man smiled at her, a nasty smile that spoke of disbelief.

"You are a high born lady, with little to no concept of what those below you suffer. Whether you know it or not, you preside over them. The very way you act, expect to be waited on and protected. You consider yourself of more value even if you don't realise it." He stared at her with such intensity Lady Bird has to look away.

"Did you kill them?" Mia asked in a small voice.

"No. They let me in." The man's deep voice seemed lighter as he moved away and back to the place he had been sitting.

"They let you in?" Mia frowned and followed him.

"After all that has happened in the last few days to your family, the king has been advised to and appointed you a bodyguard." He said calmly to the point of almost being bored.

"After all that has happened?" Lady Mia sat on one of the benches that was covered in feather stuffed cushions.

"Your father's death, my lady." The man said with a passive expression. Mia stared at him expecting more to be said; when no more was forthcoming she spoke.

"What else?"

"What do you mean; what else?" He titled his head with curiosity.

"You said, after all that has happened in the last few days. If my father's murder was the only event you would have said after what has happened. This means there is something else, so what else?" Mia demanded.

"Is that an order, my lady?" The man asked with amusement.

"If I am given to presiding over others by my upbringing and situation, then I shall issue orders." Mia replied simply, trying to look dignified. The bodyguard burst into laughter, leaning forward on his knees to catch his breath.

"What a creature you are." He gasped as he tried to regain his composure. "Other events are not your concern. You should be focused on your own safety for the moment." He warned with seriousness replacing the humour.

"Both my parents are dead; my brother is leading the king's army in a war that sees him fighting alongside the barbarian queen. My family lands have been seized by the king and will be handed out to his favourite lapdog at any given moment. I am held prisoner in the palace of the king, completely helpless to do anything for my family. The people of Afdanic are left leaderless and have lost the stability my father provided.

"I wake up every morning in fear that my brother is dead and that I will be forced to stay here for the rest of my life whilst my people are treated like cattle that can be bought and traded by the highest bidder." She raged. The man looked at her with a deadpan expression.

"You feel a sense of responsibility towards people that you have never spoken to?"

"I have a responsibility to protect those people." Mia shot back, her cheeks flushed with frustration. The man was still sitting, his back to the young lady.

"The people that your family has treated like cattle, buying and trading them to the kings army, the farms, the mills, the armoury to bring money back to your hold?" He asked with disinterest in her response. The bodyguard had no illusions as to how the nobles of Nosfa treated those that were of lower birth.

"How would you know how I have treated my people?" Mia demanded as she leapt to her feet from the soft furnishings. She had never thought before about how the people were sent to work to bring in the food, resources and wealth that Afdanic needed in order to survive.

"Your people?" The man scoffed.

Mia paused before she replied.

"My people." She said firmly. In her mind there was no doubt that she was cared for by the people of Afdanic, no doubt that they accepted her as one of their own, that she was as much a daughter of the city as a lumberjack or hunter's daughter.

"You think of them as belongings, possession that can be disposed of when you are finished with them." He said flatly, sneering at the girl as he turned his face towards her.

"No." She cried, resisting the urge to slap the bodyguard. Instead she clenched her fists and hit the table in front of her.

"You talk of them as a belonging…"

"I think of them as equals." She spat cutting off the bodyguard.

"You have never seen anyone as equal in your life, save for your own family." He said dismissively.

"You are passing judgement against my character without knowing me." Mia glared at him.

"Do you not do the same? You claim people as your own. You assume that they love and accept you as one of their own, that you share a kinship with them because of the city you share. Have you ever spoken to any one of them outside the walls of this palace or the Ivory tower? Have you ever walked through the streets of Afdanic and listened to the conversations of the people, bought things from the market and haggled over the price of goods because you have to make your money go further otherwise you can't feed your family." He asked with only a trace of emotion in his voice. Mia stood motionless staring at him.

"You cannot blame me –"

"Then who is to blame? Your father, who fought alongside men of high and low birth? Your mother, who nursed people through the plagues that raged through the city years before your birth? Your brother, who now fights with men of the country against the enemies of this nation?" He questioned her with a steady voice. Mia couldn't find any words to reply and lowered her eyes from the steely gaze of her bodyguard.

"I'm a prisoner, taken from my family." She said quietly.

"You have the ability to be better than all of those that surround you at court, to be a greater champion of your people than any that has come before you." The bodyguard sighed, his voice taking on a more comforting tone.

"Who are you?" Mia asked, confused at the sudden change in the bodyguard's attitude.

"My name is Joab; I am here to protect you from all that would seek to harm you." He said smiling slightly.

Chapter 8

Kasnata woke early.

She enjoyed walking the encampment before the dawn chorus of horns, trumpets and drums sounded rising. It gave her chance to explore without hindrance, to overhear plots and plans of inexperienced saboteurs, to talk to those who had taken the night watch and to clear her head before the start of the day.

Her meeting the night before with the commanders of her husband's forces had been as she had expected. Warmongers to a man, demanding the death of their enemy, their thirst for blood appalling in those that had barely seen war or battle before in their lives. She had listened and dismissed them all after three hours. Amalia had stood staunchly beside her as had Avner, Shamgar and Yoav. The three men were her father's most highly regarded warriors that Kasnata had appointed to command her three divisions of the Order of the Hound, the Order of the Bear and the Order of the Wolf.

They had remained silent despite disparaging remarks that were made against them and when the generals of Nosfa had departed, they had displayed more diplomacy in discussing their actions and what Kasnata should do than the queen had thought anyone capable of.

"Good morning, your majesty." Tola cheerfully greeted the queen as he walked towards her from the coral.

"Prale Adle, Tola." Kasnata replied. "I trust you enjoyed your first night in camp?" She asked with a knowing smile.

"Whenever I am given the privilege of being within a hundred miles of your majesty, I enjoy life all the more." Tola grinned as he gave the dark angel an overdramatic bow.

"**Enough flattery.**" Kasnata said with a raised eyebrow.

"As you say, my queen." Tola frowned at the sudden change in mood and tongue. "What is it you wish to say to me?"

"Besides you and I; who else knows the language of the ancients, the language of your people?" Kasnata asked, her gaze looking out across the camp, calm and serene action to any who might be watching her, but Tola and those who knew the queen it was a nervous habit. Whenever she was uncertain or found herself in a state of confusion she would adopt the expression.

"There is no one. At least not within the camp." Tola said slowly, his stomach turned over, not wanting to know why the question was being asked.

"That at least is something." She sighed. "Tola, there is something very wrong with this world. War, bloodlust, death, why is it that these have become the things that define people for greatness? Why is peace not what drives us?" She asked her eyes not shifting from gazing at the horizon.

"Your majesty, not everyone is driven by those desires. I am not and neither are you. The generals of Nosfa, they are seeking favour; some out of greed and some out of fear of what will happen to their loved ones if they find themselves displeasing the king." Tola soothed gently as he looked around the camp for anyone that might be listening.

"What of their new commander?" Kasnata asked with a sigh.

"Lord Bird?" Tola mused on what he knew of Rathe before he answered. "He is driven by duty. Have you ever heard of his family?"

"Hermia spoke of Lord Haston and Lady Marcia with great fondness, but save for that, I do not concern myself with the unimportant intrigue of my husband's court. I have other issues that occupy my mind." The queen sounded morose as she spoke.

"Lord Haston was supposed to take the throne upon the death of King Rosla. Rosla never wanted his son to be king until he had learnt the lessons he did in his youth. Mercia was more ambitious and dangerous than anyone knew and took the throne by the law of Grashindorph that guarantees his succession by divine right." The hero of the war of the east explained.

"Lady Marcia was the cousin of King Rosla though." The dark angel replied with a frown, her gaze shifting from the horizon to Tola.

"Yes, Lord Rathe has a legitimate claim to the throne; in fact after your son he is next in line to succeed King Mercia." He shrugged at the queen.

"So if his family were really after Mercia's throne, my son would be dead by now?" The queen looked thoughtful for a moment.

"It would make sense, though they could also be waiting for the moment when Mercia is dead before doing anything." Tola motioned that the two of them should walk further into the camp as shadows began to stir in the tents around them.

"True, but unlikely I feel." Kasnata pursed her lips in thought.

"Is this what has been concerning you?" He asked.

"No, having these fools in my camp doesn't bother me. My son is smart enough to know who his friends and enemies are in his father's court. No. What concerns me is why we are still fighting this ridiculous war." She spat with disgust. Warriors were beginning to stir around them and those that were awake called out a greeting to the queen as she passed.

"What about your daughters?" The hero of the east was struck by the lack of the mention of the queens most beloved children.

"My daughters are more capable than even I could credit

them." The queen said proudly. "**We are fighting here against the people of Delma and are to move against those of Vasknar once we have defeated them. It is not a war in the name of peace, but in the name of conquest and destruction.**" The frustration she felt was not concealed in her voice.

"**When is a war fought for peace?**" Tola shrugged as he was offered food from the fire of a group of warriors they passed.

"**When dictators are being removed, when the people are protected from invaders, when -**" Kasnata spoke with fervour.

"I see your point, I don't agree, but I see what you mean." He conceded as they reached the part of the camp where the warriors of the Order ended and the soldiers of Nosfa began. None of them had stirred yet from their beds.

"**How many of your soldiers have marched with my people before?**" The dark angel asked with a slight smile on her lips.

"**Less than a division.**" Tola said returning the smile.

"Then this will be amusing." Kasnata said as changed back to her native tongue. No sooner had she spoken than the low rumble of drums began. It built up gradually like thunder at the start of a storm. Then the horns began, horns that gave tune to the rumble, starting quiet and growing to a crescendo that was crown by the trumpets. Sharp blasts of the high pitched noise could pierce through the slumber of even the heaviest sleepers.

The camp of the Order emerged from their tents before the trumpets had begun to sound and most moved to vantage points where they could observe the chaos that was about to unfold in the camp of Nosfa.

It was a sound unlike any that the men of Nosfa had heard before. Men spilled from their tents, half-dressed, dropping their weapons, tripping over the ropes that held their tents, their clothing and their fires.

Rathe was awakened by the sound of the drums, his first thought flashed to it signalling an attack by the enemy. He dressed quickly, the horns adding urgency to his movements. He could hear the rest of the camp being sent into disarray by the noise, but there was nothing he could do to bring order until he was dressed and armed. As the trumpets seared through his consciousness, he was ready and stepped out into the camp.

Men were rolling around in the mud trying to finish dressing after they had fallen, tents had been knocked down and some had even caught fire.

"Tola?" The general called out, searching through the chaos for his second-in-command. The noise from the trumpets, horns and drums died and in their place the roar of voices could be heard.

"Awake, rise, battle will soon be here."

Rathe turned at the sound of the voices to see the ridge that divided the two camps swarming with the warriors of the Order. Men and women stood dressed and armed for battle, but none of them looked like they were about to engage in battle. He looked to where the queen stood, wry amusement on her face and beside her with the same look of delight was stood Tola.

"Sir." One of the men came running over to him.

"What is it soldier?" Rathe asked as the man saluted him.

"The drums, horns and trumpets aren't the enemy sounding an attack." He reported.

"What is it then?" Rathe asked, returning his eyes to the ranks of the Order.

"It is the sound of rising for the Order. I've served with them before." The soldier replied.

"They sound it every morning?" Rathe asked with a frown.

"Only when the queen is in the camp and battle is close at hand. It tells the enemy that they are coming and that their queen is with them." The soldier spoke with admiration.

"Thank you. What is your name, soldier?" The general smiled.

"Jack."

"Thank you, Jack. Spread the word through the camp that there is no cause for alarm. Find the quartermaster and give him my orders to see the camp rebuilt and repaired. I appreciate your effort." Rathe saluted and watched Jack move off into the camp.

The feeling of panic began to subside as the general made his way across the half-destroyed camp. He walked past people putting the camp back together and dowsing fires that had threatened to get out of control.

He walked over to where the queen was stood and bowed.

"Good morning, your majesty."

"General." She replied.

"I was wondering where my second-in-command had gotten to." Rathe said with a minor note of annoyance in his voice.

"Tola is a comrade from past battles. His career and advancement within the kingdom's court are something that my generals and I take great interest in." The queen said with a slight tilt of the head to Tola. Tola bowed and stepped away from the queen.

"Thank you, your majesty." Tola smiled and shrugged at the general.

"I believe you have duties to attend to Tola, General Bird, walk with me." She ordered. Rathe opened his mouth to protest but a warning look from Tola told him that he should not argue with her.

"As you wish."

The queen led the general through the camp. The members of the Order had returned to their daily tasks in the war camp having observed the entertainment provided by the men of Nosfa.

Fires were stoked, patrols were sent out, armour and weapons were sharpened, repaired and cleaned. A large man was stood surrounded by a ring of fires that were three times the size of any of the camp fires. He was roaring orders at a group of younger warriors who scurried about building the fires and carrying water and ores to where the big man stood.

"Benaiah. Our forge master." Kasnata said with affection as she noticed where Rathe's attention was drawn whilst they walked. "He has served the Order well for many years. He forges every named blade for those who earn them in battle."

"Your warriors earn their swords?" Rathe asked with interest. He knew nothing of the culture of the Order and did not believe the rumours that the king had spread about them being nothing but barbarians.

"All of my people are trained to use sword, spear and bow from an early age. When old enough to join their brothers and sisters in battle they must prove themselves worthy of having a blade forged for them. A blade that is crafted for them alone, no other is to wield it and it is named. I earned my blade at the age of twelve; most do not earn them until much later. It is called the Ralenetia Estral." She said with great affection and warmth in her voice. "It was forged by Benaiah and I had to carry the water and ore for his forge as they do now." She said gesturing at the young warriors scurrying about.

"What if they do not prove themselves in battle?" The general asked with a frown, the impression of where the barbarian rumour stemmed from beginning to form in his mind.

"It is not battle as you would know it." Kasnata said with a broad smile. "It is when they prove they can fight, stand alone on the battlefield, defeat the vicious wild beasts that live on the plains of this realm. Most are earned by killing moorin that have been raiding the farms around

Anamoore." She assured him.

"When will we be facing the enemy?" Rathe asked as they moved away from the forge.

"Soon. I am waiting for the patrol I sent out this morning to report. They should be back within a few hours. I would talk to your commanders and choose a small force to join those that my own commanders will be leading."

"How many of your commanders will be on the battlefield?" Rathe asked; pondering how many men constituted a small force.

"Four." She said without a moment's pause. "I would suggest that you choose two commanders at most, that is if you decide you do not wish to be on the field. It is going to be little more than a skirmish."

"I will talk with my commanders and have you informed of my decision within the hour." He said as he took his leave of the queen.

Odd. She thought as she watched the general walk away. *For a man so consumed with duty...* Her thoughts were interrupted by the appearance of heralds at the far edge of the camp. *So the prince is leading the army to skirmish with mine. The Delmarian people do not take this war seriously; we shall have to do our best to change their minds.*

*****

Kasna and Kia had not slept in three days. They had left the palace after the invasion and done all that they could to put as much distance between their former home and themselves as possible. No enemy had pursued them as far as they could tell, but neither girl had wanted to stop.

There had been no word or sign of the Abbott since their escape and neither girl knew how to send word to him either, so the two had only each other to rely on until they reached their mother.

"I need to rest, Nini." Kia yawned. Her feet ached and she could barely keep her eyes open.

"Okay Kit, you get some sleep. I'll stand the watch a while." Kasna agreed and watched as her sister collapsed to her knees. "I'll build a fire; will you be okay without a blanket?" Kasna asked and received snoring in reply. She looked down at her sister and smiled. It didn't take long for Kasna to build a small fire and settle down beside her sister. The quiet of their surroundings, the warmth and crackle of the fire and the weariness she felt in her bones soon had Kasna drifting off to sleep.

*****

"The prince is leading their army." Kasnata shook her head in disgust as she led her forces out of the camp towards the ridge where the Delmarian army was massing.

"They are not taking this threat very seriously." Renta agreed. "Do you think they are plotting something?"

"No. If they were, then they would not have sent the prince. They would have sent one of the lower nobles. I think their spies have reported that there is dissension amongst the army and within Nosfa's court." The queen replied.

"You think they are going to keep skirmishing with our forces trying to demoralise them until they are recalled?" The general asked of her queen.

"I do. If they want to keep throwing their forces at us, then it will be their forces that are depleted and leave their strongholds undefended." The dark angel said with conviction.

"We shall do what we can, your majesty." Renta smiled.

"I shall be relying on you. Make sure that Tola survives as well." Kasnata said solemnly as they began their descent down the hillside towards the flat where Kasnata had chosen to make their stand. Renta saluted and signalled to her division to peel off from the main force and follow her as she headed off to the left of the flat where a dense copse stood. Tola led a detachment away from the army, following after Renta.

Rathe marched at the head of his men that followed the warriors of the Order. He watched the men and women before him with some amazement. They did not march in silence, with neither a semblance of order nor discernible ranks and yet there was clear discipline, more so than amongst the soldiers of Nosfa that he led.

As they reached the flat, he watched as the warriors of the Order fanned out into their battle formation with such practised precision that it almost appeared graceful.

The soldiers of Nosfa by comparison looked to be sloppy and poorly trained, shuffling into a loose formation that had the sergeants and corporals running up and down the line shouting, bullying and pushing the men into position.

The army of Delma could be seen atop the ridge on the opposite side of the flat. They seemed to be a blazing ball of light, so resplendent was their armour in the early morning light. The dazzling brightness made it hard for Rathe to estimate their numbers, but Kasnata's patrols had confirmed their forces numbered less than five hundred.

They seemed to have been waiting for the army to arrive, as they began to advance towards the forces of the Order and Nosfa in almost the same instant that the army had filed into its battle formations. They moved slowly at first, walking at a steady pace as they traversed down from the ridge. As they reached the flat, they began to quicken their pace. The Delmarian soldiers were led from the front by their prince mounted on the only horse on the battlefield.

Excitement and inexperience seemed to get the better of him as he began to canter headlong towards his enemy causing the heralds of his army to sound the charge far too early.

Though he had been trained by some of the finest tutors of sword play that the kingdom of Nosfa had to offer, Rathe was not prepared for the panic that lurched in his stomach at the sight of the army of Delma bearing down upon them.

Kasnata stood ahead of the line, her hair braided, her armour so dark that it was almost like she was death itself.

"This is merely a skirmish. After this, the real battles will begin. Kill quickly, do not make them suffer." She ordered, her face grave, her eyes as dark and dead as her armour.

Renta had taken the far flank along with Tola and a small detachment force. The other generals of the bird divisions had remained behind at the encampment. Amalia was in command until the queen returned. Most of the colonels and commanders of the men of Nosfa had also stayed behind with the main bulk of the army.

This was Rathe's proving ground, to show the men he was fit to lead them. If he died here, then his sister's and his father's hearts would break and the plan of the king to dispose of the threat to his throne would have succeeded.

He looked at the three generals that stood behind Kasnata; Avner, Shamgar and Yoav, all steady and unshaken by the mass of men bearing down on them. There was a small portion of Rathe's mind that believed that the three generals and the queen would have been able to defeat this small force with ease on their own.

"When they reach the line of trees, we charge." The dark angel called out and was gratified by the response of swords being drawn and bows being readied. "Archers, fire."

A flurry of arrows were loosed, the front rank of the Delmarian forces fell, but the rest of the army didn't falter as they trampled over the bodies of their fallen comrades.

"Charge!"

The warriors let forth a blood-chilling roar as they charged. The sound made the soldiers of Nosfa shudder slightly and say silent prayers of thanks that in this battle at least, they were the allies.

Rathe led his men forward, the ground beneath his feet seemed to be slowing his pace; there was a bitter taste in his mouth. The world around him seemed to have muted and slowed as he charged, moments of quiet before the crunch of man against shield sped up his world.

There was confusion all about him as he tried to fight an enemy that veered away from the warriors of the Order in favour of attacking the less seasoned troops of Nosfa. He could hear men screaming, screams of pain and terror, cries of despair and pain mingling with the terrifying noise the acting men of the hound, bear and wolf made.

To see them fighting was to see men unleashed, their efficiency and brutality unmatched by any on the field. As men raised their swords against Rathe they were cut down by others. So the general stood there, dazed and confused by the savagery that was unfolding around him.

"Majesty!" Avner called out to the queen as she danced her way across the battlefield. She moved with grace and poise that looked almost grotesque amongst the midst of such suffering. Men saw her approaching and knew why she was known as the dark angel, for death approached them with her, an unbidden shadow that shrouded her and her Ralenetia Estral.

She paused at the sound of the General of Hound calling her name. She thrust her sword forwards, the blade slipping between the ribs of a man that ran screaming towards her. He died as the blade passed clean through his body.

"Rest well." She whispered as the soldier of Delma died. She withdrew her blade so her crumpled to the floor. "What is it, Avner?" She enquired as she moved through the slaughter to the side of her general.

"I feel that the young pup might be in danger." Avner nodded towards where Rathe was stood, eyes glazed over.

"He may have been trained as a swordsman," She shaking her head.

"But he will end up dead if the Prince on that skittish gelding reaches him. As much as neither of us would want to save the life of a man so close to the snake you must call husband, I don't think we could live down the shame of a child so close to a yearling boasting of how he killed a nobleman before your eyes." Avner observed as he carved his way through three men that tried to launch past the general at the queen.

"Then I shall make sure he cannot boast." Kasnata sighed. Avner laughed as he watched her move to rescue the general of Nosfa. She moved with such speed it was a fright to behold by allies as much as enemies. She was almost silent in her movements too, so light was her step. The general felt it a shame that one so gifted in battle would feel so guilty about the blood she spilt.

Yoav saw the queen moving towards Rathe and ran beside her, keeping those that would hinder her from crossing her path.

Prince Jayden Delich was a proud and arrogant man. He had told his father that he would be able to defeat the forces of Nosfa and the Order without any need for him to send Lord DeLacey on a fool's errand. His father had agreed that he could lead his army against the forces of Queen Kasnata, but only in a skirmish.

So it was here that he would prove his worth to his father. He would defeat the barbarian queen and the men of the warmongering kingdom of Nosfa and be pronounced the hero and saviour of his people. He watched the battle unfolding before him, without engaging a single foe. He watched as his men fell at the hands of the enemy and cursed his father for not allowing him to bring more men.

He cast his eyes across the carnage and noticed the general of Nosfa stood all alone and dazed in the midst of the confusion. The prince saw his chance for glory and seized it. He cried out in victory, dug his heels into the sides of his horse and charged towards the stupefied general. Rathe could not see the danger before him and did not raise his blade. The prince shrieked with sheer delight as he saw the glory he felt he was due was within his grasp. He raised his sword and brought it down, a killing blow aimed at Rathe's neck.

Kasnata flinched as she dove between the blade of Prince Delich and Rathe's exposed neck. The sword cut deep into her arm as she pushed the general of Nosfa to the floor. Behind her Yoav rammed his spear upwards into the chest of the horse of Jayden. It reared and threw the prince from the saddle onto the solid ground below.

The sickening crunch of his neck breaking as he hit the ground was lost amidst the sound of sword on steel and stone. It was at this moment that the flanking force of Kasnata's army arrived. Renta and Tola bringing fresh men to the battle causing the men of Delma to be driven forward onto the swords of those that were blocking their escape.

Rathe was shaken back to reality by the queen throwing him to the ground. He heard her groan as she felt the hot, liquid stream of blood ebbing from the cut on her arm. She was lying on him still, seemingly oblivious to the presence of the general.

"Highness, are you alright?" He stammered as he tried to manoeuvre them both to a seated position. Around them the battle was ended. Cheers came from the victorious men and women, the greener troops of Nosfa crying with relief at having survived the ordeal. Yoav was talking to the horse that lay thrashing as it died from the spear thrust he had delivered to its chest. Avner and Shamgar embraced as brothers and let forth a great cry that only warriors could understand.

"If you are to lead these men in battle, then you stand beside them and you fight. If you ever freeze again on the battlefield, I will not be there to save you and neither will any of my people." She warned with eyes marked with hatred.

Rathe was stunned by the look she fixed him with, a disgust that registered below contempt. He nodded meekly at her as Renta walked over to help the queen to her feet and bandage her arm. Tola offered a hand to the general as the two women walked away without uttering another word.

"I'm not sure I am cut out for the field of battle." Rathe sighed as he accepted Tola's hand.

"Perhaps not, but it is not something that you have ever experienced before. It will get easier." Tola offered the general some reassurance.

"I hope so. I don't think I want to live through a second if I have to see that same look of loathing on her face." Rathe shook his head with disappointment at his reaction to being faced with the slaughter and carnage of battle.

"If it is any consolation, if she gives you that look a second time, she will honour you with a clean death." The hero of the war of the east shrugged and offered Rathe a consolatory smile. "Come, there will be some celebrating in the camp. You'll be so surprised at how much fun these barbarians can be when they've come out on top in a fight."

Chapter 9

The king sat in his private chambers, his mind was dwelling on the past, nursing his hatred of Kasnata.

Mercia's hatred of his wife was not unfounded. She had been little better than a barbarian when she had first arrived at his palace gates to aid him in the war against the people of Naladi. He had been desperate when he sent out the call for help, more desperate than anyone had known.

The Naladi people were threatening to lay siege to the city and force the city to surrender whilst his nobles were off gathering forces from the provinces to fight the war. It had been a matter of life and death for the king when he had welcomed the barbarian into his home.

She had arrived with arrogance and pride that the nine kingdoms had come to associate with the people of the Order. The lack of knowledge of customs of the court of Nosfa had offended most of the nobles and caused resentment to run through the court like a plague.

He had needed her people to ensure the survival of his kingdom, to allow him to keep his throne. His mother had advised him that the people of the Order were the only way peace could be achieved, but Mercia did not just want peace. He wanted a guarantee that his throne would be secure, that there would be none who could threaten to take it from him.

Peace was a pipe dream of fools like his father. There had always been wars, fights and skirmishes, even when the council had been unified there were still countries that fought against each other, only the council did not call it war.

The devotion of her entourage was something of a marvel though. Each member that accompanied her to court was clearly strong and skilled in warfare. They walked with a presence that caused the nobles of Nosfa that had not seen war to cower and shiver at the shadows of the warriors' of the Order passing over them.

When the king had spoken to her, her voice had excited him in a way he had never imagined possible and despite her barbarism, she was beautiful. He didn't love her, he wasn't sure that the emotion was even genuine and not just the flight of fancy implanted into his brain by his mother to ensure that the line of the blood of his father was continued.

When they married, he had expected that she would allow their kingdoms to be merged, for autonomy over the army of the Order to be handed over to his direct control, for the obedience of the warriors to their queen to be his.

This had not happened; she had remained independent of him and refused to allow her armies to be used as his arm of vengeance against his enemies. He hated her for that but until she had given birth to their children, he had no way to control her. His daughters had been the true blessing in finding a weakness he could exploit in his wife. He had no use for women in his line of succession were irrelevant. Grashindorph had never allowed for a woman to inherit the crown and Mercia would not change that.

He knew his wife loved her children and that in the Order it was her daughters that would inherit the title of queen once she passed. Without them, the Order would be leaderless and fall into civil war. The Valians would rise up and claim back the throne they felt had been usurped. So he held his daughters hostage to gain the power of the armies that his wife denied him.

Yet she still managed to defy him. She went to war, but her methods were not what he desired and the generals he had sent to spy and control her had all failed. She was too unruly, too proud and uncompromising. She was not a woman he could love.

The door to his chambers opened and brought him out of his

musing. A woman walked in quietly, her steps almost silent.

"Neesa, what did you find?" He asked of the woman as she settled down next to him.

"Your intelligence reports were correct. Kelmar was at the palace. He was after your daughters." The woman called Neesa spoke with silken tones. She leant her head upon the king's shoulder as she spoke and ran her fingers through his hair.

"I see. Was he successful in killing them?" He asked as he closed his eyes and enjoyed the woman's touch.

"No, I arrived before he was able to do so. They fled into the wilds. The forces of Delma continue to search for them and my own men are looking for them." She replied, kissing his cheek.

"I see, there is no doubt they will try to re-join their mother. You should have the roads to east and to Delma garrisoned. They haven't the training to cross the wilds." Mercia reasoned as he reached over and took Neesa into his arms.

"I have work to do, my king." She protested with a smile.

"It will take more than a few hours for Kelmar and our forces to discover where the barbarian's daughters are. The rest of the orders can wait until much later. Besides, I wish to have at least one night with you before I send you to keep Kelmar at bay. I don't care if he kills the two girls, but neither he nor any of his men should live to report about it to Delma." The king said as he rolled Neesa onto her back and pinned her to the floor.

"I understand, my king."

*****

Kasna awoke with a start, the world around her was light and she cursed herself for falling asleep. She yawned and looked around to see Kia was no longer lying beside her. She felt her heart leap in her throat.

"Kit? Kit?" She cried out frantically as she searched for her. The fire had long burnt out; the ashes hadn't been disturbed, not even by the light stirrings of the wind.

"I'm here, Nini." Kia replied as she appeared from the undergrowth that surrounded the clearing where the two girls had made camp the night before.

"Where did you go?" Kasna asked as she hugged her sister tight with relief.

"I heard noises of soldiers passing by. I went to see who it was; I thought it might have been the Abbott." She replied returning her sister's hug.

"You should have woken me; we could have gone to look together. What would have happened if it hadn't been him? What if it had been the enemy? What if they had captured you?" Kasna scolded her sister as she held the shoulders of the younger girl.

"I was careful. I'm far more skilled than you are when it comes to subterfuge, as you are well aware." Kia said pulling away.

"You idiot." Kasna sighed with resignation. "I take it, it wasn't the Abbott."

"No, it wasn't. It was a trade caravan." Kia said with a sly smile.

"It wasn't an ordinary trade caravan." A new voice entered the conversation. Both girls jumped as neither had heard the stranger approaching. They turned to see a man stood leaning casually against a tree. He wasn't dressed as a soldier, or a guard, he looked more like a farmer than anything else. Kasna had her hand on her blade as she stepped between him and her sister.

"And who are you?" The older of the two princess glowered at the man, shifting her feet to a defensive stance.

"My name is Mathias. I have met you once before, but you were but babes in arms." He smiled at the two girls warmly. Kasna frowned and cast her eyes backwards to Kia, who shook her head slightly.

"Any could make that claim and we would be unable to recall them." Kia said backing away towards the undergrowth.

"That is a fair assessment. There are many who would try to deceive you with such trickery, but I am not one of them. Of course I know that any of those who would deceive you would also say that. There can be no way to convince you that I am friend. You won't even know who Tola is." Mathias smiled to himself as he spoke. "Though I suppose I could tell you of how the Abbott came to see you, of what he promised to you if you were able to escape without his help."

Kasna relaxed her stance.

"What evidence do you have?" She asked with a raised eyebrow.

"Nothing but my word. I would ask that you trust me; after all, you were both asleep for a very long time during which I could have killed you. That should be enough to buy a little trust, maybe enough trust to allow me to escort you to my village?" He said taping his chin with a boyish grin.

He wasn't an old man by any stretch, in his mid-thirties with the shadow of his youth still clinging around his eyes and at the corners of his mouth.

"Where is your village?" Kia asked moving to stand beside her sister.

"To the east of her, the village of Roenca. It's on the way to your mother, so accompanying me won't take you out of your way and I may even prove a little useful in helping you avoid those that are coming after you." He said holding out his hand towards the girls.

"What makes you think anyone is coming after us?" Kasna asked with a slight snarl.

"The palace that you used to live in being attacked last night and all those within it killed. You, scolding your sister for going off alone; only small things but enough for a man who pays attention to reach the right conclusion. Come young princesses, you'll be getting hungry soon and there is nothing we can forage in this part of the woods."

*****

The warriors of the Order were lined up to welcome the victorious queen back to her camp. The colonels and commanders of Nosfa stood with austere looks on their faces, sneering down their noses at the mud and blood smeared forces as they returned, behind them the men cheered their comrades' bravery.

Rathe walked behind all the soldiers watching them, feeling ashamed that they had acquitted themselves so well in battle where he had failed. None of them looked at him any differently to how they had before, there was no whispering behind their hands or glances thrown in his direction and yet he could not shake the guilt he felt.

He looked over to where Kasnata walked. Her arm had been bandaged and the bleeding had stopped. She walked with pride etched on every feature of her face and yet there was a deep sadness lurking beneath it. The fire still burned in her eyes that he had seen when she had admonished him on the battlefield; hatred boiling in her soul.

Tola walked beside him, the long haired Roencian was silent as they marched. He hadn't said a word since they had left the battlefield. He knew that the queen was carrying burdens that she refused to share, but there was nothing he could do to ease those burdens currently. He looked at Renta. She walked at the head of the triumphant parade. She was flushed from the thrill of battle, the joy of victory coursing through her veins.

As Renta reached the centre of the camp she stopped, the rest of the warriors of the Order halting in unison. The soldiers of Nosfa watched with great interest, some knowing what was about to happen, others feeling the prickling excitement of anticipation. The warriors were silent, even those within the camp barely made a sound as they drew breath.

"Arala, cactesna ans col hesta. Loa dasmalda fei col fienesca. Arala, rolma mocda rist sangla, Kasnata!"[1] The members of the Order spoke with one voice and cheered as they finished. The ranks dissolved in celebration, the warriors left in the camp rushing to greet their friends that had survived. They embraced one another and saluted, their noise of jubilation growing louder by the second.

All celebrated save for Avner and Kasnata. Rathe watched as the two moved quietly towards the wagons that the soldiers of Nosfa were bringing in behind the army. The general saw there was nothing close to joy on either of their faces.

Avner pulled back the linen that covered the top of the wagons. Underneath it lay the bodies of the fallen soldiers from the forces of Nosfa and the Order alike. Kasnata stepped forward and took each body from the wagon in turn, carried them to the tent of the priestesses and priests of the religions of Nosfa and those of the goddess of the Order, Arala.

Avner stood guard by the wagons until all but the last body had been removed. Kasnata did not pick up the last corpse; instead Avner took him up into his arms and carried him to his own quarters. Rathe watched with a confused expression as he realised that the last body was that of Prince Jayden Delich.

"Tola, why is the general carrying the body of the Prince of Delma to his tent?" The general asked quietly.

"General Avner is the father of Queen Adina Delich; Prince Jayden was his grandson." Tola said as he looked away from Lord Bird.

"His grandson? Avner is going to war against his own family?" Rathe looked at the general of the Order of the Hound with confusion.

---

[1] Arala, grant us your favour. This glorious victory won for your favour. Arala, watch over and bless our queen, Kasnata!

"He loves his daughter. She married the king of Delma to bring peace between the Order and the kingdom of Delma, which worked until King Mercia decided that he wanted the lands of Delma. The king of Delma is a more proud man than any I have ever met. He sent a messenger to Kasnata telling her that he understood what was going to happen and told her that he forgave her for all the harm she would do him in warfare, as he hoped in turn that she would forgive him." The hero of the war of the east looked over to where Kasnata stood, her eyes fixed on the horizon.

"You know far more about the Order than I would have expected of anyone outside of her trusted people." Lord Bird looked at Tola with a raised eyebrow.

"Then there is much you don't know about me." Rathe's second-in-command shrugged. "Excuse me, sir, there is celebrating to do." Tola smiled and disappeared into the throng of celebrating warriors before Rathe could speak.

Rathe watched in amazement as the men of Nosfa that had been in battle joined with the warriors in the cheering and embracing. He heard music strike up, drums, horns, trumpets and strings; fires were lit, meat and drinks were brought from seemingly nowhere and dancing began.

He had never seen such dancing before. It was not like the stiff dancing of the court of Nosfa, but was an expression of joy without reservation. Rathe was hypnotised by the movements. The men spun, lifted and carried the women; their feet moved quickly, tapping out the beat that the drums played. Those that were not dancing clapped along to the rhythm, cheering at particularly exciting moments – girls being thrown into the air and caught again, men back-flipping over another. The general found himself drawn towards the festivities, as so many of the men of Nosfa who had not been in the skirmish were. Most had joined in the clapping; a handful that were brave enough had joined the dancing.

Tola and Renta were dancing close to the bonfire that stood at the centre of the dancing, the two skirting dangerously close to the flames. Some of the men not dancing had taken up staves, the ends coated in pitch; they held the ends into the smaller fires and began to perform intricate routines of skill with the weapons.

Avner was absent from the celebration, but all of Kasnata's other generals – Shamgar, Yoav, Marissa, Amalia, Kia, Hesla, Quisla, Misna – were at the heart of the dancing. Even forge master Benaiah was enjoying himself by throwing his wife, bowmistress Serra, around the fireside dance floor as throw she weighed no more than a feather.

The music changed from fast-paced to a slower, more rhythmic tune. The dancing changed almost instantly, none of those involved missing a beat. It was then that Rathe noticed the queen. She had moved through the crowd without attracting any attention. She had changed from her battle armour into silks that floated over the contours of her body.

Rathe watched as the other dancers moved to one side and left the floor open for the queen. She began to slide with slow purposive steps, her arms exaggerating every move she made, silk flowing in ribbons from her wrists and round the top of her arms.

"The dance of the dead."

Rathe looked to his right to see General Avner had emerged from his tent.

"I'm sorry, about your grandson." Lord Bird muttered.

"Thank you. He was an impetuous youth, he shouldn't have ridden to war, but he wanted to prove himself so much. I will not stay for most of the entertainment the festivities will provide, but this I could not miss." Avner said gruffly.

"What is the dance of the dead?" Rathe asked as he shifted his attention back to Kasnata's dancing.

"It is the dance that offers tribute to those who fell in battle, both on the side of our allies and that of our enemy. It offers absolution for those who have spilt blood, a release from guilt and a chance for friends and family to see their loved ones into paradise. That is why I had to be here." Avner spoke softly, the old man's eyes glistening with tears. As the two spoke, the generals that had been dancing stepped forwards and joined the queen in the dance. The movements repeated every sixteen bars, the speed grow with each repetition.

"Does the queen have to lead the dance?" The young general was mesmerized by the movement of the queen.

"No, there is no requirement for her to take part. Her father and mother never took part in the dance, but she, my dear lady, she holds the lives of people more dearly than any of our line. Her most high majesty, first of our blood, fire of our souls, she always leads the dance, even if she has been severely wounded, she still dances the first sixteen bars." The admiration for the queen was clear in the general's voice.

"She really is a great leader then?" Rathe said with a smile.

"She is. The next dance is the dance of the warrior, normally it would be me that would dance with the queen, but today I must prepare my grandson's body to be returned to my daughter and son-in-law. You should dance with her instead." Avner said with a smile.

"I don't think so. She looks at me with such hatred, especially after the battle. I disgraced my family and my country." Lord Bird shook his head in disgust.

"She doesn't hate you. If she did, she would not have saved you. She has let cowards and weaklings that her husband has sent before die in the most dishonourable circumstances. You have not yet done anything to place yourself in her bad graces. Dance with her, you'll see." Avner said with a wave of his hand. He pushed the young general forward into the mass of bodies that now danced. The music changed again, a song of drums and horns that stirred the blood.

Kasnata looked up as the music changed, expecting to see Avner moving towards her, but instead she saw him stood beyond the dancing. His face was pale, his eyes glassy with tears. He nodded to the queen with a smile and gestured to where Rathe stumbled through the mass of bodies that had begun the dance of the warrior. She smiled in acknowledgement and returned the nod.

"You should follow my lead." Kasnata said softly as she took Rathe by the hands. She closed her eyes for the briefest moment at the touch of his hands, the gentleness that she could sense there as well as the strength. It was a strange sensation, one she had never felt when Mercia had taken her hand.

"I have never done this before." Rathe mumbled trying to conceal his embarrassment.

"Don't worry, the steps are simple. Just don't trip over your feet." She smiled kindly.

Chapter 10

Jephthah and Layla had been rivals since the day the Abbott first brought Layla to serve Lady Hermia. The shadow and the shield. Both had been raised from birth for the task, giving up their freedoms for a life of service, a life of laying down all they had for the sake of one greater than they.

Before Layla's arrival, Hermia had never had a shadow before. She was a noble woman, born to a duke from a nation that had been destroyed by the war. Her mother was a woman that had been the childhood friend of Haston's father. Jephthah had been her sworn guardian as his father had before him, his family raised to serve as shield's to her father's house.

When Hermia had married, Jephthah had been at her side, protecting the queen as he had done when she was but a lady. Shadows were not used by the noble houses; they were not needed to protect any save the royal house.

Rosla had insisted that Hermia should be awarded her own shadow to protect her as well as her shield. For many years, Hermia had resisted, her strength of faith in Jephthah's abilities enough to sooth her husband's worries if all but temporarily.

It wasn't until the Abbott had arrived with Layla and presented her as the shadow to the queen that Hermia finally conceded. The Abbott was known as a man of great foresight, who knew more than any mortal should about the rising storms and trials that would sweep the land.

He would appear with tidings at the bleakest of hours, bring gifts that would seemingly be unimportant until days, weeks, months or even years later when their purpose would become clear. He would never speak directly of anything that would occur. He would not speak in riddles; it was almost as if he was there to prepare people for what was to come. He never gave instructions to be followed, but merely provided tools to be used as the recipient saw fit.

So when he had appeared with Layla, the wisdom of her arrival prevailed upon the queen.

Jephthah had been less than enthusiastic. He had treated the arrival of Layla as a personal affront to his dignity, a comment on his ability to protect and serve the mistress he had spent his whole life guarding.

Layla had been told of her duties in more detail than anyone knew. She had been told that she would have to protect the queen from many individuals, some of them she had been told by name and given the discretion to action to neutralise the threat they presented before it materialised or to wait and react to the course they chose.

Many men and women had disappeared in the kingdom over the years. Some at the hands of the king, some at the hands of the desert folk, so none would attribute another disappearance to the hands of Layla or the name of the queen.

The shadow had never revealed to any what she had chosen to do and the extent of the protection she had provided the queen. A good shadow was one that was never seen to work, a good shadow managed to maintain the peace of the household and the happiness of a kingdom.

She was aware that Jephthah found her presence intrusive. On the day she had arrived he had made it clear that if she betrayed the queen or allowed any harm to come to her, then he would make his vengeance against her swift and all those that she held dear. It was a threat that had never concerned Layla. She knew her duty and was more prepared to carry it out than the shield knew.

In protecting the queen, their paths rarely crossed. Jephthah was the public face of her protection, intimidating those who held grudges against the crowd by snarling and displays of strength in competitions.

Layla would move through the people, listening for mentions of the queen, threats and thoughts that would lead to actions. She spread rumour and propaganda to the people. She kept her eyes and her ears open in the palace. She trusted no one. Not even the king.

For the shadow and shield to work together was something of a precedent. It would require concessions on both parties' parts and had it not been the Lady Hermia asking them to, it would have been an impossible feat.

"Have you ever looked for a mole before?" Layla asked innocently as the two sat in the hall of the Gibborim.

It was a tunnel that contained tables and chairs, a bar and musical instruments; for all intents and purposes it was the banqueting hall, the assembly chamber and the inn combined into one.

Around the two agents of Hermia the daily life of the Gibborim buzzed. Men called to one another, drinking pints of mead and ales that they brewed themselves in the tunnels that ran beneath the hall. It was not a brew that could match those that the larger breweries of the city created, but for the outlawed men and women of the Gibborim, it was the best they could hope for.

Women moved between the tables call out to one another, trying to find the material for the latest patterns they had traded with one another. Children played with toys, games of adventure, leaping across table tops and spilling the mead and ale under foot. Food was carried in and out by those that had gone hunting in the desert and forest to the south of the city; having used the older tunnels to go under the walls and avoid detection.

"No, this is not the work of a shield. It is the work of a shadow, the work that should have already been done. No mole should be allowed to exist in such a place." Jephthah snarled at Layla. She sneered in response and subtly knocked the table, so the tankard of mead that Jephthah was about to place upon it, missed and spilt across the floor. "Woman, you'll pay for that."

Layla grinned and flicked a coin at the shield.

"That should more than cover it."

Jephthah reached for his behemoth blade and swung it in a smooth motion at the shadow. Layla, expecting the retaliation flipped backwards, her body spiralling gracefully through the air with ease, avoiding the reach of the giant man's sword.

"Wench!" He shouted. The shadow grinned in response, raising her eyebrows and flicking her gaze around the assembled people.

It wasn't uncommon for fights to break out within the Gibborim hall, in fact during the later hours of the day the fights were common place as drunkards picked meaningless battles with each other.

It was well known throughout the Gibborim that Layla and Jephthah were not the best of friends. Their rivalry had led to violent outbreaks on more than one occasion, but normally these altercations were fist fights. To see Jephthah with a drawn sword in a public place was unheard of.

Layla hadn't drawn her daggers, instead she crouched, her body tense and ready to react to the slightest movement that Jephthah made. She looked like a cat waiting to pounce. Her every breath seemed measured as she judged the next movements that the shield would make.

"Someone got out of bed on the wrong side this morning." She teased him with a patronising smile.

"I've been waiting for so many years to do this." He growled with satisfaction.

"Waiting for what? To be embarrassed by a woman in public? I thought that would have happened on more than one occasion. After all

I've met your wife and daughters." The shadow laughed. Jephthah roared and launched himself towards where Layla was crouched. She giggled with glee at the chance to fight and easily dodged his attack. "Temper, temper."

"My sword is going to wipe the arrogance right off your face!" The shield swung his sword and cleaved through the table that Layla had landed on after his last attack. "Stay still you stupid woman."

"Why? I like my blood and flesh where it is. If I stay still you'll rearrange it all, not to mention make more of a mess than you already are." The shadow shrugged as she taunted the shield.

People screamed as the fight between the two servants of Hermia escalated. Some of the children had started crying, mothers ran to them to move them out of the path of destruction Jephthah was carving.

Layla was evading the strikes of the shield's blade without breaking a sweat, her ability to predict the man mountain's every move seemed uncanny to any watching, but it was merely a matter of timing as far as she was concerned.

Outside of the Gibborim hall, the noise of the fight could be clearly heard. Helez and Asahel were sat engaged in a game of chess that had taken the two men three days to play so far; neither man was willing to give ground and concede defeat.

"Sirs, you must come quickly something terrible is happening!" Bracha, Jephthah's wife, shrieked as she came running from the hall in search of the two men.

She was a stout woman, not easily given over to panicking, but both men had known her to shriek over the smaller boys of the underground trying to steal her apple pies. She was good natured and highly maternal; not a man under the age of thirty didn't think of her as their mother in the underground world they had created.

"What is it?" Asahel asked as he looked up at the woman he

respected almost as much as the Lady Hermia.

"Jephthah, he's fighting Layla. The two of them are tearing about the Gibborim hall." She gasped with genuine fear grasping her eyes.

Without a word, Helez and Asahel leapt to their feet and abandoned their game. They ran through the tunnels, Bracha shouting after them, but what she was calling out, neither man could hear.

"What can they be thinking?" Helez growled to his friend. Asahel shrugged in response and shook his head,

"I doubt either of them is thinking much of anything. We should send word to Hermia; we may not be able to stop them." The older of the two men thought as he looked around for someone who could help them.

People were crowding outside the hall, most too afraid of getting caught in the crossfire to step inside. Helez and Asahel fought their way through the throng. As they moved forward, Helez saw his sister, Ilana, trying to fight her way forward too.

"Ilana, go find Hermia, tell her to come." Helez shouted and waved his sister away.

"No, brother, I will not run off as a messenger when I can do things to stop others from being injured." Her pale blues eyes flared at her older brother's suggestion.

She was a slight in figure as he was broad. Their sandy hair and bright blue eyes they held in common, a trait that was unusual in the people of Grashindorph. Ilana was only a head shorter than her brother, taller than most of the women of the kingdom.

Helez always felt that though his sister was blessed with some extraordinary traits, beauty was not one of them. Her face was squashed and fixed in a permanent pout, but she was barely fourteen and there was time for her face to fill out and for the childish pout to be replaced.

"Ilana, do as you're told for once!" Asahel shouted as he reached the front of the crowd. He scowled at the young girl's obstinate attitude. The girl squeaked at the look that the darker skinned man gave her and nodded meekly before disappearing the opposite way through the crowd.

"She's still in love with you then." Helez said wearily, shaking his head in mock despair. He was fifteen years the senior of his sister and Asahel was another four beyond him. He knew his dark eyed and white haired brother-in-arms didn't return Ilana's affections, but this did not discourage her from following the poor Asahel around the tunnels and often into darkened corners that had to be fled from with some speed.

"She'll leave it alone soon enough, when the boys her own age begin to mature, you'll have to chase them away from her with as many weapons as you can carry." Asahel assured his friend.

The two men entered the Gibborim hall to see half the tables had been reduced to splinters. Groups of people cowered in corners, ducking at every loud noise and scurrying away the moment Layla and Jephthah got too close.

Layla had still not drawn her daggers; her face told the two shield warriors that she was clearly enjoying the challenge of avoiding Jephthah's attacks. The man mountain was swinging wildly, cursing and charging with reckless abandon. At least that is how it appeared.

Helez shot Asahel a side glance, who nodded in response. Both men had spent years being trained by Jephthah and afterwards, fighting beside him. They knew his fighting style, they knew the difference between controlled movements and when he had given himself over to his rage.

What both could see before them was not the effect of bloodlust or wrath, it was controlled, every movement calculated. Each step he took was planned; his blade was the perfect extension of his arm, there were no gaps in his defence, no opening for Layla to use to counter attack.

"Well I'll be." Asahel said in wonder.

"I never thought I'd live to see the day when they'd work together. I don't know what they are working on, but my my, that is some show they have created." Helez sounded genuinely amused.

"Well I hope they realise, they'll be the ones clearing up all this mess." The darker skinned man whispered. The two laughed and went in search of some unbroken furniture they could use to view the spectacle of shield vs. shadow until Hermia arrived.

*****

The sun had set on the forward camp of the Order and the men of Nosfa. The colonels and commanders that had stood apart from the celebrations had returned to the quarters, most assumed to rest, but Yoav saw a much more sinister purpose to their early departure.

The general of the Order of the Wolf was suspicious by nature. He had seen more than his fair share of betrayal in his years fighting in both Jadow's army and now in Kasnata's. It was said that he had seen the darkest secrets that the soul of a person can possess and become so hardened and cynical that no act of depravity could shock or surprise him.

In truth, his cynicism was little more than harbouring distrust for those around him, protecting his battered old heart from the pain of betrayal this late in life.

He had trained all of the men in his camp to place loyalty to their queen and to those they fought beside above all else. He taught the by rule of the pack, any that chose to go against their brothers would be exiled by them. Training with men of such devotion meant that it was easy for Yoav to see spineless treachery in others.

He saw it in the colonels and commanders of Nosfa as they slunk away from the festivities and snuck through the night. These actions were not the actions of men that could be trusted. So he followed them. His ears pricked to the slightest sound around him, his eyes scanning for shadows and movement in the poor light.

*****

The watch of the Order had not abandoned their posts around the camp as the celebration of the victory had begun; indeed extra warriors had come forward to fill the gaps that were left in the defence of the camp by the soldiers of Nosfa finding the fireside, dancing, food and drink more appealing than century duty.

They stood tall, their focus on protecting those that had fought and won for the glory of their queen and the Order. The sounds of merriment were filtered out, all distraction were. It had been Queen Tsmara that had trained those that stood watch; it had been her desire to create a safe camp for those that fought for and beside her that had led to the creation of the almost unshakable watch.

They were not warriors that belonged to any specific division; they were not commanded by any of the generals, but instead reported directly to the queen. In battle they were the entourage of Kasnata, her personal guards; that would try in vain to keep her from harm. More often than not, the queen would lead the charge into the worst of the fighting leaving the watch to follow and try to keep up.

It was a long standing joke within the Order that the queen needed so many guards because she was infinitely more reckless when faced with an enemy than any of her line had been before her. In truth it had been the last command Queen Tsmara had given to her warriors of the watch before she had died.

"Look after my daughter. Her path will be marked with far more danger, subterfuge and treachery than any since Princess Ina."

The queen's words had shocked all of the watch. Princess Ina had been murdered by her older sister, Valia, who had been driven mad by bloodlust. Ina and her older sister Dana had been held hostage by Valia because she believed the rest of her family was plotting against her. Valia had murdered her infant sister in full view of her father, brothers, sisters and her grandfather, Queteria.

It had been this that had sparked the civil war that had spilt the Order into the faithful and the Valians. Valia was defeated and her sister Mala became queen; Kasnata's great, great grandmother.

The wounds were still raw that one of the Order could treat an innocent child so violently. Dana had died at the hands of Valia as she tried to take vengeance the instant the traitor had taken the life of their youngest sibling. Their names were rarely spoken of because of the pain it caused.

The watch held it as a sacred duty above all others to protect the life of their queen who was to suffer so much for the sake of their people, so they stood with pride, not begrudging their brethren the merriment they now indulged in.

*****

More wood was heaped on the fires. Those that had remained behind at the camp whilst Kasnata had led a small contingent to battle had employed their time by preparing for the evening, for the celebration of a victory that was to be won.

Foraging parties had been dispatched to gather five times the amount of wood, three times the amount of water and six times the amount of meat that the camp would need on any other night.

It wasn't arrogance or certainty of victory that made those of the Order who had not ridden to battle go to such extravagant lengths, but rather a hope that it would be a celebration; not a funeral procession that returned to camp.

No words had been spoken regarding the skirmish since the contingent of warriors had left first left camp. No worries were shared, no doubt was allowed to linger. The men of Nosfa had spoken of nothing else.

The small number of veterans amongst the soldiers told tales of past battles, of friends they had lost, of loved ones left behind. Some wished their comrades would not return; the commanders Mercia had placed to report back to him upon General Bird's death were amongst those wishing death upon their countrymen.

The soldiers thought the warriors cold and unfeeling for ignoring the battle being fought. The warriors felt the soldiers callous and cruel to wish to live in the pain of others whilst men and women were dying on the battlefield. It was this that caused tension to fall in the camp.

Shaul and Methanlan had not left the soldiers of Nosfa known as Jack and Harry since their first meeting. Their orders had been to remain with them until Kasnata wished to see them. Shaul had sat and listened by the fireside, saying nothing during the discussions of past battles. Harry had reminisced with Methanlan about the past battles they had shared, listing names of faces they had never seen again.

Shaul could see the comfort the men around him took in the stories, that their names would not be forgotten by their friends if they did fall to the enemy. But the Queterian could not shake the feeling that the men sitting around waiting whilst there was work to be done was disrespectful to those that fought. That their brothers-in-arms would return, exhausted from battle, and yet have work to do before they could rest.

His mind wandered to thoughts of those he served with in the Order of the Bear, to General Shamgar. The tiny man that was more ferocious than a man of twice his size. He carried a claymore that in the hands of any other man his size would have been comical.

Shaul smiled inspite of himself at the memory of the first time he had met the general. It had been a few years ago, the new recruits had lined up for inspection after they had completed the training to join the Order of the Bear. Only the legend of Shamgar was known to the men, so when they first saw him, many of the men had laughed, some had made an attempt to hide it, but all laughter had died when the general had attacked.

All those that laughed lay on the ground, groaning within a blink of an eye. It had been a sharp lesson in humility.

He taught his men to not trust appearances, to judge their enemy on his ability not what he or she looked like. Methanlan and Shaul had learned these lessons best of all. It was for this reason that Kasnata chose them to infiltrate the ranks of allies and trusted them to report all that they found.

The awkward feeling Shaul felt had remained until Renta had appeared on the horizon leading the army contingent and Shaul had spotted General Shamgar marching amongst the throng.

He didn't like the sense of fear or relief that the thoughts of General Shamgar had brought, he had glanced at Methanlan and was gratified to see the same emotions reflected in the eyes of his friend.

This is going to be harder than I thought.

Chapter 11

The dancing did not stop after the sun had set. The dance of victory had followed that of the warrior. It differed from the others as the men and women of the Order danced separately, only uniting as one upon the last beat.

Rathe found something exciting and intoxicating about the experience. He had danced with the queen for only the dance of the warrior. He'd never imagined that a people that were so competent engaging in war could be capable of such beautiful expression of soul.

Seeing Shamgar, Serra, Amalia and Benaiah celebrating, allowing themselves to drop the severe expressions he had seen them wearing was enough to make the young lord feel at ease amongst these people.

He was not the only one. More of the men of Nosfa were joining in the dancing, forsaking observing from the edge. As the dance of victory had ended, the generals had left the floor and the young warriors took the centre stage. There were no other formal dances to be done, but instead it was a time when the thankful joy each felt at having survived another battle could embrace it fully.

Some of the married couples retired early, to spend what remained of the night lost in one another, glad that they had lived to hold each other again. Kasnata had been dragged back to dance after only a few moments break; her people eager to see their queen enjoying herself after she had won her victory.

It was hard for her, she wished more than anything to be able to quietly depart and go to Avner, to comfort her stalwart friend in his grief. She knew the general did not blame her for the death of Prince Jayden but the queen still felt responsible for it.

She had intended to capture the prince and send him back to his father alive to sue for peace, but that would not happen now. There had been only a handful of men left of the Delmarian forces by the time they had surrendered that were now kept by the watch.

The watch guarded the prisoners, fed them and protected them from any retribution drunk soldiers tried to take for their fallen comrades. There had been a small number of casualties on the side of the Order; most were injuries that could be treated on the field.

Sixteen warriors had died. Their friends and family now attending them; preparing them for the funeral pyre that would mark the end of the celebrations the following morning.

Two hundred of the men of Nosfa had fallen and four hundred had been injured and treated. A handful of them had developed fevers and there was doubt that they would live to see the dawn. The healers of the Order had advised that they not be confined to beds, but instead allowed to experience the merriment that belonged to them as much as it did to any other in the camp.

It was an odd mix of feelings. Rathe had never imagined that war would be so complicated and did not want to know how it felt to carry guilt of having killed someone added to what he already felt; but he knew that he would. It was kill or be killed.

As his thoughts wandered he found his eyes drawn back to the queen. He smiled absent-mindedly as he wanted her dance. There was an honesty in the emotions she expressed as she moved, a release, possibly her only release, for everything she had to hold inside; everything she had to keep hidden in order to lead her people.

He blushed as he thought back to how it had been to dance with her, to feel her heart pounding, her breathing laboured with exertion, the heat of her body close to his. He understood why Mercia had once desired her as a woman. She was unique, complicated, intelligent in ways that Rathe had never realised a woman could be.

He had spent his life surrounded by the stupid women of court, their minds consumed with finding a wealth husband, advancing their position in life, the gossip of court and fashion. Of all things he had heard talk of, fashion was the one that Rathe never wanted to hear of again.

He was sure that his mother had never been so shallow and was certain that his sister was not. But he was without them both now. He shook his head as thoughts of exile began to encroach on his thoughts of the queen.

Kasnata could feel his eyes watching her. It was something she had developed as a warrior, the sense of knowing when you are being watched. Goosebumps rose on her flesh and her cheeks flushed. Had it not been for the effort of dancing, she was sure it would have been noticeable.

She caught Amalia's eye as they met and span together down an alley created by the men. The general smiled at her queen, a smile that told Kasnata Amalia knew the queen was being watched so intensely and the queen was enjoying the attention.

Kasnata raised her eyebrow slightly in response and the two danced apart. It hadn't been since her youth that she had felt so lost in her emotions when it came to a man. Even in the early days of her courtship with Mercia, he had never brought feelings of excitement to her heart in the same way that Rathe watching her did now.

Whether these feelings were enhanced by the danger she knew surrounded the general, the queen could not tell. But what she was sure of was that the risk to her children was not worth indulging her own desires for him.

The watch sounded a deep horn. It blasted four times. The dancing members of the Order all parted around the queen, making way for her to depart.

Rathe looked confused as a rotund man with rosy cheeks collapsed next to him.

"Ah, young general!" He exclaimed with delight. "I'm Oswin, swordmaster of the Order." He cried embracing Rathe as though he had known him all his life.

"Swordmaster?" Rathe asked, only half-listening to what the older man was saying.

"Ah, I should have thought, I am a man that trains all those born of our blood to use swords and other weapons. Some of our techniques are extremely complicated, our people their whole lives learning them. Even King Jadow spent hours every day improving what he knew about the art." Oswin said proudly beaming.

"I see." The general replied, still watching the queen.

"Visitors have arrived." Oswin said with a knowing smile.

"Excuse me?" The general said, giving his full attention to the swordmaster for the first time.

"The horns sounded the arrival of visitors to the camp. The watch keep them outside the camp until the queen has given them permission to enter." Oswin replied taking a swig from the tankard he clutched in his left hand.

"Who would be visiting the camp?" Rathe asked as the dancing resumed.

"There are several people who often ask for permission to enter, on this occasion it is likely that it is envoys from Delma requesting the release of prisoners and the return of the prince's body." The swordmaster sighed.

"Why is it that we did not require leave to enter the camp when we arrived?" The general asked.

"You were not visitors. Your arrival was expected and you were followed from the moment you entered the camp until you met with the queen. There are many protocols that are involved in a camp that is as large as this one; I doubt you will ever discover all of them." Oswin said with a knowing smile.

*****

Kasnata walked through the camp without an escort. There was no need of one. She reached the watch commander, who saluted and led the queen to where the visitors awaited.

It was a small group, mostly children. All of them were dressed in little better than rags and looked half-starved. The oldest one of their number was barely sixteen and badly injured.

"Majesty, they say they are from the village of Ashpa, to the south of Olney." The sergeant reported as Kasnata approached.

"Have they said what happened there?" The queen asked, keeping her eyes of the children.

"Yes, highness. They say that the forces of Delma rode through their lands and burnt their village. They did not want to leave it standing as a free city to offer aid to our forces." The sergeant said with a sad look in her eye.

"Have you sent a force to scout for the village?" The queen replied.

"Yes, my queen." The watch commander said, dismissing the sergeant.

"Very well, take the injured ones to the healers. Assign a small guard to keep them there until they are healed. The rest need feeding, from what I hear, it's three days walk from here to Ashpa. Send four of the watch to escort them. Find them beds and we shall see what can be done when the scouts return." Kasnata ordered. The watch sprang to work without a word. "Keep them out of sight of the funeral pyre, that is not something any of them need to see if their village has been destroyed." She said quietly to the watch commander.

"Yes, highness, we will do what we can." The watch commander agreed with a stern expression. "No child should have to witness such destruction."

"Too many have seen it these last years." Kasnata agreed.

*****

Tola and Renta lay in each other's arms. They could hear the music and noise of the festivities faintly from the corner of the camp they had retreated to. Renta's quarters were too close to the fires, so they had stolen away to Tola's on the far side of the Nosfa encampment.

"We should go back soon." Renta sighed happily as she lay listening to the beat of Tola's heart inside his chest. It was a comforting sound to her, one she had missed in the time they had spent apart.

"We have time yet; there are four hours yet before the pyre needs to be built." Tola replied kissing the top of her head. He rested his on hers and closed his eyes. It was rare to find a woman that could understand his life so completely and make no demands of him.

The feel of her skin had not changed, nor had the sensations he felt when he made love to her. The same desire for the touch of her lips on his, the same need to have her, to hold her. The same desperation to possess her completely for fear that the next moment they would be apart again.

"We will be missed if we are away too long." Renta argued as she let her fingers explore the familiar contours of his belly and legs.

"Let them miss us." Tola half-moaned as he felt the surge of desire rising again.

"You will find yourself in trouble with your superiors." Renta warned as she encouraged him with her fingers and lips.

"They can kill me if they deem it necessary." He struggled to draw breath as he grabbed hold of the woman and rolled her onto her back. He felt her fingers dig into his flesh, pulling him closer to her, raking at his back as he ravished her. He felt her teeth against his neck, the soft groans urging him to continue.

Renta pushed herself against Tola, gasping moaning, she could feel one of the Roencian's hands controlling the movement of her hips, moving them in time with his. The other was in her hair, his arm around her back keeping her body pulled in close to his.

She felt her passion for him growing with every passing second, his grunting gave rise to more pleasure. She knew what he enjoyed and desired in her without him having to articulate it. Her lips searched hungrily for his and when they met, she rolled him onto his back, their bodies not parting for even a heartbeat.

Their union was the only thing she wanted. Whenever there was war, battle, she knew she would see him, allow herself to be drawn into his bed. It was dangerous for them both. The king had decreed it to be treason for any of the men of Nosfa to fraternise with those of the Order. But she knew Tola did not care.

He had been her first and only lover. He had begged her on many occasions to marry him, but she had refused. Her heart had longed for her to agree, but she would not sign his death warrant but her consent. Their encounters could be smoothed over and a punishment less severe awarded to him if they were discovered, but marriage did not afford such leniency.

She had never dared to ask Tola if there were other women. She did not want to know, could not face knowing. She didn't feel jealousy when she saw the women of the caravans that followed the army of Nosfa trying to seduce him. She blocked out those emotions. She knew that if he died in battle whilst she harboured any feelings of resentment towards him, it would torture her for the rest of her days. So instead she chose to love him, trust him and enjoy what they had.

*****

Yoav suspicions were not unfounded. The colonels and commanders of the men of Nosfa had not retired to their beds. Instead they sat in the tent of the lieutenants.

"He didn't die." The canvas of the tent was too thick to discern faces, only silhouettes cast by the single torch they held.

"No. I was certain he would." Yoav crept as close to the tents as he could without making those inside aware of his presence.

"Some of the men say he froze during the attack, that he was a sitting duck and the queen interfered."

"She saved him?"

"Prince Jayden was bearing down on him and would have cleaved his head from his shoulders, but the barbarian knocked him to the ground and one of the others killed the prince's horse."

"The prince was thrown from the saddle and broke his neck." The conspirators' voices were low, but Yoav could discern seven different voices.

"The king will be disappointed."

"It can't be helped, but it being the queen that saved him; that at least holds promise."

"Yes, we'll report to the king and see what he wishes us to do. If needs be, we can ensure his death at the hands of the barbarians."

"You mean we have her violated and present the general as the guilty party?"

"Yes, they would believe us; to them we'd have no reason to lie about it."

"The way he has been looking at her, the way he danced with her. It is believable he would forcibly take what she would not freely give."

"True. Is there anyone of a similar enough height and weight that would do it?"

"There are two. If we are agreed on it, I can speak to them tonight. The deed can be done by morning."

"Do it. The sooner the general is the dead, the better."

Yoav resisted the urge he felt to slice through the fabric of the tent and slaughter all those that sat inside. Instead he crept silently back away from the conspirators' meeting place and went in search of the queen to warn her and the men and women of the watch.

*****

Avner sat in prayer for the soul of his grandson. He had spent many hours choosing what he would say to his daughter and son-in-law about his death. He had considered offering them his life in exchange for the one that was taken, but asking a daughter to take the life of her father was as grotesque to Avner as taking the life of grandson had been.

Yoav spear had killed the horse that threw him, but it had been Avner suggesting the queen save General Bird that had led to the spear. He knew soldiers died in battle, that warriors would not live forever and that death in battle was an honour over time ravaging the body; but still he had never wished to see it happen to any of his line.

He felt the cool air of the night across his neck as the flap to his tent opened and closed again.

"Good evening, majesty." He said without opening his eyes.

"General." She returned with a half-smile. She moved to sit beside him and chose her words carefully before she spoke. "I cannot say that his death is shameful. We both know what happens in war. But I am sorry that it was my doing. I would have given anything to spare you this."

Avner felt tears begin to stream down his face.

"The fault is not yours, highness. Nor is it Yoav's. The burden of his death falls to me. It was I that saw the general was in danger and suggested that it be you that rescue him. Had I done it myself, Jayden would not have charged. He would have lived." The general of the Order of the Hound sobbed.

"You cannot know that. A stray arrow, his horse being spooked, anything could have caused his death in that place. You were not to know that this was the consequence of your warning. You should not bear this sorrow in your heart." Kasnata soothed earnestly.

"Thank you, highness." He said with a slight smile.

"One day, you may actually believe what I have told you. I have made arrangements for use to deliver the body to the queen. She expects us in four days at the four pillars." The queen said patting the general's arm. "We shall be a small party, but he shall reach her safely. We depart when the funeral pyre has burnt to ashes."

Avner nodded, not trusting himself to speak. He was grateful to the queen for her kindness and her mercy to his family. He could still remember the days when his daughter had taught the young queen how to throw a spear when on horseback; the irony of the memory not lost in the rose tint of history.

"I shall leave you to your grief. Though, you are expected to light the pyre. Until sunrise." Kasnata bade him goodnight without waiting for him to respond.

She stepped back out into the night and smiled to herself. The sounds of the merriment were a welcome contrast to the tears that Avner shed over his departed kin, though she could not shake the feeling of sadness that rested in her soul. It was an oppressive feeling; one that could be masked with smiles and laughter, but in quiet moments would show itself without bidding.

"How is he?"

The queen turned to see Rathe stood not far from her. His face held the same guilt over Jayden's death as she felt in the pit of her stomach.

"He grieves for one he loved and takes all blame upon himself. He would not have you, Yoav or I shoulder the burden of Jayden's death." She said gently, offering him a smile.

"I would like to offer him my apologies." Rathe stuttered slightly, feeling the colour in his cheeks rise at the kindness in the queen's voice.

"He will accept them, but not tonight. When he has sought forgiveness from his daughter, then I shall take you to speak with him." Kasnata's tone was firm but no less kind.

"Thank you." He said, bowing slightly. The two stood there in an awkward silence. Neither one could bring themselves to turn away from the other. So they remained, as two statues, unmoved by the breeze that carried the sound of laughter to their ears.

Kasnata closed her eyes and tried to picture the faces of her children, to summon the memories of their voices to her mind, to remind her what she risked if she did anything to displease her husband.

Rathe could see the conflict swirling inside the queen and felt the same in himself. His sister's life was at stake if he angered Mercia, and yet part of him didn't care. Part of him only cared that he had found a woman more interesting than anyone he had ever met and he wanted to know more.

"My queen, I would never do anything to cause you pain, to disgrace you in anyway." He blurted out, the words feeling clumsy as they passed his lips. Kasnata opened her eyes and looked at the young Lord with surprise. She tilted her head as she regarded him, not sure of why he had spoken.

"I am your queen." She said softly, sadness pouring from her.

"It is my place to serve you." He stated rushing forward to kneel at her feet.

"You are a bold man." The queen spoke as she tilted his chin upwards so she could look into Rathe's eyes.

"I offer you my apologies for my behaviour today. It was inexcusable to react so in the face of the enemy. I beg your forgiveness and that you would grant me the honour of continuing to serve you, in whatever way you see fit." There was desperation in his voice and eyes, a pleading not to be parted from her.

"You have been forgiven and your plea is granted." Kasnata smiled warmly, though her eyes were still wreathed in sorrow.

"You were injured because I failed to act, because I was too weak." He chided himself and looked away from the woman.

Kasnata dropped to one knee and placed her hands upon his shoulders.

"Whatever action was or was not taken, injuries in battle occur. I long ago accepted this. I may not have been born of Nosfa, but I am its queen and if I can save the life of even one person in forfeiting my own, I would gladly do so." She said with conviction.

"Is battle always so horrifying?" Rathe asked in a small voice, looking back at the queen with hope.

"Yes and more so. Those that take pleasure in it often find even more grotesque ways of inflicting pain on those they call enemy."

Rathe could see the ghosts of many battles haunting the queen. Though she was well practised in warfare, it was evident to the general that she found no joy in it. Her hands still rested on his shoulders, the touch of them was reassuring to the general.

Tentatively Rathe reached out for her, his arms encircling her waist. He expected her to withdraw, to find her hands moving to stop his, for her to question him. But she did not. She offered no resistance as he drew her into his arms, hers moving to encircle his neck.

The two knelt in the darkness, holding the other silently. Neither wanted the other to let go.

"Your sister is in danger?" The queen whispered in his ear. He could feel her lips moving and her breath softly caressing his skin.

"Yes." He breathed into her neck, the sensation causing the queen to shudder slightly. "Your children are hostages?"

"They are." Kasnata felt tears begin to fall as she spoke. Rathe could feel her body trembling as she sobbed and so held her tighter. He felt her pulling away and so released her. To his surprise, she did not pull away, merely moved so he could hold her to his chest as she cried. He rested his head upon hers and held her until her crying ceased.

"I'm sorry." She breathed and pulled away from Rathe's chest.

"What for?" He asked as he released her.

"I should not have wept." Kasnata shook her head and wiped her tears from her eyes.

"Have you ever cried about it before? Your children, I mean." Rathe shifted his weight so he moved from his knees to sit on the ground and stare up at the stars.

"No." She admitted as she sat back on her haunches.

"Then you have no need to apologise to me." The two fell silent again. The queen stared at the ground in front of her, the general focusing his attention on the sky.

"Thank you." The dark angel muttered after a few minutes had passed.

"You are welcome. Can I ask you something?" Rathe asked tentatively.

"Yes, though I cannot promise I will answer." Kasnata said candidly.

"Why did you save me from Prince Jayden?" The general let the question hang in the air without an answer for a few moments before he began to shift nervously.

"Avner saw you were in need of help." The queen shrugged without looking up.

"The general asked you to save me?" Rathe frowned.

"No, he made several rational points as to why I may want to save your life." Kasnata smiled to herself and chuckled slightly.

"And these rational points are what convinced you?" He pursed his lips and lay back crossing his arms behind his head.

"Rationality is not something I can admit to possessing when on the battlefield. If I had been rational I would have let you die. A man who does not fight on the battlefield causes the death of men that try to protect him. If you do not find the will to fight from somewhere, you will be as useful to me as the spineless oafs that my husband has sent to spy on me in the past. Rationality was the last cause of my actions, if it had any influence at all." The queen sighed.

"I see." The general sounded indifferent to her response.

Kasnata looked up and studied him as he stared at the night sky. She wasn't entirely convinced that he wasn't a spy. Tola's opinion of him was undecided, and that spoke more to him being a man that was out of favour with the king rather than him being a spy.

His lack of experience on the battlefield told the dark angel that he was nothing more than a spoilt noble of the court. Most of them had never seen battle. There were a handful of generals that knew about war, but they had all served under King Rosla and Mercia did not trust them. They had advised him against war, against expanding his lands, against senseless fighting. Mercia had taken this as cowardice, doubt in his leadership; the poisonous beginnings of a threat to his position as king.

They had all served with Haston Bird, friends, brothers-in-arms, a bond that Mercia was convinced was deeper than their loyalty to the crown. He had removed Haston from his position as general as one of the first acts as king, isolating the next in line for the throne as much as he could from any military power.

Two of his veteran generals had been killed in the war of the east and most that had remained had retired, unwilling to take part in war when their advice was cast aside so easily.

So the lesser sons of the noble houses were sent to command armies with no experience of battle, no knowledge of how to lead men. Their main orders had been to monitor the queen, to report back all that they could about her treason against Nosfa.

The true control of the troops belonged to the colonels and commanders of the men of Nosfa; soldiers that had made their careers in battle. Kasnata could not remember the last battle in which one of Mercia's generals had fought before Rathe had arrived.

He was an oddity that she found herself trusting, despite any reservations she had from her first meeting with him.

"Is that why you were so angry?" Rathe asked rolling onto his side to look at the queen.

"No. I was angry because you had no business being in battle if you were not going to fight. Much like Prince Jayden had no business being in battle. His arrogance and lack of experience caused the deaths of most of his men and his own." The queen said frowning.

"The only way to gain experience is to be in battles." The general countered.

"You need to find someone to teach you if you really want to learn to be better in command." Kasnata said as she stood up. "I should be returning to the celebration. There is only so long before my absence cannot be explained by greeting camp visitors." The queen excused herself and left the general on the ground thinking about how strange life had become.

Chapter 12

As dawn approached a group of warriors left the fire side and walked to the edge of the camp where they started to build the funeral pyre. A typical funeral pyre stood at sixteen feet wide, sixteen feet deep and six feet high. It was built like a lean to with a floor of wood that was three feet deep. The bodies of the dead were carried inside of the structure before it was lit and laid at the centre.

It was set alight by torch bearers that were led by General Avner. The High Priestess of Arala then led prayers for the dead until the pyre had burnt to ashes. This marked the end of the battle celebrations and the normal routine of the camp would recommence.

Renta supervised its construction, after she had lost her sister in battle a few years before; she had ensured that she was the one that oversaw the creation of the funeral pyres. Tola had gone in search of General Rathe as he had not been seen for a few hours.

The dancing still continued. The battle stamina that the warriors possessed put to good use in sustaining them through the many hours of dancing. Benaiah and Serra had taken over leading the dancer when Kasnata had departed.

Yoav had returned to the fireside to discover his queen absent. He saw Oswin and Shamgar sat drinking and made towards them. The two men were laughing raucously, the ale in their tankards being flung over the ground.

"You better be more sober than you look." The general of the Order of the Wolf barked at his friends as he approached.

"Yoav! Where have you been? There is drinking to be done and you, my friend, are far behind!" Oswin laughed as he stood and gave Yoav a giant bear hug, his tankard spilling what remained of his ale down the Yoav's back.

"You fool." Yoav scolded him, pushing Oswin off him and slapping the swordmaster.

"What has put you in such a bad temper?" Shamgar asked as he inspected what remained in his tankard.

"Conspiracy. Where is General Bird?" Yoav asked; his normal sense of humour absent.

"Somewhere in camp. He was here when the queen went to greet the visitors the watch were holding, but I've not seen him since." Oswin shrugged and tried to drink from his empty tankard. Finding it empty he threw it aside and made to take Shamgar's from him.

"You'll need to be faster than that!" Shamgar roared as he dodge Oswin's clumsy attempt at thievery with ease. "What conspiracy, Yoav? You're beginning to get suspicious in your old age."

"Beginning? Wolfblood has been suspicious since the day he first crawled howling out of his mother." Oswin laughed and slapped Yoav on the back.

"The snake, his loyal men are planning to attack the queen and blame it on General Bird so that our people will lynch him." Yoav growled, his yellow teeth barring at the idea.

"So Wolfblood has been following our not so trusted allies about the camp again." Shamgar sighed as he drained his mug and threw it aside. He stood and yawned. "Well what do you suggest that we do?"

"Tear the blaggards to pieces!" Oswin shouted, fumbling as he tried to draw his sword.

"The queen will be safe enough, when she has met with the visitors she will be back to the fireside. The general on the other hand, should have one of us with him at all times." Yoav smiled at Shamgar, who nodded. Oswin let go of the hilt of his blade and it slid back into its scabbard.

"Not one of our people who call us liars if we vouch for the general's lack of involvement in any attack on our dark angel." Shamgar agreed.

"Then what are we waiting for? Time to find the general!" Oswin yelled and charged off into the camp.

"Does he know that Lord Bird went that way?" Yoav asked as he watched the swordmaster running off through the crowd that was still celebrating.

"No." Shamgar said with a wry smile. "He went that way." The general of the Order of the Bear pointed in the opposite direction to the one Oswin had run in.

"Then that is the way we should go." Yoav sighed and shook his head at Oswin as the swordmaster disappeared from sight.

*****

Tola found the general before Shamgar, Yoav and Oswin did. Oswin had run round in circles for twenty minutes and then forgotten what it was he had been running in circles for. He had sat back down at the fireside and found more to drink before falling into a light slumber.

Shamgar and Yoav had disappeared from the fireside just before Kasnata and Rathe returned.

Tola had left Renta to her work on the funeral pyre and found the general sat at the side of one of the smaller fires.

"You seem sullen." Tola observed as he came to sit beside the general.

"The queen thinks I have no place on the battlefield without anyone to learn to lead from." He sighed as he stoked the campfire with a larger piece of unburned wood.

"You haven't grown up in war; it is not unreasonable to think you could benefit from being taught about battlefield leadership." Tola shrugged.

"Who would be able to teach me? None of the commanders of Mercia's army have that ability, nor would they want to see me gain any influence over the troops."

Tola sank deep into thought. Kasnata would not teach the general, she had enough to worry about without adding an apprentice in warfare to those burdens. Marissa, general of the Phoenix division was a possibility but it had been several years since Tola had held an amicable conversation with her. Amalia was not just the general of the Kestrel division but aide and bodyguard to the queen, though no one had ever officially given her either position.

Renta would teach Rathe if Tola asked, but command of the cavalry of the Order was very different to any other position of command throughout Celadmore. Quisla as the general of the Vulture division was in charge of the main force, but with such a large group under her command, Tola feared Rathe would become lost amongst their number.

The fire crackled as his thoughts were disturbed by approaching footsteps.

"A merry search through the camp we have had trying to find you young pups and here you are back where we started!" Shamgar laughed as he sat down next to Tola.

"A lesson in waiting before acting could be learnt from this, you haven't seen Oswin have you?" Yoav asked as he sat beside Rathe.

"No, he is probably lying drunk somewhere." Tola shrugged with a smile. "Why have you been looking for us?"

"That is a long story of deceit, corruption and treachery that would take too long to tell." Yoav said thrusting his hands towards the fire to warm them.

"And a man who is far too suspicious for his own good." Shamgar whispered to Tola so Yoav could not hear him.

"I see. By happy coincidence, I have something that I would ask one of you." Tola said slowly.

"Oh? What favour do you need now? How have you offended our wonderful female generals this time?" Shamgar yawned.

"For once, I haven't offended them. I've only really seen Renta so I couldn't have affronted them all." Tola said, feigning offence.

"Are you being chased by assassins?" Yoav asked with a weary tone.

"That only happen once and that was only because they thought I was someone else." Tola said with indignance.

Rathe listened to the three men around him. The two Queterian generals teasing Tola told him that there were many times the hero of the east had fought beside these men, bled with them, mourned with them. He was treated almost as if he were one of their own. It did not seem to be a courtesy that was extended to him due to his relationship with Renta, but rather an honour he had won.

"It's happened at least three times that I know of!" Shamgar said clapping Tola on the back.

"Anna and Cara asking Misna to send her troops after me doesn't count!" Tola half-shouted with exasperation.

"Anna is the swordmistress, Cara I the horsemistress and General Misna is the head of the Kasnata's infiltrators and assassins." Yoav whispered to Rathe when he noticed a brief look of confusion flutter over the young general's face.

"And I thought trying to remember all the different lieutenants in King Mercia's army was hard enough." Rathe replied in an equally quiet voice. Yoav laughed in response.

There was a warm and friendly atmosphere between the four men, despite Tola suspecting that the two generals of the Order joining them was not something they had done out of a need to strengthen ties of friendship.

"The queen has told General Rathe that he would benefit from being taught how to lead on the battlefield." Tola explained, cutting off Yoav and Shamgar before they could bait him again.

"Has she now?" Shamgar said with a strange expression on his face. "How interesting." He was no longer paying any attention to Tola but focusing it instead on Rathe, who shifted uncomfortably under the small man's gaze.

"She has, but there is no one suitable within our own ranks to teach him." Tola replied innocently.

"What a pity." Shamgar's tone suggested he thought the exact opposite. He shifted his eyes to Yoav who nodded ever so slightly.

"What do you think you are more like, boy, a bear or a wolf?" Yoav asked clamping his hand on Rathe's shoulder.

The young general looked at Tola, who had begun to innocently whistle and look anywhere but in Rathe's direction. Shamgar was smiling, his eyes shining with excitement and an edge of an emotion that Rathe couldn't name, but looked like menace.

"A wolf." Lord Bird stuttered slowly.

"Aha ha!" Yoav slapped Rathe so hard on the back that the young general fell forward onto his knees. Shamgar's face had fallen in disappointment.

"You cheated." The small man accused Yoav with glaring eyes.

"How could I cheat? It's the boy's preference! I'm sure we will find him in need of gaining some invaluable experience fighting beside you though Cave Dweller." Yoav teased his friend and comrade.

"Go howl at the moon Wolfblood." Shamgar growled.

"You are more like a wolf? Well time shall tell. You'll be learning from me boy, or should I say pup. You'll spend every moment at my side that I tell you to and only when I am done with you can you crawl into your bed and nowhere else. You'll stay away from those awful caravans that follow your army too. Are we clear?" Yoav asked hauling Rathe to his feet.

"Yes, wait, I'm learning from you?" Rathe couldn't quite believe his ears.

"That you are, pup. And from this point onwards, you'll call me sir or Wolfblood." Yoav ordered.

"You'll have to learn to speak our language too, can't spend all day repeating ourselves. We'll start now and find you a teacher who can spend their evenings teaching you when we aren't training you." Shamgar grunted, still unhappy that the young general wasn't going to be training in the Order of the Bear.

"You're right, Cave Dweller, remember these two words – sir is remento and Wolfblood is Camhelta." Yoav said steering Rathe away from the fire.

"Lady, where are you taking me?" Rathe asked, his tongue tripping over the unfamiliar word remento and coming out as remen instead.

"Many a man has died for calling me a lady, pup. You should also know Camsa too, that's your name now after all." Yoav said pushing the general ahead of him. Rathe blushed slightly at his mistake. "Remento not remen."

"Sir, where are we going?" Rathe tried again.

"We are going to the funeral, pup. It's as important to understand the effect that battle has on the lives of those that survive it as much as how to act during them." Yoav explained. Tola and Shamgar had stood and started to follow the two men.

"Why were you, Oswin and Wolfblood looking for us?" Tola asked Shamgar in a low voice.

"We weren't looking for you, just the general." Shamgar replied in the same pitch. Tola stood dead in his tracks and stared at the small man.

"What happened?" The hero of the east's lips had drawn themselves into a thin line; his eyes betrayed fear and every muscle in his body had tightened.

"The commanders below you, they are all picked by the king, correct?" Shamgar asked stopping a few steps ahead of Tola.

"They are." The Roencian confirmed; his stomach sinking as he spoke.

"Do you trust any of them?" Cave Dweller asked.

"No." Tola said with realisation starting to creep over him.

"Then keep your guard up. I am not sure how safe you will be when I tell you what we know." Shamgar said; all traces of his humour gone as he began to explain what Yoav had overheard.

*****

Avner did not miss the funeral pyre.

Renta had completed the pyre with time to spare and spent the remainder of the celebrations sat in silent prayer for her sister. As the light of dawn began to leak into the ink black of the night sky, people began to filter down from the fireside to stand vigil around the pyre.

When the last notes of music had played, those that had retired from the celebration returned to witness the closing of the festivities, only the watch and the colonels and commanders of the men of Nosfa were absent.

Rathe stood beside Yoav, Tola and Shamgar behind them. Tola could feel his heart pounding in his chest, his eyes not moving from where Kasnata would appear at any moment. The mixed crowd of soldiers and warriors were waiting in silence. No one dared to breathe as they waited for the sun to rise from its bed.

The moment it had stirred, Kasnata appeared flanked by twelve warriors bearing torches. Behind them was a procession that was formed by the families and closest friends of the fallen carrying their loved ones to the pyre. By the pyre there stood four men holding the structure of wood that would be placed over the door into the pyre before it was lit.

Wolfblood explained the importance of the ceremony to the young general as it unfolded, the history of the Order and how the customs of the celebrations had developed.

The queen reached the pyre and stepped to one side. She raised her voice and began to sing, a sad song that seemed designed to rip out the heart of even the most hardened person.

Rathe could feel tears beginning to fall down his cheeks as he listened, even though he could not understand what she sang.

"Let them be laid down, let them find their rest. They have warred for long enough, they have earned their place. Let your hand guide their way, let their feet carry them true. They are weary from battle, they have shed their blood. Let them be laid down, let them find their rest. Let the honour guard ride out to welcome them in, let the gates be flung open, let them come home. Let them be laid down, let them find their rest. They have warred for long enough, they have earned their place. Let your hand guide their way, let their feet carry them true. They are weary from battle, they have shed their blood. Let them be laid down, let them find their rest." Her voice was haunting, the rhythm she sang in slow.

As she reached what Rathe assumed was the end of the song, the bodies of the fallen were brought forward by the families. The voices of all the warriors of the Order were lifted to sing.

Some of the men of Nosfa were moved for tears, some burst into laughter they couldn't supress, the shock and depth of the emotion being shown through the singing making it impossible for the soldiers to control their reactions.

The song was repeated with differing harmonies until the last of the family and friends of the dead had emerged from the pyres. Kasnata stepped forward and drew her sword.

"We live by the will of Arala, we die by the sword. Let those we give to her flames be welcomed into her arms and find peace." She said loudly, her voice echoing across the crowd causing some of those gathered to shiver. The torch bearers stepped forward, led by Avner. They knelt as a unit around the pyre at equal intervals and placed the torches against the pyre.

"By the will of Arala, by the will of fire." They said in unison as they stood and stepped back from the pyre, fire already spreading across the structure.

The High Priestess stepped forward to stand beside the queen and began to pray. She led the prayers until the last of the fire had been extinguished. As the flames died, the warriors of the Order silently turned away from the ashes and moved to go about their daily tasks.

Avner waited for the queen to join him before he stepped away from the burnt out pyre.

"Let us depart." She said gently as she took Avner's arm.

Chapter 13

Ariella was a member of the Order. She had been born to a pair of very well thought of warriors. Her father was an aide to King Jadow and her mother had been a weaponsmith, but they had both died because of Queen Kasnata.

They had been amongst the first to die when Kasnata had married Mercia and been sent to fight on his behalf and Ariella bore a grudge against the queen for this. Had she not been so foolish in marrying a man to try and bring about peace then her parents would still be alive.

It had been during her grief that she had been recruited to the Valians. It was not because she felt that the line of Valia were the true rulers of the Order, it was because she hated the queen and wanted to see her suffer for her mistakes.

She had begged the Valians to allow her to assassinate the queen, but they had refused and asked her to work with one who was far more patient that she was. She was ordered to bide her time, wait until the time was right, until all had been prepared. It had taken all her restraint to do so, but she was now so close to her reward.

She walked through the camp of the Order, a smile she couldn't supress was spread across her lips.

"Ma'am, you sent for me." She saluted as she stepped inside the tent of the woman she had been told to report to by the Valian that recruited her.

"The queen will be away from the camp for several days, if not a few weeks. Whist she is gone her dogs will be less vigilant. With the refugees in the camp we also have the advantage of blame for strange occurrences being easily passed to them. We have time to accelerate our plans and place you in a position where you can remove her. Her daughters are in no position to take the throne and so the power will be passed to one who is respected by all and seen to be the logical choice to guard her throne until her daughters can take it." Eagle General Hesla turned from the maps she was studying to face Ariella.

She had a nasty expression of malice fixed on her sharp features, her red hair pulled back into a high ponytail. She was known throughout the Order for her steadfast support of the queen, that her loyalty to the crown was unflinching.

"You think they will appoint you as steward?" Ariella asked, not wanting to take anything for granted.

"Yes. They will. There is no one else they can be sure will not decide they should keep the throne for themselves. As soon as they name me steward I shall hand the throne to the line of Valia, then the true heirs shall have taken the Order back from the usurpers." She spat with satisfaction.

"Then I shall get to work." Ariella bowed and stepped back out of the Eagle general's tent. She needed to move closer to the queen, to have access to her without arousing the suspicions of Kasnata or of Raven General Misna and Kestrel General Amalia.

It was not an easy task, but it was possible. Acting as an emissary between the commanders of Nosfa and the queen was the most obvious role she could take and gain the access she required in a short space of time. What made this even easier was the rumour that was circling the camp; a rumour that General Shamgar was looking for someone to teach the language of the Order to the general of the men of Nosfa.

Ariella now had permission to take action, so she moved through the camp looking for General Shamgar and hoping that no one else had volunteered for the task.

*****

Rathe was exhausted. He had never had to work so hard in his life as he did under the command of General Yoav. He had begun by testing the abilities of Rathe by presenting him to swordmaster Oswin, horsemaster Horace and bowmaster Wist.

The three masters had put the young lord through the most rigorous feats of skill that Rathe had never imagined could possibly have existed. By the end of each test he could barely stand and yet each of the masters had barely broken a sweat.

Yoav had found it entertaining for reasons that Rathe could not understand. When the tests had been completed, Yoav had put Lord Bird in charge of all the menial chores that the Order of the Wolf had to complete in the camp. Rathe could not see the benefit of becoming the servant of the warriors, but he dare not question the general in case he sent the young lord back to the three masters for more testing.

Shamgar was his constant companion in the evenings, barking instructions at him in the language of the Order, trying, somewhat unsuccessfully, to teach him the basics of communication.

All this had afforded Lord Bird little sleep in the few days that Kasnata had been away from the camp. Tola had taken over the duties that Rathe had been neglecting during his training with Yoav, but made sure he informed his commanding officer of everything he needed to know.

Tola had just finished reporting to Rathe when Shamgar had arrived for their nightly teaching session.

"I have some good news for you, pup." Cave Dweller barked as a greeting as he entered without waiting for Rathe's permission.

"You do?" The young lord yawned.

"This will be the last night that you and I are to go through this hellish exercise." Shamgar said with more relief than he intended.

"Why?" Rathe said with a similar amount of relief.

"Because you are to have a new teacher. Ariella came and

volunteered for the thankless task today. I was only too happy to let her have the job. So let's get on with this last tortuous evening and be glad that we'll be free of each other tomorrow." Shamgar said gruffly.

*****

The journey to the four pillars was a slow but uneventful journey. Avner rode beside the wagon that carried his grandson's body, Kasnata next to him. There were six other warriors that had been chosen by the general to accompany them to the meeting.

There would be no trouble from the Delmarian forces whilst they carried the body of Prince Jayden. Most bandits had been driven out of the area by the threat of being caught between the two armies. The six other warriors presence was more for appearances sake than for safety.

The party had been silent as they travelled, the sombre nature of their current task weighing heavily on each of them. It had started raining two days before and there was no place to find shelter from the downpour between the camp and the four pillars.

On the fourth day they reached the four pillars and found the heralds of Adina, Queen if Delma waiting for them. Through the rain, on the far side of the four pillars, the travellers from the Order could see a pavilion had been erected and a group of twenty or so soldiers were crowded around the makeshift throne at its centre.

"Hold here." The herald instructed as the warriors approached.

"Herald, be warned, this is my grandson and that is my daughter, I will not be delayed if you are here to question my honour." Avner warned with a growl.

"You are enemies of my kingdom, protocol must be observed." The herald said without a hint of fear.

"Your entourage will wait here, only the queen and the general may approach with the body of our prince. Then the price of his death will be agreed upon." He was not a large man, nor old. Avner did not know what it was this that made the herald so foolish as to talk down to warriors after two days of journeying in the rain, but he was not going to allow the insult to his queen or his honour stand in such a place.

In a single fluid motion Avner drew his blade and brought it arcing down through the herald's neck. The head of the herald slipped from his shoulders and bounced across the ground, his neck spraying arterial blood over the queen and general.

"I am glad to see diplomacy isn't dead." Kasnata said dryly as she nudged her horse, Red Hare, forward; Red Hare delicately picking his way over the corpse of the herald.

"I apologise for the mess, your majesty." Avner said wiping his blade.

"That is quite alright, Dog of War, it is always good to intimidate the enemy at parlay." The queen smiled as she focused her attention on the pavilion in front of them.

"Just remember that the enemy here is my daughter and one who trained you as a girl, my queen." Avner cautioned the dark angel as he sheathed his sword.

"She has been a palace brat too long, old friend, she has gone too soft feeding on food that she has not had to hunt, not having to dress herself or train. I would be very surprised if she even knew how to hold a sword now." Kasnata said with some disgust.

"You think she has changed that much?" Avner asked as his horse, Just Nuisance, caught up to Red Hare.

"When was the last time you saw her?" Kasnata asked, not shifting her eyes from the pavilion.

"When Jayden was born. I've been fighting these pointless wars since then." Dog of War said with a slight amount of regret.

"When you last saw her, did she travel with a pavilion and an armed guard of twenty men?" The dark angel was calculating the average age of the men surrounding the queen of Delma as they drew nearer.

Behind the general and queen, the six warriors and wagon were following. None of them had even flinched at the sight of the herald having his head parted from his body. A few had been surprised that the general had made the death so painless for the young upstart, but they had other business to attend to at present that did not include teaching manners to the enemy soldiers.

"No, she didn't." Avner admitted.

"Did she have a spineless herald stand to greet the enemy and issue pathetic demands to warriors that have fought more battles than he has seen years?" The queen continued her questions in tones growing quieter as the passed the first of the four pillars.

"No." Dog of War smiled.

"We hold here. Make camp. Here we stay until they come forward. They have made several mistakes, the worst of which belongs to Adina." Kasnata ordered with a wry smile.

The six warriors saluted and silently went about the business of creating camp. Avner laughed and sat down beside the wagon.

"She made the mistake of sending a herald?" He asked of his queen with amusement.

"She made the mistake of going soft and insulting her father." Kasnata said smiling down at the general.

"So you'll make her come out in the rain and meet between the second and third pillar?" Dog of War grinned, showing his yellowing teeth.

"I'll make her kneel in the mud and beg forgiveness if I have to." The queen shrugged. "She has grown too proud, you could see it in her son and her country will burn and die because of that pride. If she can learn some humility, then maybe, just maybe some of the people of Delma can be saved from the fires of war."

"You would never let your people die without a fight. She is merely doing what she thinks is right." Avner said trying to bait the queen.

"I married a man to stop war and now we have warred almost constantly since that day. If I would not let my people die without a fight, Mercia would be cold in the ground and my children would be alongside him. I have made many mistakes in my life, dear one, but I will not give up hope that each day I cannot wake up and save my people, the people of Nosfa and all the other peoples of Celadmore from this hell that man has created for himself." The dark angel spoke with passion and fire that she rarely let shine through her impenetrable emotional defences.

"And you will start this day with my daughter, because she should know better?" The general asked lightly.

"Yes."

The six warriors worked tireless so that the camp was set within two hours of the groups' arrival at the four pillars. The eight of the party sat around the fire once the foraging had been done and shared stories of home, of life and of love.

Kasnata sat and listened silently to her people talking. She never told stories at the campfire, just sat and listened to the voices of her people, smiling at the joy they had, the safety they lived in and certainty they felt. Certainty in her leadership, certainty in freedom and certainty in victory.

The rain didn't stop for days.

The warriors of the Order didn't care; they had lived in far worse conditions for far longer than a few days. The Delmarian queen and her men were as soft as Kasnata expected. They could not hunt or forage what they needed, the men were little better than palace guards.

After two days of sitting in the rain under a pavilion that was not water tight, without food or space to lie down and sleep, the mood of the

Delmarian's was not a happy one. The corpse of Prince Jayden was sat in the rain, crows trying to tear through the sheet that covered it to get to the flesh beneath.

After four days, Queen Adina walked forward and waited between the second and third pillar. She walked out the moment the sun rose and stood there. Kasnata smiled to herself at the sight of the queen and then ignored her.

All day Queen Adina stood there in the pouring rain, her men cowering and mewing under the pavilion, wanting to return to the comfort of the city of Delma. As evening fell, Kasnata and Avner approached where Adina stood.

"Your arrogance has not diminished." Adina spat at Kasnata as she reached where the queen of Delma had waited for hours in the rain. She was shivering, her clothes soaked and the chill of the northern wind digging into her bones.

"You'll speak with a civil tongue, girl." Avner warned his daughter.

"You no longer have the right to talk to me like that." Adina scowled at her father.

"Do you know the history of this place?" Kasnata asked brightly, her head tilted up so the rain ran down her face, her eyes closed and her lips parted slightly to catch the water.

"What?" Adina snapped at the warrior queen.

"The four pillars. Do you know why they were built?" Kasnata asked again, her tone still light.

"No, and I fail to see -" Adina began but was cut off by the dark angel raising her hand.

"The four pillars were built when there were only four kingdoms. The rest of the land was divided into tiny settlements, the people not yet ready to step out of their villages to see cities. The four kingdoms had been at war, but famine and drought were causing all of the kingdoms to die. They couldn't continue to fight against each other anymore so the kings and queens all met here. It was the central point of neutral ground that none of the kingdoms owned." Kasnata explained. She started to walk over to where the pillars were.

The pillars where circular discs of black stone that were stacked to create pillars. Each had a crest carved into it at roughly eye height. The crests all looked slightly different, but they were worn down now so whatever they once looked like, they were now little more than curved lines in a random pattern.

"They met here and brokered peace. They promised each other that they would never raise war against one another as long as these pillars stood. We call it the four pillars, but they called it the Spire. There was a monk that was asked to bear witness to the peace and he was appointed the guardian of this place. To show they all agreed to hold the peace they carved their kingdom crests into the pillars." Kasnata smiled as she stroked her fingers over the crest of the second pillar.

"What does this have to do with me?" Adina asked, her patience worn thin after little food, sleep and standing for hours in the rain.

"Delma was one of the nations to agree to the peace. It was Delma, Nosfa, Vasknar and Zin." The dark angel said sadly and sighed as turned back to face Adina.

"So why are Nosfa attacking Delma now?" The queen asked impatiently.

"Because it was Delma that broke the peace, they attacked and destroyed Zin. Not a trace of the kingdom is left save for the crest carved on the second pillar." Avner growled.

"It was Delma who broke the peace, Delma that forsook it's oath to maintain the peace. It was greed and arrogance that drove them. Be careful you do not sacrifice your men for your own pride and greed." Kasnata warned. She signalled to the six warriors to bring the wagon forward and present the body of her son to the queen.

"Break camp." The queen of the Order commanded.

"Where is his horse?" Adina demanded.

"Dead. His horse threw him, that's what killed him." Kasnata didn't even look at Adina as she spoke.

"You still have to answer for his death and the murder of my herald." Adina tried to grab for Kasnata's arm. Avner was quicker than his daughter; he reached out and seized her by the wrist, pulling her round to face him.

"I spent all of the celebration of victory praying for and mourning the loss of my grandson. I came here prepared to offer my life in penance for his death to my daughter who I imagined would be heart broken. Instead I arrive here to find the girl I raised is no more. Here stands the Queen of Delma, a spoilt palace brat. It is no wonder your sound was so arrogant. He was no general. He had no reason to be on that battlefield. He is dead because he was stupid and as arrogant as you have become.

"You sent a herald to greet your father bringing you the body of your son. You demanded a price for life of a man killed in war from your father and the queen of the people you were born of. You have disgraced me; you have disgraced your mother." Avner paused as he tried not to let his emotions overwhelm him.

"You cannot talk to me like this, I am not a child." Adina spat in the general's face as she wrenched her arm free.

"No, you are a queen now, not a child any longer. At least you are not my child any longer." Avner said with anger burning in his eyes.

"Avner…" Kasnata tried to stem the words of Dog of War, but he would not be pacified.

"Adina, you can no longer call me father, and your mother is no longer yours to call by name. You have made where you stand perfectly clear." The general turned away from his daughter and walked back to where Just Nuisance stood pawing at the ground with his hoof.

"Run back to your city, Adina. Bury your son. We will see you there soon enough." The dark angel followed in the footsteps of the general. The camp was being packed away faster than it had been erected.

Adina stood there watching the people she had once called family as they got onto their horses and rode away. The twenty men she had brought with her had not stirred from underneath the pavilion that merely strained the rain now. She looked at the pillars and felt a chill run down her spine and thought, for the first time about the future of the people of Delma.

*****

Ariella was a much better teacher when it came to the language of the Order than Shamgar was. In eight days she had managed to teach Rathe the basics of the language.

He was pleased with his progress and that Ariella was his teacher, for no other reason than she was not Shamgar. Yoav was bad enough to suffer under during the day, but having to be tortured by Shamgar at night had almost been too much.

"You should try and practise on the men you spend your days with." Ariella encouraged him as she readied to leave him for the night.

"I'm not quite ready to face that kind of ridicule." Rathe half laughed.

"You have learnt more than you think." She assured him.

Horns sounded outside in the camp.

"Visitors?" Rathe asked as he saw a brief frown flicker across

Ariella's face.

"No, the queen is back." She replied with a forced smile.

"I see, then I should go and greet her." The general stood and walked past the Valian into the camp.

There was a lot of movement for the late hour. Many had been stirred from their beds by the sounding of the queen's return and were hurrying through the camp to greet her.

Rathe decided to wait for her in her tent rather than joining the throng that would be milling around her from the edge of the camp until she retired.

He found it odd that such a large number of people would gladly stir from their beds to greet their leader. In Nosfa none of the people would rise to greet a returning lord or even the king if he was arriving after they had gone to bed. He chuckled to himself at the thought of it as he ducked inside Kasnata's tent.

"Most people would ask permission before entering."

Rathe nearly cried out with surprise at the sound of Kasnata's voice.

"How are you here? You just arrived, the horns…" Confusion was etched on Rathe's face.

"I arrived an hour or so ago. The horns are the general returning with the guard sent with us. I came back earlier because a messenger found us on the road." Kasnata was sat at the small desk in her tent. She was not dressed in her armour but instead in loose silks that fell in layers over her body.

"A messenger?"

"Yes, he was sent by my husband. With the news he brought, I felt it best to return here quickly." Kasnata said indicating that Rathe should sit at one of the chairs that stood a short distance from her.

"Is it your children?" Rathe asked with concern as he sat.

"No, he makes no mention of them." She said quietly. "Rathe, your father was killed by a bandit attack as he was taking the road home between Grashindorph and Afdanic." Kasnata said gently.

Rathe stared unblinking at the queen.

"No." He said flatly shaking his head. "That can't be. You're wrong." He drew breath sharply and bit into his lip.

"My lord." Kasnata spoke softly as she moved from her chair to kneel in front of the general. She reached out and took his hands in hers.

"He can't be dead." He said stubbornly as tears began to roll down his cheeks.

"He is. I'm sorry." The queen let the general fall forwards into her arms as he began to cry. She rocked him as she comforted him, his denials slowly being replaced by his weeping.

Rathe buried his head in her shoulder as he mourned his father. He wasn't even aware it was the barbarian queen that held him; he was so consumed with grief. Thoughts rolled around in his head. What would happen to his sister now his father was dead, what would happen to him, what would happen to Afdanic and the Ivory tower.

For half an hour he wept as Kasnata held him, the queen not tiring of his grief. It took half an hour for the shock to fade, for Rathe to regain control of his thoughts and realise that he has clinging tightly to the queen as she soothed him.

"I'm sorry, my lady." He said without thinking as he drew back from her. Kasnata was struck dumb by his knowledge of her language she blinked at him, speechless.

"You know my tongue?" She asked in disbelief. Rathe looked as surprised as Kasnata had, then nodded slowly.

"A little. Wolfblood has ordered that I learn it whilst he is teaching me to lead on the battlefield." He offered the explanation as he dried his face of the tears that had been there.

"I see." Kasnata said with a half-smile. "Who has been teaching you?" She seemed amused at the prospect.

"Shamgar did to begin with but a girl named Ariella has taken over."

"I am glad that my people are taking such care of you." The queen said as she rose to her feet. "And he wants you to call him Wolfblood." She sounded entertained but Rathe made no comment on it. "You have no need to be sorry, though."

"I don't?" The general had never known a monarch of any people to allow their subjects to touch them, let alone collapse into their arms to be comforted in grief.

"You have lost your father; your grief is necessary and understandable. What kind of heartless monster do you think me to be to not allow for that?" She asked sounding hurt.

"I don't think you are a monster." Rathe blurted out quickly. "I think you are nothing like any other ruler in this realm, that you are far more caring and understanding than most people let alone leaders. You are not at all like you are reported to be." He blushed deep crimson and let his voice trail off as his thoughts caught up with his speech.

"Thank you. I think you should rest; you have had a terrible shock today. If any other messengers arrive I will wake you, but for now, return to your tent and sleep." She said gently without looking at the general.

"Yes, you're right. Thank you, your majesty." Rathe bowed and left Kasnata's tent.

Chapter 14

The scouts that had been sent to Ashpa had returned a few hours before Kasnata had. They reported to Amalia that the village was as the children had described. The general had passed the information to the queen, who had granted the children leave to stay in camp until arrangements could be made for them.

The queen retired to bed dismissing all other reports until she had rested. She was used to travelling, to making camp and sleeping in less than ideal circumstances; but there was something that was comforting about sleeping within the walls of her tent amongst the furs that comprised her bed. She always seemed to sleep better amongst her furs, even than she did in her bed on Anamoore.

The moment she laid her head down and wrapped the furs about her body she would drift off to sleep. It was rarely a deep sleep, her senses sharper than most even when she was sleeping, but there were nights when exhaustion would have her sink into a slumber she would not easily wake from.

The first that she knew anyone else was in her tent was the sensation of weight pressing down on her body. She opened her eyes to find a figure pinning her down, his breath hot on her neck.

She didn't scream. Instead she flung her bodyweight to one side, the surprise at the unexpected movement caused the figure to roll off the queen and lose his grip on her wrists.

The queen did not wait for the man to recover. She sprang to her feet and sped to where her sword hung as she slept. She drew it from its scabbard and turned to face the figure. After a moment of deliberation, the figure ran from her tent, the risk of her skewering him not worth the reward.

Kasnata breathed heavily as she dropped her sword. She felt the surge of adrenaline coursing through her veins, causing her heart to pound and her hands to shake. It had been a long time since she had felt that way, not since the first night that Mercia had taken her against her will.

There had been nothing that she could do then, she had been lucky this time, he had not expected her to wake up when she did, nor had he realised that she was awake when she did stir.

She waited until her breathing had returned to normal before she picked up her cloak, threw it around her shoulders and walked out into the night to find the watch commander.

It did not take long for the watch commander to organise a camp search for the man that had tried to force himself on the queen. None amongst the Order had any information for the investigators, but the commanders of Nosfa had been very quick to place the shroud of suspicion over General Bird.

The watch commander did not report to Kasnata before she had the general arrested, she waited until the queen had slept for a few hours before bringing her the news.

"Who gave you this information?" Kasnata asked with disbelief as the watch commander stood before her.

"The colonels of the men of Nosfa all agreed that he was the man that matched the description of the man who attacked you." The watch commander said firmly.

"The height and weight? There is only one man in their number that matches the approximate height and weight? Ridiculous." Kasnata laughed hollowly.

"Majesty, my responsibility is to protect you. If you order his release I will have it so, but I advise against it. If his own men do not believe that he is above this, I beg you not do so." The watch commander spoke earnestly as the flap to Kasnata's tent was opened and Yoav barged in.

"I will not apologise for interrupting as I am not sorry that I do so, but I will ask you stay my execution until I have spoken." Wolfblood roared as he marched towards the queen and watch commander.

"This is not your concern, general." The watch commander warned.

"Like hell it isn't!" Yoav shouted.

"Lower your voice." Kasnata warned gently.

"Majesty, if you ever were to believe anything I was to say to you, then believe this. It wasn't the general that attacked you." Yoav went down on one knee before the queen. Kasnata raised an eyebrow with interest at the sudden show of respect.

"And what makes you so certain, Wolfblood?" She asked trying to sound aloof.

"I followed the colonels and commanders on the night of the victory celebration. They were conspiring to frame the general. They were to arrange for a man of the same build to attack you whilst you were alone and he had no one that would vouch for him that your people would believe. They then expected we would kill him for attacking you." Yoav reported, snarling as he spoke.

"I see, and you heard this?"

"I did."

"Well there we have it; it is not just blind faith on my part. Bring him here and fetch Misna." Kasnata waved that the watch commander should leave. The warrior bowed to her queen and moved to carry out her instructions.

"You were going to free him anyway?" Yoav asked unable to hide his shock.

"This evening, he received a message informing him his father had been killed by bandits. I knelt with him in my arms for half an hour this evening as he grieved. The man who attacked me did not have the same breathing rhythm, the same touch or the same smell as the general." Kasnata shrugged with a smug smile. Yoav laughed and rose from his knee.

"You always did know how to surprise me."

It did not take the watch commander long to return with Rathe. He was pale and shaking, this night having turned his world upside down more than once. Upon seeing the general stood in front of the queen, even more colour left his face.

"Majesty, I -" He began, but Kasnata raised her hand to quiet him.

"Peace, your colonels do not like you very much. If it were not for them we would not have arrested you." The queen said lightly.

"You don't think it was me?" Rathe looked between the general and the queen, not quite sure he understood what Kasnata was saying.

"They were conspiring against you, on the implied orders of the king. But even if we did not know that, her most high majesty did not believe you guilty in the first place." Yoav beamed as he untied the hands of the general.

"You should be careful." Kasnata warned him. "There are many that would seek to do you harm in your own ranks as well as spies of the enemy that are in both camps. Do not trust anyone who has not earned it, not here. Yoav, would you see him settled?"

Yoav nodded and showed Rathe out of her tent.

"She cares too much." Rathe said in a quiet voice as Yoav walked him back through the camp.

"She always has. It is one of her greatest strengths, though she considers it a weakness." Wolfblood said with a sad smile.

"She is right, there are too many that would exploit that." Rathe said with disapproval.

"There are many who already have and yet, the world still continues to become a better place every day because she is that caring."

Yoav said in a brusk voice. "Try not to worry too much about her and rest. You are excused duty tomorrow."

"Why?" Rathe asked with a furrowed brow.

"Because today has been a hard day for you and even General Avner was excused from duty for a few hours when his grandson died. I am sorry about your father." Yoav said gently as the two reached Rathe's tent.

"I see. Thank you. What will they do now?" He asked as he paused by the entrance.

"Misna will prove once again why it is she that is invaluable to the queen." Yoav said over his shoulder as he walked back towards his own quarters.

It did not take Misna long to discover who the true culprit of the attack on the queen was. His punishment was swift. Execution. The man was dragged out to the spot where the celebration bonfire had been built and there was run through with six spears by six men simultaneously. His death sent a message to all those that plotted against the queen. As she watched the execution, even General Hesla felt a momentary twinge of fear, but not quite enough to shake her convictions.

*****

The village of Roenca was larger than either princess expected. From the ridge that overlooked it, they could see it spread for two miles in each direction from a central point that looked to be a plaza.

It should have been a town or small city given the size of it but the Roencians managed to convince every lord that had visited them that it was still a village and avoided paying the higher taxes that were due for a town or city.

As Mathias led the girls closer, it became clear that much of the village was dedicated to lumber. The Marsden forest surrounded the village in all directions meaning that they could do little farming. Most of their food camp from hunting the beasts that lived in the words and money was brought into the village through the sale of lumber to provinces and traders that were lacking in the resource.

They passed two large buildings that looked to be house, but in fact were filled with cut logs and planks awaiting collection. A handful of children were playing in the street, but at the sound of the approaching travellers, they vanished and a few moments later a bell began to peal.

"What is going on?" Kasna asked. She still didn't trust Mathias and was not convinced he was not leading her into a trap.

"The country is at war. When unexpected visitors arrive there is always a small amount of fuss, after all it is not unheard of for scouts to find villages and deliver ultimatums of destruction to the population." Mathias said with a smile as he walked down the wide street that led to the plaza.

Kasna and Kia took in their surroundings as they followed Mathias at a distance of three sword lengths behind him. The buildings were simple in design, nor crude, but built for function rather than for beauty.

The houses that held wood seemed to stand further apart from the others, buckets of water, sand and damp earth stood at each corner of the buildings. Kia could see the logic in this. If a fire were to start in one of the houses, the blaze would become an inferno in a short space of time. An inferno would not only destroy the village's income and the village itself but also the forest that surrounded Roenca.

As they drew closer to the plaza, they could see a well was stood at the centre of the town. It was much bigger than any well either of the girls had ever seen. It looked more like a small walled pond than a well. The children were sat on the wall watching the girls approach with suspicious eyes. In front of them stood a man clothed in what looked like a very loose fitting dress. Kia giggled at the sight and whispered to her sister, who started to giggle too. Mathias stopped and turned sharply.

"It is a robe, not a dress. He is the village elder and leader, so be respectful or you will wish I had left you back in the wilderness." Mathias hissed at both of the girls. Kia nodded to show she would be as respectful as possible, her giggling subsiding.

Kasna however gave Mathias a challenging look, her lip curling up slightly as she bit back a retort she knew would have been scolded for had she been back in her prison of a palace.

"Welcome home, Mathias!" The village leader stepped forward and embraced the chaperon of the two princesses.

"I am glad to be home, Akiva." Mathias replied as he returned the embrace of his leader.

"And who have you brought with you?" Akiva asked as he stepped past Mathias to look over the two princesses.

"The daughters of Kasnata, if I am not very much mistaken. They were at the edge of the forest just to the south of Abergorlech." Mathias explained as Akiva studied the princess.

Kasna looked upon the village leader with the same suspicion she viewed Mathias with. There was something about the two men that the older of the two sisters couldn't explain, something that was almost too convenient about their presence. Mathias' knowledge of events and plans that no one had mentioned also set Kasna on edge.

The heir to the throne of the Order merely stared at Akiva, her eyes cold and her expression severe. The leader of the village looked at her expectantly, but when she said nothing, he moved his attention to Kia.

"We were asked to accompany Mathias here; he didn't offer any explanation as to why we may want to visit this place." Kia spoke with all the practised formality of a royal child. She tried to match her sister's expression and cold eyes, but could not.

"Well I would assume that is because you have both been here before, you were no more than small babes at the time, but your mother is known by all here and counted a friend. If you are escaping your father in order to join her, then we would be honoured to assist you. Please, I will have Nasus and Haras show you around the village and then help you to gather whatever supplies you might need for your journey." Akiva said with a smile.

The children that had been sat on the wall leapt to their feet and disappeared, returning a moment later with two young women that looked little older than teenagers.

"What now old man?" The blonde girl that the children had fetched asked in an annoyed tone.

"I'm glad to see your manners are not improved at all, Haras." Akiva said shaking his head. "You are such a tiresome child, even when a guest."

"We aren't here to answer to your every beck and call as you are well aware." Haras said turning her nose up in the air.

"Behave yourself, sister." The darker haired girl spoke, ashamed of the other girl's words.

"Nasus, you are too obliging." Haras shot back, scowling slightly.

"Akiva, what is it you wanted to see us for?" Nasus asked ignoring her sister's glares.

"Nasus, you are the light to the dark of your sister. It would seem we have some guests. Mathias found them in the forest. Would you be so good as to show them around the village and find whatever supplies they need for their onward journey? There should even be some horses that can be spared if you speak to Isaac." The village leader said warmly.

"Of course, we would be more than happy to oblige." Nasus said with a smile, whilst Haras' expression told Kasna and Kia that the opposite was true. "Please, follow us, we can get acquainted." Nasus indicated that the two princesses should follow her as she led the way down the eastern path of the village.

Akiva and Mathias watched them go until they were out of earshot. The two men turned and walked towards one of the houses that lay on the opposite side of the plaza. The buildings were constructed from wood and thatch and affectionately called rowdanes by those that lived in them as no other settlement had buildings quite like them.

If fire broke out in the village they could be pulled down and dragged out of the fire to help control it and stop the spread of the flames. Yet they were strong enough to survive the rain and the cold winters.

The two ducked inside the rowdanes and sat down either side of a low table.

"The palace was empty when I reached there." Mathias said leaning forward on his elbow.

"Were they all dead?" Akiva asked with a furrowed brow.

"There were lots of bodies. The servants were all dead, most of them seemed to have been dragged to a single point and executed." Mathias sighed. "There wasn't any sign of any bodies of the attackers, though there were some pools of blood that had no bodies."

"I see." Akiva said thoughtfully. "The princesses were unharmed?"

"They seem to be. Whether by skill or luck they managed to escape." Mathias sighed and shook his head.

"Do you know who it was that attacked the palace? Was it Mercia?" Akiva asked as he stood and began to pace around the rowdane.

"No, it wasn't Mercia. If it was then I don't think the servants would all have been killed." Mathias replied as he watched the village leader pacing.

"If the servants couldn't be trusted, he would have had them killed." Akiva observed as he made his way over to the window.

"True, but I don't think it was Mercia." Mathias shook his head.

"Then who?" Akiva stared out at the village. It was quiet on the streets at the moment. The children had gone back to playing at their post. Nasus and Haras had taken the two princesses to the east and would be keeping them occupied for a while.

"I don't know. I was hoping they would show themselves as we journeyed her, but it wasn't to be." Mathias said drumming his fingers on the table.

"Is it safe to send the two girls off on their own to their mother?" Akiva turned round to face the younger man.

"Probably not." Mathias shrugged.

"Can you send for Tola?" The village leader sighed as he considered the small number of options available to him.

"He has to serve in the army in the war against Delma; he can't just drop what he is doing and come to collect them." Mathias said with exasperation. It always seemed to him that the moment there was a problem in Roenca; the village leader would want to send for Tola. He was Mathias cousin and as close to him as a brother, but he often felt like he lived in the other man's shadow.

"I see. Haras and Nasus are more than capable of doing so, but we need their skills here more than the two princesses do." Akiva drummed his fingers on his chin in thought.

"I will go." Mathias said. It was not a suggestion, more a

statement.

"You are not an escort; you have not been trained as such." Akiva said dismissively

"No. But I do have skills that can protect them." Mathias said standing. He kept his tone calm, but his frustration could be read by the older man in the lines of his body.

"I cannot risk losing you. You are too important to protecting our work here." The village leader said trying to dissuade the younger man.

"If the princesses don't re-join their mother then all of this will be for naught. Even if those that are trying to capture or kill the princesses now are stopped, it will not be long before Mercia has them disposed of." Mathias shrugged.

"You will go whether you have permission or not, so I will grant it though I question the wisdom of it." Akiva sighed and shook his head. He turned back to the window.

"I will go and make preparations then." Mathias said with a smile. He left Akiva alone in the rowdane, the village leader unsure he had made the right decision.

The east path of Roenca was lined with low, long rowdanes that turned out to be healing houses. As Nasus and Haras had led the two princesses down the road, the number of people walking about and into the village increased. Kia could hear the screams of those having limbs removed almost half a mile away.

"What is this place?" Kasna asked as they were shown all the different wounded that were being healed. Some were villagers, some soldiers of Nosfa and others were soldiers of Delma.

"It is a refuge. We treat all wounded here, no matter their country." Haras said shortly.

"And there have been no consequences to this?" Kia frowned as she noticed one of bandages on a wounded man's arm needed changing.

"None. The soldiers all know they are guests here and that any aggression or violence towards each other or any of the villagers will mean that they are sent away, along with all their countrymen." Nasus explained as she analysed another patient's arm wound to see if it had closed properly.

"Is that why you are both guests here?" Kasna asked the two women.

"It is. We are here to help treat the wounded and when this pointless war is ended we will return home to our father." Haras said pointedly. Kasna opened her mouth to respond but she was cut off by Kia jabbing her in the ribs.

"Show us more." The younger princess said with interest. Nasus looked at the girl with searching eyes before slowly nodding and leading her to where the healers were at work with the latest refugee arrivals to the village.

*****

By the time Hermia arrived at the Gibborim hall, the only furniture that remained intact were the chairs that Asahel and Helez were sat upon. The two had found some ale and were sat drinking as they watched Jephthah and Layla fight.

"Separate them." Hermia said with a grim expression on her face. Helez spat out the ale he had just sipped from his tankard.

"He kill crack us like eggs." Asahel protested, but was cowed to silence by the cold stare that Hermia fixed him with. The two men sighed and slowly stood.

Circling away from the direction Layla darted in they managed to catch the shield of Hermia off guard long enough to disarm him. Jephthah roared and swung his giant fists at his two protégés.

"Enough!" Hermia shouted after her anger got the better of her patience. "You should be ashamed of yourself, Jephthah." The former queen scolded him.

"She started it." The giant man couldn't have sounded more like a child being told off if he had tried.

"What could she have done to provoke such a reaction?" Hermia asked fixing eyes will with ferocity on the man mountain.

"She made me spill my ale." Jephthah said quietly.

"You destroyed this hall and brought chaos to the Gibborim because she made you spill some ale?" Hermia asked in disbelief. She closed her eyes as she fought to control herself. "How could you forget your place and responsibility so easily?"

"I'm sorry, my lady." Jephthah said as he hung his head.

"As am I." Hermia said sadly. Jephthah looked up sharply when he heard the tone in her voice. "Jephthah, I do hereby revoke your status as shield of the lady of the Gibborim. You are dismissed from my service." The queen mother said firmly.

Helez and Asahel looked at one another with shared looks of astonishment. Layla's face remained a passive mask that none could read, whilst Jephthah went almost purple in colour.

"Helez, Asahel, you shall assume the duties that were formerly the province of Jephthah. I name you shields to the lady of the Gibborim. Serve me well." Hermia said before turning on her heel. "Layla, see that this is cleaned up and repaired."

Jephthah roared and swung at the shadow again. Layla dodged easily and shook her finger at the man mountain

"Now, now." She mocked him.

"I swear by all the powers I possess and by all those of the Gods themselves, I will have my vengeance on you for this Layla." The former shield was savage with rage as he stormed from the Gibborim hall. Helez and Asahel shrunk away from their former teacher as he passed.

*****

For the second time that day, the peal of the bell brought the village leader to the plaza.

"Akiva, troubling rumours have been circulating the area." The Baron of Fintry greeted the leader of Roenca with a look of contempt barely masked by the false civility he practised.

"What rumours do you find so troubling? The ones that say the king send soldiers to attack and murder his own daughters or the rumours that say they survived the attack?" Akiva asked with the most innocent air he could muster.

"The rumour that your village is harbouring enemy soldiers. What is even more concerning is that amongst them could be men linked to the murders at the palace of Abergorlech and the kidnapping of the princesses." The Baron said with a smug expression of victory.

Akiva stood expressionless in front of the baron. He knew that there was a small possibility that the baron was right, but the look the lord of Fintry wore told the village leader that any enemy soldier that the baron came across would be taken as a suspect. None of them would be safe and the village of Roenca would be torched, it's people tortured for harbouring enemy soldiers. In all likelihood Akiva would be arrested and executed for treason.

"Let your men begin searching. If there is any truth in these rumours it would be troubling indeed." Akiva said calmly as he went in search of Mathias.

*****

The burial of the dead of Nosfa had taken considerably longer than Kasnata had expected. It was the responsibility of the lower commanders of the army to instruct their men on how and where to bury the dead after a battle. With over two hundred bodies to bury and a suitable grave site to be found, it had taken a few days before they were able to begin the work.

Until they were the army could not move forward. This was problematic for the queen, not because she was desperate to engage the forces of Delma in battle again, but rather that the longer the army was camped in one place, the further the foraging parties had to travel to find food, wood and water for the camp.

This would mean that as the army moved forward, the foraging party would have to travel closer to the enemy increasing the danger for those the queen sent out. It also increased the risk of malnutrition and starvation for the army.

On the third day after Kasnata had returned, Marissa brought the queen news that one of the foraging parties she had sent out had been attacked by deserting Delmarian forces. Two of the party had been taken hostage so Kasnata had order Yoav to assemble a small force to ride to rescue them.

Yoav had chosen sixteen men, including Rathe to form the rescue force. Marissa had also volunteered some of her forces to assist in the rescue but Kasnata had opted to go herself instead.

The foraging party had been to the northeast of the camp when they had been attacked. It had only taken four hours for the rescue force to find the tracks of the deserters.

"You should have stayed behind, majesty." Wolfblood growled as they followed the trail left by the deserters.

"Why are you fussing now, old man?" The queen asked playfully. Being out of the camp after foiling the plans of her husband had put the queen in high spirits.

"You have spent little time in the camp as it is, your people do not need you to constantly prove yourself in unimportant conflicts." The general said gruffly. The path the followed grew ever narrower as they followed it into a narrow canyon. Rathe listened trying to pick out words he understood from their conversation.

"Saving one of our number from the hands of the enemy is not unimportant." Kasnata chided the general.

"It is not something that you should be doing yourself, majesty, as you are well aware." Yoav replied with a mild tone of irritation.

"Wolfblood?" Rathe interrupted the queen and general's conversation.

"What is it, pup?" Yoav growled at the general who rode ahead of them.

"The trail disappears after this point, there's no sign of anything having passed any further north in quite some time." Rathe explained. Yoav rode up to where the young lord had dismounted and was examining the ground. It took only a moment for Yoav to know that Rathe was right.

The sound of war cries ringing off the canyon walls caused some of the horses to rear and bolt with their riders. Soldiers poured from every direction and clashed with the warriors of the Order.

Rathe steeled himself for what was to come. It was not glorious or pretty as he made his first kill. He held his sword steady as a foolhardy man had run straight onto the blade.

He could feel the warm sensation of blood flowing from the wound down his sword and onto his hand. He felt dead inside as he watched the life leave the eyes of the man who had run headlong into death.

Kasnata was not far from him, trying to fight her way to the side of the young general. She was lethal in her precision, even when facing such overwhelming numbers. Yoav and his men were roaring and howling as they attacked, each of the howls and the roars was a different command and response.

Kasnata smiled at the sound, it was not necessary in most battles, but when it was the Order of the Wolf fight as one unit, one force, it was a sound that had caused many to flee the battlefield in fear.

As well trained as the warriors of the Order were, the sheer numbers were taking their toll on the fighters.

"Majesty!" Wolfblood shouted over the noise of the battle.

"I'm here, general." Kasnata shouted back. "There is too many of them, we need to retreat."

"As you say, highness." Yoav agreed and howled three times. "Pup, come, time to go." He called to Rathe.

"Yes, sir."

"They've sealed off the canyon; we'll have to find another way out." One of the warriors of the Order of the Wolf shouted as he tried to break through the lines of the enemy.

"Come with me." Kasnata had broken through the enemy to where Rathe was battling. His defences had been breached several times but none of the injuries were life-threatening.

She grabbed his wrist and pulled him from the fight, forcing him to run beside her.

"What about the others?" He gasped as they fled from the battle.

"They will retreat and return to camp." The queen replied. Her breathing was laboured and she was running slower with every step. The canyon twisted and turned, but eventually opened out into scrubland.

The light was fading as Kasnata finally allowed the two to stop running. Rathe collapsed to his knees with exhaustion, Kasnata was clutching her side as she tried to catch her breath.

"We need to find somewhere to hide. They will be following us and neither of us has the strength the fight." Kasnata dropped to her knees beside Rathe.

"Majesty, are you okay?" The general asked. The queen was paler than normal and her skin was covered in a light sheen of sweat.

"We need to get to that dense foliage." She replied, trying to stand, but her legs would not take her weight. Rathe managed to catch the queen before she could fall.

He supported her weight as they moved to the patch of dense foliage that lay ahead of them. When they were hidden in the thicket, Rathe lowered the queen to the ground. She was barely conscious and cold to touch.

"Are you bleeding?" He asked her as he took off his cloak and wrapped the queen in it.

"I think so. One of them struck me from behind; I think they have pierced my armour. You'll need to remove my breastplate." She groaned.

"Majesty?" Rathe stammered.

"You'll need to take off my armour to see the wound. If it is still bleeding, then I will not live very long. If it has closed then I will need food, water, warmth and rest to recover. Your wounds will need cleaning too." She said quietly, the strain of talking weighing heavily on her body.

With shaking hands, Rathe unbuckled the armour of the queen and slowly peeled it off her body. He saw the wound on her back, it had closed itself, but the padding that protected her skin from the armour was soaked in her blood.

"You've stopped bleeding." He sighed with relief. He placed his cloak around her shoulders and gentle lay her down on the ground. It didn't take long for him to build a small fire that would not be noticeable from outside the thicket, but big enough to keep the queen warm.

"My supplies of food and water are with Red Hare." Kasnata yawned as she curled up in Rathe's cloak and drew as close as she could to the fire.

"I left mine the food on my horse too, though I have some water here. What happened to the horses?" Rathe asked trying to keep the queen awake.

"Some of them will have been cut down by the enemy, but most of them will have run from them. They will find their way back to camp. We should think about our own survival." Kasnata's eyes were closed.

"Here you should drink this." Rathe said as he picked the queen up into his arms and poured water into her mouth a little at a time. "Food will be scares here. But I am sure there will be some muntjacs that I can hunt whilst you rest."

"It's so cold here." The queen shivered.

"Try to get some sleep." Rathe soothed as he stroked her hair. The queen rolled in his arms so her head was buried in his chest. The general smiled as he held her.

His heart pounded as he watched her drift off to sleep. Gently he laid her down next to the fire where she would be safe and warm enough until he returned from hunting.

He could feel some of his wounds burning under his clothes. They needed to be cleaned and dressed, but finding food to help the queen recover was his first priority.

He stroked her hair absently as he moved to stand and kissed her cheek without thinking. She murmured his name in her sleep and smiled. As he moved through the thicket he cursed himself, when he had met the queen he had known she was beautiful and he had felt lustful tugs on his heart. But the feelings that prompted his slight affectionate acts of fondling her hair and a kiss on the cheek were symptoms of emotions that ran far deeper.

Emotions that a lord should not have for his queen; emotions that an unmarried man should not have for another man's wife.

Chapter 15
2430GL 3rd Wentrus

Red Hare was the first of the party to arrive back at the camp of the Order. His arrival provoked a mild panic to run through the more inexperienced soldiers.

General Kia sent out scouting parties to try and discover what had happened. They found no trace of the queen. General Yoav arrived back at the camp with most of his warriors still breathing and most of the horses were with him

"What happened out there?" Renta asked as the generals sat in counsel with Tola.

"It was a trap. I don't think they kept the women they captured alive, just took them so we would search for them and killed them when they knew the plan had worked." Wolfblood said with disgust.

"We should have seen this coming." Misna growled, more admonishing herself than anyone else.

"Do we know what happened to the queen and General Bird?" Tola asked. When Rathe had not returned with Yoav the colonels and commanders of Nosfa had all but jumped for joy. Their lack of concern and lack of respect for the general had put Tola in a bad mood.

"No. If the enemy had killed her, we would know about it now." Amalia observed calmly.

"She has not come back though and that means she cannot. We need to appoint a steward to the throne. The princesses are held as prisoners and cannot take over from their mother and if she is dead then we need to be prepared." Hesla said matter-of-factly. She managed to keep her lips from curling into a smile but her eyes were shinning too brightly when Amalia and Misna looked over at the General.

"And who would you suggest, Hesla? Yourself?" Quisla asked in a condescending tone.

"If I was asked to, then I would do so." Hesla said with a shrug. Avner and Shamgar exchanged a sceptical glance.

"No." Amalia and Misna spoke as one. The others turned to stare at the two women. The infiltrator commander and the intelligence commander both united in thought and speech.

"I agree. It has barely been two days. If she were injured she would need to recover first. We wait until we know." Avner said in support of Amalia and Misna's sentiment.

"The child refugees have offered to go in search of the queen and the general. They know the land to the northeast; they wish to repay a debt of kindness they feel they owe to Kasnata for allowing them into the camp." Kia said slowly.

"Well that sounds like a fine idea. There are eight of them so there are too many to be the prey of bandits but too small a number to attract the unwanted attention of the Delmarian army." Shamgar said with enthusiasm.

"I will see to their departure." Marissa stood as she spoke; she wanted to be out in the fresh air as soon as possible.

She closed her eyes as she stepped out into the cool night that had settled around the camp. It been unbearably hot as Sagma/Sumar had turned to Antompne but now the temperature had changed as Wentrus arrived and Marissa much preferred Wentrus.

The queen had been missing before, she had always returned to be scolded by the older generals for irresponsible behaviour, but she had never disappeared in a war before. She had always ridden home again.

The thought that Kasnata was dead burned in the Phoenix General's chest, a pain she wanted to reach in a pull from her body. Marissa was not a woman to cry, she was a woman to act. It had taken more self-control than she thought she possessed to not draw her sword and carve into Hesla's flesh what Marissa thought of appointing a steward to the throne.

She was glad to see that Misna and Amalia were united against the Eagle General. Marissa strode through the camp to where the refugee children were billeted.

The eight children had recovered quickly from their ordeal, the younger ones that had been half-starved still looked underweight, but they were much healthier than they had been.

"The generals have agreed that if you wish to search for the queen in the northern wilderness then we will give you leave to search and any provisions you require." Marissa said as she entered the tent that they slept in.

The children all leapt to their feet as Marissa entered, the sound of armour clanking brought a smile to the Phoenix General's face. They had arrived in rags and now each wore a full complement of mismatched heavy armour. She passed no comment on what they wore or how they had acquired it.

"You have six days. If you cannot find her by the end of six days return and report." The general was firm in her instructions though she wanted to tell the eight children to search for as long as it took.

The children all nodded in acknowledgement and followed Marissa to select their horses.

The other generals had all returned to their own tents after Marissa's departure. There was nothing more for them to discuss and most had not slept for the last few days needed to rest.

Misna was one of the few who did not retire to her bed. She waited for an hour before she went to meet with Amalia. The two had not spoken about whether a steward should be appointed before they had held counsel.

After they had both stood against Hesla's suggestion, Misna wanted to find out what had motivated Amalia to speak out.

"You are worried then?" Amalia greeted Misna as the Raven General entered her quarters.

"You know I have never trusted Hesla." Misna shrugged as she sat down opposite the Kestrel General.

"No, this is true. There are few who share your opinion of her, but it would seem that you are not as wrong as I wanted to believe." Amalia pursed her lips as she offered Misna something to drink.

"She has always been too vocal in her support of the throne." Misna said with exasperation as she refused the drink she was offered.

"She has always expressed where she stands more loudly than any other." Amalia agreed with a grim expression.

"Too loudly. The louder someone shouts their support for something, the less I believe it." Misna said flatly. Amalia looked at her friend.

"You think she is still alive?" She asked changing the subject.

"Kasnata won't have died so easily. Either she or the general will have been injured and needing the time to recover before returning." Misna said with complete confidence. "Hesla knows that better than anyone, she could have sent out her troops to search for the queen without any inconvenience and yet she never volunteered them. Instead she suggests a steward for the throne, a position she has always said she is perfectly suited for." There was disgust rife in her voice.

"She was too quick to suggest a steward. Quisla has her eye on her though. After all that business with Quisla's husband and Hesla, she has never trusted her since." Amalia observed as she sank back in her chair.

"No, but we should all be vigilant. I do not think that Hesla is as true to the throne that Kasnata sits on as she would be if those descended from Valia would be." Misna tapped her fingers on the arm of the chair.

"If you are right she will not be alone. We must all remain watchful."

Amalia said pointedly.

"Do you think we can trust General Bird?" Misna asked leaning forward onto her knees, her fingers steepling as she brought her hands together.

"I think he does not wish our people or Kasnata any harm, but he could be more dangerous because of that." Amalia mused, "Why?"

"We assume he has been alone with the queen for the last few days and yet no one seems too concerned about it. He seems to have the trust of a lot of very suspicious individuals. If I were an assassin or a spy, then that is how I would infiltrate our people." Misna observed with a shrug.

"You are an assassin, spy and infiltrator." Amalia said with a raised eyebrow.

"Then perhaps we should be more mindful of General Bird than we have been."

*****

Mia was happier than she had been in months. Joab's presence in her life was a blessing she had been longing for. He was more intense than any man she had ever known. He challenged her every word and made her want to scream with frustration, but she finally had someone to talk to, someone who did not run to the king with her every thought and secret.

Joab was surprised by the young lady. She was smarter than he would ever give her credit for. She was unafraid of arguing with him and had not been taught the same diplomatic ways of hiding anger as the men of Nosfa's court.

When she was angry she would lose all her abilities to debate and throw insults at the bodyguard. Joab had never laughed so much in his life than he did with Mia.

She was becoming more aware of the world the longer she spent with the shadow. She knew the names of her maids and guards, of their families, of the problems they faced in their day-to-day lives. One day she would be a good leader of her people.

What Joab found hard about protecting Mia was how the king treated her. Mercia would ignore her for weeks on end and then would arrive at her rooms. Her maids were ordered to leave and Joab was told he would not be needed until the morning.

Her guards would be shaking with rage as Joab was removed from the room, knowing what the Lady Bird would have to endure at the hands of the king. When Joab returned to her the morning after these nights he would find her bruised, bloody and her spirit broken. Often for days she would sit and cry, not wanting Joab to be in the same room as her. On other days she would weep bitterly into his arms as he stroked her hair and soothed her.

There were days, when she was so broken she could not even cry; that Joab considered telling her that her father still lived. But he knew that the risk to the Gibborim was too great to be worth the brief joy it would bring to his ward.

Joab cursed the king and swore oaths to see Mia freed from this place not matter what it took.

*****

"What are they doing?" Kasna hissed as she watched the Baron of Fintry's men searching the buildings, coming closer to the rowdane filled with enemy soldiers.

"Looking for the men in here." Nasus replied, her lips set in a thin line if disapproval.

"Why?" Kia asked as she finished changing the bandages on the man that lay closest to Kasna.

"Because the place where you were held was attacked and you were not amongst the dead. They are looking for the men that did that and trying to find where you have been taken." Haras snapped as she strode down the rowdane.

"It wasn't any of these men." Kia looked worriedly over the faces of the injured men.

"It doesn't matter." Nasus shook her head. "They are looking for someone to blame, another way to manipulate your mother."

"Then we shall tell them, they are wrong." Kasna said firmly. She was about to stand when the sound of approaching hoof beats heralded the arrival of Kelmar.

The Baron of Fintry was waiting in the plaza; he did not sully his elevated status with such tiresome things as searching when he had men to do that for him. He was sat on the wall of the well when Kelmar arrived.

Kasna and Kia snuck from the rowdane and carefully picked their way between the searchers and the buildings, following Kelmar. Nasus had disappeared in search of Mathias and Haras remained behind to defend the injured men from the Baron of Fintry's men.

"What a pleasant morning this is." Kelmar greeted the baron with a tone that suggested that their meeting was anything but pleasant.

"You!" The baron exclaimed with wide eyes, nearly falling into the well as he struggled to his feet. "Kelmar, you -" He stammered, unable to form the words that circled around his mind.

"I am here, I am the one that attacked your secret palace of Abergorlech and now I am searching for your princesses as they managed to elude me. It would seem that the most competent people in Mercia's court are, in fact, his exiled daughters." Kelmar mocked the baron as he sat astride his horse.

"You! It was you?!" The baron screeched. "Men to the plaza!"

The baron ran a few steps in each direction looking for his men appearing at his all, but none of them came.

"They are dead, Fintry." Kelmar said with a cruel smile as he nudged his horse forward so it could drink from the well.

"No, you couldn't, how did you reach here with no one recognising you, you're the Regent of Delma, you couldn't." The baron was fast falling to pieces.

Kasna looked at her sister who nodded to show she had heard who the man that had raided their home was.

"I could and I have, you really aren't at all able to process these events. Such a pity. You should run home, baron, run back to your master and tell him that I will see his daughters dead and buried." The Regent of Delma waved away the baron, who screamed, seized the reins of his horse and ran from the plaza.

"Now, princesses, I know you are here and I know you can hear me. You will turn yourselves over to me, give yourselves up or I shall be forced to burn this village to the ground to ensure you do not escape." Kelmar shouted loudly.

Kasna and Kia exchanged worried glances but before they could act, Mathias stepped into the plaza with Nasus beside him.

"You have no business here, regent." Mathias sneered at Kelmar as he approached. Nasus remained at the edge of the plaza, some slight movement between the buildings distracting her attention.

"Assassin, you show your face in daylight, away from cover. How careless. No Akiva to greet me? Your hospitality is slipping, friend." Kelmar snarled through a smile.

"We greet visitors, not invaders." Mathias shot back. He circled to the left of Kelmar, his eyes scanning his surroundings for any signs that Kasna and Kia were about to do something stupid.

"Then you should not have taken my prize. I know they are here, if you deny it you are wasting my time." Kelmar sighed, growing bored with dealing with Mathias.

"They are a prize?" Mathias asked with a wry smile.

"Yes, my prize." Kelmar narrowed his eyes at the assassin of Roenca.

"If they are a prize, then fight me for them. If you win, you can take them. If I win then I can keep them." Mathias offered casually.

"If only I could. Killing you would be a highlight in this unusually frustrating day, but their capture and execution is too important to leave in the hands of a single duel." Kelmar said smugly as he gathered the reins of his horse.

The Regent of Delma made to rein away from Mathias, but the sound of the air being sliced and his horse rearing and screaming in pain caused Kelmar to be thrown from the saddle. Mathias watched as a shadow dodged past him and leapt on top of Kelmar.

"Witch!" He shouted as the woman grabbed him round the throat. It did not take much effort for the regent to throw the woman off. "Neesa, I should have known you would not be far away."

"Then you should have been more mindful. I cannot let you harm the daughters of my master." She said sweetly as she recovered from being flung across the plaza.

"Neesa." Mathias growled.

"Ah Mathias, how is your mother? Does she rest well now?" She said callously. Mathias scowled and spat at the woman.

"So this is what it comes to? Fighting two assassins in order to kill two princesses?" Kelmar asked with resignation in his voice.

"It would seem that way." Mathias' lips curled as he spoke.

Neesa laughed and launched herself at Kelmar as she pulled two throwing blades and threw them at Mathias.

Nasus had vanished from the plaza. Kasna and Kia watched the fight below them unfolding. It was ferocious and underhand. It was nothing like the elegant tutoring they had received, more like a fight between thieves in the street. It was chaotic, even to the two girls watching.

Buildings were being destroyed by the fight, creating dust and obstacles around the plaza and in the confusion of the brawl, the two princesses lost sight of Mathias.

"We have to leave, now." Mathias appeared behind them, his side bleeding heavily and a deep cut across his eye meant his face was covered with fresh blood.

He seized the girls by the wrists and dragged them hurriedly through Roenca to the edge of the village. Nasus was stood with their horses, bundles of food and skins of water.

"Thank you." Mathias nodded to the dark haired woman who smiled.

"Be careful." She whispered and waved as the three mounted and disappeared into the wood.

Chapter 16

Snow had begun to fall in the northern wilderness. Rathe had managed to find rabbits, hares, pigeons and muntjacs in the scrubland to hunt. It had years since he had ventured into the forest that lay outside the walls of Afdanic to hunt with his father, but he could still remember how to track and trap.

Kasnata had survived the first few nights because the general of Nosfa had held her between him and the fire whilst she was wrapped in his cloak. There had been little reason to build any form of shelter because of the cover the dense thicket naturally provided.

There was a small stream that Rathe had found to provide water. Kasnata had explored the thicket and found lots of plants that could be used to fight the infections that caused her fever to remain high and those that had begun to fester in Rathe's.

The general had briefly cleaned his wounds, but he had been more concerned with ensuring Kasnata's survival and had ignored his own wellbeing. The queen had noticed that the general's health was deteriorating and whilst he slept she had treated his wounds properly. Rathe had woken to find his head resting in the queen's lap as she attended to the wounds on his face.

He found his feelings for the queen intensifying during the time that the two spent in the wilderness as she recovered. As the nights grew colder they spent more time sleeping in each other's arms, their shivering bodies hold tight to the other under their cloaks.

Rathe had watched her as she grew stronger. She repaired her armour and weaponry, prepared the food that he foraged and cooked without an utterance of complaint. They had used the time to help Rathe speak more of the language of the Order and he had become more and more fluent as time had gone on. Kasnata had been impressed by how quickly he was able to pick up the language.

It was an existence that the general would have been happy to continue. On their fifth day of living in the ticket, Rathe returned to find the queen dressed in nothing but his fur cloak. Her clothing had been washed, the blood having stained the padding would not wash out, but it hung drying beside the fire.

The general had been embarrassed by the sight of the queen, and she had enjoyed his embarrassment.

"You have had little to do with women." She observed as he stood there unsure of what to say or do.

"No, the women of noble birth in Nosfa do not interest me." He replied, staring at the floor as he placed the days hunt by the queen.

"None of the serving girls piqued your interest?" She asked with a smile.

"We had more respect for women in my home than to take any woman to bed that we pleased." Rathe sat beside the fire and warmed his hands.

"I see, that is respect that Mercia was never taught." Kasnata said with a warm smile. "You should let me wash your clothes too; the dirt in them will not be helping your wounds to heal."

Rathe flushed scarlet at the suggestion. Kasnata laughed kindly and moved around the fireside to sit beside the general. She took his arm and wrapped it around her shoulders and in turn encircled his body with her arms.

Rathe closed his eyes as he pulled the queen close to him.

"You have never known a woman's touch?" Kasnata asked softly as she listened to his heartbeat racing.

"No." He admitted. "I wanted to be in love, to be married, to only know the touch of my wife." He explained. Kasnata smiled sadly and sighed.

"I understand." She said quietly as she began to pull away from the general.

"I didn't mean...please..." Rathe didn't know what to say to the queen as she moved.

"You should hold onto what you want, do not let go of it easily." She told him as she began to sort through the food he had brought.

Rathe smiled to himself. The queen had her back to him as she prepared their meal. Her heart had sunk in her chest when she had heard Rathe explain his lack of experience. She had once felt the same as he did, but that had been taken from her by Mercia.

She skinned the two rabbits he had brought, taking care to save the fur so it could be used in clothing later, as she had pulled the skins she imagined that it was her husband's neck in her grip and gained immeasurable satisfaction from the act.

"Did he really take that much from you?" Rathe asked as he slipped his arms around her waist. Kasnata sighed and let herself fall back against his chest. He buried his face in her hair as he held her and felt her fingers stroking his arms.

"He took more than I can explain." She closed her eyes as Rathe held her and felt him kiss her neck. "You shouldn't..." She began as she turned in his arms and was surprised to find his clothes were lying on the floor behind him.

"I am in love." He said simply, he wasn't blushing as he spoke. "I know you cannot be my wife, but I do love you." He was earnest as he gazed into her eyes.

Kasnata did not know what to say to the general, she was struck dumb by his words and close to tears. She had enjoyed the time the two had spent together the past few days and felt desire for him, but she was not sure that she could ever love after the pain that Mercia had put her through.

Rathe smiled at her as her stroked her face and kissed her. The touch of his lips on hers was gentle, a glancing caress that sent a shiver down the queen's spine.

"I am not letting go of what I want." He whispered as he pulled her body as close to his as he could. "Though you will have to be patient with me." He tilted her chin upwards so he could kiss her again.

"When we return to camp, we cannot…" The queen protested, but was silenced by Rathe kissing her more passionately than before. Kasnata allowed herself to be rolled onto her back, the general's body pushing down on hers.

"I know." He told her as she kissed him. "But I will not stop loving you." He promised.

*****

The eight children of Ashpa rode north to where the canyon met the scrubland. There were few places that the queen and general would be able to find food, shelter and water in the northern wilderness outside of the small settlements.

The tracks of the soldiers told the children that they had abandoned their search after three days but that they had been unsuccessful in capturing the two missing warriors.

Upon riding past the thicket that the queen and general camped in the horses became excited and agitated.

The sound of spooked horses caused Kasnata to stir from her contented slumber. Rathe still slept, his body exhausted from exertion, his soul at peace. Kasnata smiled as he stirred and tried to pull her body closer to his.

"Wake up." She whispered as she kissed his cheek. "There is

movement outside."

Rathe sat bolt upright and quickly scrambled for his clothes. Kasnata was dressed before Rathe and slowly made her way through the foliage to look out at whom was passing so close to their hiding place, the general not far behind.

"Your majesty?" A small voice called out. Kasnata frowned as it sounded vaguely familiar to her. "Marissa sent us."

"The children." She whispered to Rathe who smiled. He stepped out of the foliage first to see the eight children mounted on horses of the Order with Red Hare and Ebony being led beside them.

It had been less than six days when the horns of the camp sounded the return of the queen. Hesla had been surprised but had seemed to be overly relieved that Kasnata had returned.

The children that had gone searching for the queen were rewarded for their actions. They were named the Eight, to be trained by Generals Misna and Marissa, for what, no one was told save for Misna and Marissa.

On their first night back amongst the camp of the Order, Kasnata lay down amongst her furs and sighed. Movement next to her made her smile as she rolled happily into the arms of Rathe.

"I thought this could not continue when we got back." He whispered as he held her in the darkness.

Kasnata kissed him in response.

*****

Amalia stood in Kasnata's tent and waited for the queen to rise. She made no comment on the general who lay beside her leader, his arms holding her tightly to his chest.

"My lady, he is here." The Kestrel General said quietly as Kasnata stirred.

"Is he in the war room?" The queen yawned as she gently removed herself from Rathe's arms. The general snored loudly and rolled over as Kasnata rose.

"He is." Amalia confirmed as Kasnata dressed.

"Thank you."

Amalia saluted and left the queen to make her way to the war room. It was still dark as Kasnata stepped out of her tent. The camp was quiet as she picked her way across it.

As she walked into the war room she saw the cassocked man sat at the foot of her throne.

"It is good to see you again, Abbott." Kasnata smiled. The Abbott rose and bowed to the queen.

"It has been too long, Venia." He said with a smile.

"What news do you bring?" She asked with a yawn. She still felt the pain of the wound from the sword strike to her back. It would never fully heal but she grew stronger every day and the pain of it lessened.

"Your daughters are safe for the moment. They have escaped from Abergorlech where the toad was holding them. Mathias took them to Roenca. He is bringing them to you, though he may need some help." The Abbott grinned.

He watched as relief flooded over the queen. She sank slowly to her knees and sobbed; tears of joy with a smile on her face.

"Thank you." She gasped through tears.

"You are welcome, my queen." The Abbott offered her a hand to help Kasnata back to her feet. "But you should know that Kelmar, Regent of Delma is chasing them. He killed all in Abergorlech to try to take your daughters before they could escape."

"Kelmar? Why? He has been a friend to my people, not an enemy." Kasnata looked up sharply as she regained her feet.

"Cassandra is trying to discover why. But he followed them to Roenca and threatened to burn the village unless they were handed over. Neesa was there too." The Abbott said calmly trying to soothe the worried queen.

"She was trying to kill them?" Kasnata frowned and moved to drink from a jug that stood on the table by her throne. It contained wine that she gulped from without pouring into any of the goblets that stood by it.

"No, it seemed she was there to protect them, to allow them to escape." The Abbott replied with a sombre tone.

"That doesn't make any sense." Kasnata spoke to herself more than she did to the Abbott as she thought. "Amalia!"

"Yes, majesty?" The Kestrel General stepped into the war room and saluted sharply.

"Wake Tola and Renta, I have a job for them. Ready their horses and supplies for three days."

"Three days?" Amalia asked with a furrowed brow. Tola and Renta being sent out on any mission did not need supplies.

"Three days." The queen confirmed. If her daughters were with Mathias and they were being chased by Kelmar they would not have time to forage or camp properly. The supplies should be enough to keep them from starving whilst Mathias, Renta and Tola brought them home to her.

"I also have a gift for you, highness." The Abbott said as he drew Kasnata's attention back to him.

"A gift?" She asked, only half listening.

"Yes, highness." He said kindly. From beneath his robes he brought a black staff. It was carved with runes that stood proudly on the surface of the black stone. He offered it out to the queen on open hands.

"What is it?" She asked as she ran her fingers over the surface of the staff.

"Something that Kania had made for you. You are far more powerful than you know, but you shall discover in time. When you are ready Cassandra will come for you." He said as she took the staff from his hand. It felt warm in her hand and lighter than she had expected.

"Thank you." The queen smiled. But the Abbott had gone.

*****

It was the dead of night when Joab was sent for by the king. He was taken to a small room he didn't know existed in the palace and was told to wait. The king arrived a few moments later and told him that Joab was to leave the palace within the hour.

Rumours had been growing within the kingdom that a revolution was stirring and that they were to start by killing the Lady Mia. Mercia could not allow a revolution to occur and so he was sending Mia to Fintry where she should be safe from the assassin's reach.

Joab had felt relief at being able to remove the lady from the reach of the king, even if it was only for a short time. He had woken her gently and told her they were leaving. Her maids had been woken and were preparing her bags that would be sent after her with her guards and maids in the morning.

They left within the hour under the cover of night and journeyed to the south. It would take a week or more to reach Fintry on horseback so supplies had been packed for them on their horses.

Joab had no way for sending word to the Gibborim that he was leaving the city with the Lady Mia, but he would find a way to do so when they had left the danger of the city behind. The shadow knew there was no danger posed to Mia, but he relished the opportunity to save her from Mercia.

They passed the city of Afdanic and Joab watched the Mia as she stared at the walls of her home with a pained expression. He wanted to take her into the city, to let her reassure her people, but he knew that it would mean the king would punish her more than he already did.

They made camp just to the south of the city with snow light on the ground. Mia was not used to travelling or sleeping outdoors especially in such cold conditions. She shivered as she huddled close to the fire draped in her own furs as well as Joab's.

The shadow did not seem to mind the cold; he did not shiver or complain even when away from the heat of the fire.

"We shall be in Fintry soon, my lady." He assured her as the two finished eating.

"That is fine, at least I am away from the king," She smiled though her teeth chattered noisily.

Joab was going to move to her side to keep her warm with his own body heat but a noise in the forest caused him to leap to his feet.

Mia had not seen Joab fight, she only knew the side of his nature that provoked and taught her to see the world beyond the one she had been raised in. His reactions were like lightning; Mia had not even heard the sound that had provoked the reaction in her bodyguard. She watched as he stalked towards the trees like a cat stalking birds along a rooftop.

"Who are you?" A voice called from the treeline. Joab didn't answer; Mia could not even see the shadow anymore, he had from the ring of light that the fire provided. "Woman, who are you?" The voice asked more impatiently.

"A traveller." She said with surprise. She had assumed that the voice had been talking to Joab.

"From where?" The voice spoke again, this time from slightly closer.

"What concern is it of yours?" Mia said defiantly, her teeth still chattering in the cold. There was no response but a horse squealed. There were sounds of a scuffle breaking out amongst the trees and two girls rode forward into the light of the fire.

The two looked no older than ten years old, but had more weapons than Joab carried strapped to their backs. Mia jumped in surprise and alarm at their sudden appearance.

"Who are you?" The lady asked, her voice betraying her fear.

"Travellers." The older of the two girls replied sharply.

"It's okay, Mia." Joab said as he appeared behind her, beside him walked another man who led his horse.

"I should have recognised your voice." The man said laughing slightly, wiping blood away from his lip.

"The same could be same about me, Mathias." Joab grinned patting the man on the back. "This is Lady Mia Bird."

Mathias bowed to Mia and offered her a smile.

"My Lady Bird, may I be allowed to introduce their royal highnesses, Princess Kasna Nosfa and Princess Kia Nosfa." Mathias said pointing at the girls in turn. Mia stared wide-eyed at the two girls and hurriedly curtsied.

"Where are you headed?" Joab asked Mathias as the princesses dismounted and made their way to the fireside.

"To the north, to wherever Kasnata's war camp is. Her daughters want to see their mother." Mathias said casting an affection eye over the girls as they sat down.

"I see." Joab steered Mia back to the fire and sat her down, standing behind her to keep the wind from her back.

"Where are you taking the lady? Eloping together?" Mathias teased his friend. Mia's eyes flared with fear as she shrank back into Joab's arms as he knelt to comfort her.

"It's okay." He whispered to her. "It is a complicated, but we are headed to Fintry where she will be safe from those that wish to harm her; at least for the time being." Joab said without moving his eyes from Mia's.

"I see." Mathias said thoughtfully.

"They're going to where my brother is." Mia said softly.

"I know." Joab smiled trying to reassure the lady.

"Could they tell him I am safe?" She asked, hope filling her eyes.

"Mathias?" Joab asked his friend, knowing that no matter how quietly Mia spoke, Mathias would still be able to hear what she said.

"Who is your brother, my lady?" Mathias asked as he checked the horses.

"Lord Rathe Bird, he is the general in charge of the men of Nosfa in the queen's camp." She said still facing Joab.

"Then I shall inform him you are safe and well." Mathias bowed. The Roencian glanced at the tent that stood slightly to the left of where Mia sat. "May I ask a favour in return?"

"What is it?" Joab asked.

"Could the princesses share the Lady Mia's tent tonight? It has been a few days since they had slept in any form of shelter." Mathias inclined his head towards Kasna and Kia who were yawning as they fell asleep in front of the fire.

"Mia?" Joab asked gently and Mia nodded her agreement. "Agreed." Joab looked at Mathias who shook the princess awake and coaxed them over towards the tent. "It's probably time you went to sleep as well." Joab said gently stroking Mia's hair.

Silently she rose from the fire and disappeared after the princesses to the relative warmth of the tent.

"Who is it you are saving her from?" Mathias asked as sat beside Joab and the fire.

"The king." Joab said kicking one of the logs on the fire with frustration.

"I see. Have you thought about taking her to her

brother?" Mathias stretched and yawned. He had spent a long time without sleep.

"I have, but every time I have thought of it, the threat to the Gibborim stops me." Joab sighed.

"I doubt the king would discover that there is a revolution being planned by all the outlaws he has created because you and Lady Mia have runaway to reunite brother and sister." Mathias laughed at his friend's paranoia.

"Maybe, but there are rumours or revolution already circulating in the city; there is even a mole within the Gibborim." Joab shrugged.

"In that case, you and the lady running off to join her brother, is not going to arouse suspicion." Mathias lay back and supressed an involuntary shiver as he felt the cold of the snow seep through his shirt.

"You just want some company so you don't have to spend all night awake guarding the princesses." Joab teased his friend.

"True. You stay awake for the first half of the night, then wake me and I will take the second half." Mathias waved his hand lazily in Joab's direction as he drifted off to sleep.

Chapter 17

The Guardian of the Wilds had spent too many wasted days discovering very little. It frustrated her a great deal as time in these matters was not her friend.

She had been to the record holders in the city of Mocandella to discover what she could about the significance of the cities of Delma and Benadrocca. Both cities held secrets that their inhabitants knew nothing about, but there was so many that as the years passed, Cassandra found it hard to remember them all.

She had been to the Laviant Abbey before Mocandella. There were records there that contained all the prophecies that had been handed down from the Goddess Arala since people had first walked across the face of Celadmore.

There had been nothing there about Mercia, Kasnata or their children anywhere in the prophecies. So Cassandra had travelled to the city of Mocandella to look at the records of the cities. She had spent weeks reading through the smallest, trivial details of both cities and could feel her patience wearing thin.

Both cities had been built at the same time as Grashindorph, but Benadrocca had been populated only by the guardian of the realm and a man named Epoch. The guardian of the realm no longer dwelt there but Epoch still remained as the cities leader.

Launching an attack against the city would be tantamount to suicide even for Kasnata, but it would not have surprised Cassandra if that is what the king had in mind.

She was sure that it was Delma that was important to Mercia, but why was still a mystery. She needed to access the library of Grashindorph to find what she was looking for without attracting too much attention.

Something still bothered Cassandra about why the king was keeping the princesses alive. In order to control Kasnata, he need only threaten the life of Leinad and she would bow to his wishes. She knew that the king did not love his children, but there were was no other reason she could think of for needing to keep Kasna and Kia alive and away from their mother.

The library at Grashindorph was filled with more knowledge than even Cassandra and the Abbott could take in. It lay beneath the castle of Grashindorph at the heart of the city and was the same size as the ground floor of the castle. As the castle was not used by the king as his residence it made it easy for the Guardian of the Wilds to slip unseen into the building.

It took her two weeks of reading old tomes in languages no longer spoken and searching through records that only three other people in the realm could understand before she found what she was looking for.

It was not where the Guardian of the Wilds had expected to find the information. The volume she found the information in was a text on the magics of the dead religion of the realm of Oran. It was a book that should not have even existed on Celadmore.

The book spoke of portals that could be opened by using the blood of the Goddess and transport people from one realm to the other. Cassandra's heart had stopped beating as she read the tome. There was no way that Mercia could know why the city of Delma had been built and it was even less likely that he knew that the blood of the Goddess flowed in the veins of his daughters.

There was something amiss. If it was Mercia's plan to open the portal, he had not forged the plan by himself.

*****

When Joab told Mia that they were to travel with Kasna, Kia and Mathias to Kasnata's camp, she had been happier than he could have ever have predicted. She threw her arms around his neck and kissed him fiercely. The shadow took this to be a result of the overwhelming joy she felt rather than any amorous feelings.

Mathias was glad that he had someone to share the watch with and the princesses were glad to have a girl who was slightly older than they were to talk to about Grashindorph and its palaces. Both men were surprised at how quickly Mia, Kasna and Kia became friends. After a few hours it was as though the three had known each other all their lives and the horrible events that had marred their childhoods were nothing but distant memories.

"**They don't trust you, do they?**" Joab asked Mathias as they rode.

"**Not even close.**" Mathias grinned. "**The lady seems to have complete faith in you. Does she know what and who you really are?**" The assassin had always had a carefree nature that was at odds with his profession.

"**No, she doesn't. The time to tell her is not right. She doesn't know that her father is alive either, but that I will tell her and her brother when I can be sure that Mercia's spies will not be there to overhear.**" Joab confided in his friend.

"**So what are you to her?**" Mathias asked with an ulterior motive.

"**I am her bodyguard, her sworn protector against assassins.**" Joab said pointedly.

"**Okay, I take your point.**" Mathias said as he held up his hands in mock surrender.

"**What about the princesses? Do they know who you really are and why you are helping them?**" Joab asked as the girls all giggled and glanced back at the two men.

"I do dislike it when women do that and two of them are barely girls." Mathias said dryly. "No, they don't. They have no memory of anything that happened in the early days. They are allowing me to escort them for now and when we reach their mother then if they need to know, she will tell them." He shrugged.

"Do you think that we're being followed?" Joab asked as he changed the subject.

"Yes, but whether it is Neesa or Kelmar, I can't tell." Mathias said with his lips set in a thin line.

"We won't be able to escape them; they will keep tracking us as long as we are without Kasnata's protection." Joab shook his head as he thought. "How long until they have caught up with us?"

"A day, maybe two at most." Mathias looked at the three girls that rode ahead of them. "We can't let any harm come to them."

"No, we won't." Joab assured him.

It took less than a day before Kelmar could be seen by the fleeing travellers. He rode with a party of eight other soldiers that, to Mathias' eyes, looked to veterans of war. There was but a few hours until he would be upon them and there was nothing that could be done to outrun them.

*****

Tola and Renta had left as soon as Kasnata had told them of Kasna and Kia's escape. Tola was anxious to see his cousin again and even more anxious to see the daughters of Kasnata back with their mother.

They rode without stopping, knowing that as long as the princess were free of their father they would be hunted by Neesa and by Kelmar until they were safe with their mother.

"How will we find them?" Renta asked Tola as they rode. "They won't know we are coming and we are coming from the wrong direction to pick up their trail." The Condor General observed.

"If Mathias is bringing them to the camp then we will be keeping off the roads." Tola explained. "But the princesses have not been raised to cross the wilderness as we have. There is only one route they can take that is easy enough for them to navigate." The Roencian said with a smile. All his years of war had taught him the value of knowing the lay of the land. "They'll try and keep to as sheltered route as possible. As soon as they reach a plain, they will be vulnerable to attack."

"It won't matter with Kelmar and Neesa." Renta said as they rode towards the southern reaches of the Marsden forest.

"What makes you think that?" Tola had not considered there would be any immediate danger to the princesses whilst they were in the Marsden forest with Mathias to protect them.

"Now, Mathias, I know the princesses are with you, the longer you keep up this pretence that they are not, the more annoyed and bored I will become." Kelmar had sent men ahead of the travellers to flank them and all that Joab and Mathias could do to protect the women was hide them.

"I think your position in the Delmarian court has gone to your head." Mathias replied with disinterest.

"Excuse me?" Kelmar had not expected to have so much trouble dealing with the Roencian.

"You seem to be under the impression that your mood state I something that I am concerned with."

Joab had always found Mathias' glib nature irritating, but seeing it being used against someone like Kelmar was something he found strangely enjoyable.

"Wherever you have hidden them, my men will soon find them and when they do I shall kill all of you." Kelmar sneered, his face contorted by his anger. He was a man that enjoyed the comfortable life he had created for himself and that life did not include chasing children across the wilds of Celadmore.

Joab had not said a word since Kelmar had arrived. He leant against a hollow tree and seemed to be disinterested in the whole affair. Inside the tree, the three girls waited and listened. It had been Kasna's idea when she discovered the tree. At Abergorlech, the hollowed out tree had hidden both Kia and Kasna from all but the Abbott for months. There was no reason to believe it couldn't do the same for them now.

"Your friend doesn't talk much, does he?" Kelmar asked Mathias.

"No, he doesn't. I wish you would follow his example." The Roencian quipped and Kelmar snarled in response.

"You've hidden those girls somewhere close by and if you will not hand them over then I shall burn them out." He hissed, the Regent's eyes flaring with rage. He raised his hand and three of his men brought forward torches.

"No." Kasna shouted. She climbed up the inside of the trunk and leapt to the ground. She had her sword drawn and was seemingly prepared to fight Kelmar for her freedom.

"Excellent. Kill her." Kelmar no longer had any patience for capturing the princesses, he wanted them dead.

Men began to converge on Kasnata. Joab stepped to her side as Mathias found his path to her blocked by Kelmar. Arrows sliced through the air and hit one of the men in the shoulder. Kasna looked up expecting to see her sister sat at the top of the trunk with her bow drawn. She was not there. Instead Renta stepped forward.

"Coward." She offered the word as a greeting to Kelmar, laced with contempt and disgust.

"Renta!" Mathias sounded genuinely happy to see the woman.

"Take the children and go." She ordered. "I will deal with things here."

Joab did not need to be told twice. He hoisted Kia and Lady Mia from the hollow tree and made for the horses. Kasna tried to stand beside Renta, but Mathias picked her up and carried her, kicking and screaming from Kelmar's sight. Any movement that Kelmar or his men made to go after the princesses was met with Renta blocking them.

"You foolish woman." Kelmar said shaking his head.

"Don't worry; I'll soon catch up to them when I am done with you." Renta said confidently as the first of the men of Delma attacked.

Tola was with the horses that the travellers had abandoned not half a mile to the west of where Kelmar had caught them.

"Where is Renta?" He asked when he saw his cousin approaching.

"Covering our escape." Mathias replied as he swung himself into the saddle.

"You seem to have picked up some strays." Tola said with a raised eyebrow.

"It is nice to see you too." Joab replied with a sarcastic smile.

"We can do introductions later, we need to leave. I am not sure how much time Renta can offer us." Mathias said urgently. Joab and Tola exchanged a confused look, but did not argue.

"Follow me." Tola led the party out of the clearing and out on to the plains of the east.

*****

Haston awoke to the now familiar sound of life and bustle in the Gibborim. It had been odd at first to hear sounds of town life echoing through the tunnels of the old sewer system. It brought back an odd mixture of memories for the old lord.

He had spent months exploring and living in the tunnels during his youth when he and Rosla had been impetuous and ignoring the kings orders. They had never been told to explore the tunnels for signs of the enemy but the two boys had known better and disappeared down into the sewers.

Time had proven the two to be right, the invasion of the desert bandits had been foiled by their disobedience to the king, but it had not saved them from being punished. Their punishment had been to work in the marketplace as apprentices to each of the tradesmen for two years.

Neither of the young nobles had thought it would be a difficult time, they saw it as a period when they would be free of the pressures of nobility and schooling. Instead they soon learned how difficult working for a living was and how the people struggled and suffered during the dark, sparse winters and how they rejoiced in the simpler things in life.

Rosla and Haston had grown into men in the two years they spent as apprentices, their childish, spoilt nature had been beaten out of them by the blacksmith's iron and learning about the people they would lead.

The Gibborim reminded him of the tradesmen that he had lived and worked with. They had the same way of enjoying life, of finding joy in such small events, of not letting the difficulties they faced every day destroy the happiness they could find. They were good people.

Haston found himself being gradually accepted by the people and treated less like an outsider every day.

"You would not think you were a lord." Haman smiled at him as the two came across each other in the market.

"Not now I have changed my clothes." Haston had grinned as he shook hands with the head of the Gibborim.

"You seem to be comfortable amongst the people, rumours of your two years of exile with the king are clearly more reliable than the rumours we have been feeding to the king." Haman was an agreeable man.

He had the best interests of his people at the centre of his focus.

"I would hope so; I would hate to think you were feeding accurate information to him." The two men had laughed politely with the other at Haston's joke for a few moments.

"Come, Hermia wishes to talk to you." Haman said as he led Haston through the market to a tunnel entrance the lord had not come across before. Haman heaved it open and followed Haston inside, closing the door behind them.

"It seems like we are getting close to finding our mole, so Layla tells me." Hermia greeted him from deeper inside the tunnel. There was very little light cast, what small amount was being created by the torches that Hermia had stationed either side of her.

She was sat in a crude wooden chair with a small wooden table and three other chairs around it. She was alone; there was no sign of Asahel, Helez or Layla. Jephthah had not been seen in her company or in any company since he had attacked Layla in the Gibborim hall.

"Please sit down." Haman said as he walked past Haston and sat beside Hermia. Haston approached slowly not sure why he had been summoned.

"We wanted to have this conversation with you when we first found you, but there was some concern amongst the people that it would put them in too much danger to blindly trust you." Hermia began as Haston sat down.

"But they seem to have found a way to see me as less of a threat?" Haston asked with a sceptical expression.

"Quite simply, yes." Haman shrugged.

"You are aware that those gathered here are believed to be dead or exiled by most of the population of Nosfa. There are a few here that were born amongst the Gibborim and have never seen the surface of Celadmore, but for the most part, we are the enemies of the king." Hermia began. It occurred to Haston that though she was vehemently opposed to her son and how he chose to rule, though he had plotted to murder her, though he had seized the throne against the expressed wishes of his father, that Hermia still loved her son and everything that she did to move against him hurt her immeasurably. The Lord of Afdanic watched her carefully as she spoke, the lines on her face unable to conceal her sadness.

"Yes and that you have formed a resistance force against his rule." Haston confirmed.

"It is more than a resistance force." Haman said with a grin.

"There have been rumours of revolution circulating in Grashindorph for the last ten years. No one has paid any attention to them save for our paranoid king. We have been building our force for revolution, we are going to remove Mercia from power and install Leinad on the throne." Hermia said proudly.

"The royal line will not have been broken, the tyrant king will be exiled to the pleasure of his queen, his fate shall be left in Kasnata's hands. Advisors shall be appointed to Leinad from amongst the people as well as the court and peace shall be brought to realm for the army of Nosfa shall not march and Kasnata will be free from Mercia's control." Haman finished. There was fire burning in his eyes as he spoke and fervour in his voice.

Haston sat unmoved regarding the two revolutionaries that sat before him. He understood the need for such secrecy when there was a mole in the Gibborim and also if he stood against their plans, they could easily dispose of him without witness.

"You believe that Mercia is paranoid and that those around him remain ignorant to the danger?" Haston asked slowly as he weighed the wisdom of his actions and words.

"Yes." Hermia said confidently. There was no doubt in the old woman. She was resolute and certain in a way that Haston had forgotten a human could be after years of living under the fear that Mercia's reign had brought.

"Then I am with you as soon as you can guarantee that my daughter is safe." Haston said spreading his hands as he waited for a response.

"She is away from the king in the hands of Joab." Haman smiled warmly. "He sent word that he was ordered to escort her from the city as there was a threat against her life. They make for the camp of Kasnata to reunite brother and sister."

Relief washed over Haston. Tears came unbidden to his face and streamed down his cheeks. Here amongst the Gibborim he had finally found the hope he had been searching for since the death of his wife.

"Thank you." He breathed.

Haman and Hermia began to discuss the plans for revolution earnestly but Haston was barely listening as he thanked the gods that his daughter had been spared and that his son still lived.

*****

Kasnata had awoken to find the roof of her tent heavy with snow. Wentrus was upon them and food was becoming scarce. There were few villages that would help the army now, those that had once provided food had been destroyed by Delmarian soldiers, the survivors having fled to the safety of the city of Benadrocca.

The other villages and towns belonged to the crown of Delma and would not help the enemy that brought war to their lands. There were two options open to the queen. The first was to order the army to disband, to return home for the cold season and return when Spregan chased away Wentrus. The second was to press forward and lay siege to the city of

Delma.

The army would be able to steal all the food provisions it needed from those trying to take food to the city, from the towns and villages that would no longer have the protection of the army and the farms that would billet the men of Nosfa who had done nothing but complain about the snow.

"What are we to do, majesty?" Quisla had stood before her and asked every morning. The general knew that the queen must decide soon to move forward or allow the army to return home until the new season.

"First I wish Benaiah to devise something different for our camps. Canvas is not secure to sleep under, though it is easy to pack and transport. I want something that is equally easy to transport but more secure." The queen said as she stared up at the tent around her.

"Ma'am?" Quisla was confused by Kasnata's ramblings about their shelters.

"As we head further north, the snowfall will be higher, the drifts will be bigger and the cold will be greater. Our people will not survive the campaign or siege if we do not have something better than canvas." The queen said with a smile. "Talk to Benaiah first; tell him he has two weeks whilst we move on the city. When we arrive I wish to see what he has to keep the army alive. Then pass the order to break camp, we leave in six hours."

Quisla smiled warmly at the queen.

"As you wish, my lady." The Vulture General dropped to her knees before the queen and kissed Kasnata's hand.

As Quisla passed the order to break camp, excitement surged through the Order and dread through the men of Nosfa. There was a flurry of activity, all save for Benaiah. The forge master sat and smoked a long pipe whilst he thought. His forge was dismantled and packed by those that were apprenticed to him as he pondered upon the problem of crafting new shelters for the people of the Order.

Ariella was largely ignored as she moved through the camp. Since his return to the camp, Rathe had informed her that he had a new teacher for his evening language sessions and would not need her help any longer. The Valian had imagined slitting the general's throat as he spoke and watching the blood slowly drip down over his armour.

She had lost the position she needed to be in, a position that gave her access to the queen without arousing suspicion. She had gone to Hesla to appeal to her for help in gaining access to the queen, but she had refused and dismissed the hot-tempered girl.

In the business of the camp being broken, Ariella became aware that this was one of the few times that protection around the queen would be at a minimum. Whilst the camp was being broken, the watch were busy ensuring that no outsiders attacked without warning, the generals were busy overseeing differing areas of the camp were taken down and packed properly whilst the queen walked the camp.

She would never have an opportunity like this again. Ariella knew she had to act quickly. She strode through the camp looking for any sign of the queen, her mind forming a plan as she walked.

It was not a hard thing to find the queen amongst her people and in killing her it would make no difference if her death was witnessed or not. Once the queen was dead, the true heirs could seize the throne, it wouldn't matter if they knew it was Ariella that had killed Kasnata or not.

The queen was a warrior, a strong and talented fighter that had fought in and survived many battles. Killing her in a duel would not be very likely, taking her by surprise was Ariella's only chance.

The Valian drew her hunting knife from the belt around her waist and concealed it along her forearm, the hilt clutched tightly in her hand.

The queen was stood with the horses, Cara and Horace were checking over the horses to see which of them were suitable for riding and if any of them were lame.

Kasnata was stood with Red Hare; she was brushing his coat until his chestnut coat shone like molten fire and his black mane and tail looked like silk. He was the perfect image of a war horse to all of the Order and Kasnata treated him as an equal to her children. She was stood alone save for the horse. Beside Red Hare was a jet black mare that did not look like a horse bred for war, she was a soft creature that was bred to carry spoilt children, not warriors.

As the queen finished grooming Red Hare she moved on to lavishing attention on the mare. Ariella listened as the queen spoke to the horse, calling it Ebony and treating it like a pet rather than a partner for battle.

Ariella approached slowly, her movements slow and deliberate so she did not spook the horses. The queen didn't hear her approaching as her mind was focused on other things.

Rathe stepped into the corral and walked over to where the queen stood. The Valian watched as the two talked and saw the general slip his arm around the shoulders of the queen to move her hair away from her neck.

The two were oblivious to everything going on around them. It took Ariella four steps to reach the queen, the sudden movement caught Rathe's eye and spooked Ebony. The panicking mare backed into some of the other horses, the terror of the mare spread through the corral causing horses to rear, buck and kick.

Kasnata stepped sideways to avoid Ebony and Ariella narrowly missed stabbing the queen in the back. Rathe drew his sword and lunged wildly at the Valian. Ariella jumped backwards out of his reach and tried to run from the growing danger of being surrounded by frightened horses.

She turned and found herself in the path of Red Hare. The horses reared and brought its giant hooves crashing down onto the skull of the Valian assassin.

Cara and Horace were shouting for help to calm the horses as Kasnata patted the neck of her battle partner. She knelt down beside the body of Ariella and shook her head.

"Get Yoav." She said quietly to Rathe.

"Are you alright?" He whispered as he placed a hand on her shoulder.

"Yes, thank you. Please, get Yoav." She replied quietly.

The horses had been calmed by the time Yoav followed Rathe back to the corral. Misna and Amalia were there arguing over who was responsible.

"Highness, you sent for me?" Yoav announced his arrival, stepping between Misna and Amalia, forcing the two women apart.

"Yes." Kasnata said smiling with gratitude. "I want you to do something for me."

"What is it you need, my queen?" Wolfblood asked as he looked down at the corpse of Ariella.

"I want you to find out who she reported to in the camp. She tried to kill me and didn't care if she was caught. There will be someone else involved. Misna and Amalia can't agree to work together, so I want you to do it. If you need any help then I would suggest you talk to the Eight." Kasnata said in a low voice so the two quarrelling generals couldn't hear her.

"Of course, my lady, though how can you be sure that I can be trusted with this? Would it not be better for the Eight to investigate without me interference?" Yoav did not make the suggestion because it was a task he believed to be beneath him, on the contrary an attempt on the life of his queen was the most serious offence he could think of, but he also knew that he was fallible.

If any action he had not taken or taken had contributed to the attack being possible, then he wished to be punished for it, not able to wash over his guilt and hide his complicity.

"No, I want you to investigate." Kasnata smiled. Her smile told the general that she knew what he was thinking and that she had the utmost faith that he was not involved.

Yoav looked between the queen and Ariella and nodded.

"As you wish, majesty."

Chapter 18

Ilana was sick of being treated like a child. She had been born in the tunnels, one of the Gibborim that had never seen the world that lay beyond the sewers. Being the younger sister of Helez was no easy task for a young girl to live with. He had an overprotective attitude that drove her to distraction, no boy her age would come near her for fear that he would run them through. Especially since both their parents were dead.

He was always an important man within the Gibborim, one that protected Lady Hermia and knew of things far beyond the roof of the sewer. Since Ilana was small, Helez had told her stories of what life was like in the city above before they had runaway to the sewers and how they would rise up again one day to remove the king so they could go back home.

It had been eleven years since he had started tell those tales to her and now she was fourteen, she felt she had waited long enough for the Gibborim to rise against the king. She had argued bitterly with Helez about it long into the night and questioned Asahel over it. Neither man would tell her anything about the revolution nor when it was to start.

She felt so helpless and excluded from all that was happening in the Gibborim that she began to believe that the revolution was never going to happen, that it was false hope being fed to those who would believe it whilst maintaining the equilibrium of power.

She was sat by herself outside the Gibborim hall when Bracha found her. Jephthah's wife had spent very little time speaking to others in the Gibborim after Jephthah had been dismissed by Hermia and no one had seen Jephthah.

"You seem sad today, Ilana." Bracha said as she sat down beside the young girl.

"I am frustrated." She shrugged. "Nobody listens to me or lets me help and Helez is always lying to me."

"Helez lied to you?" Bracha asked as she put a motherly arm around the girl's shoulders.

"He keeps telling me that there is going to be a revolution and it's all lies." She said kicking some small chips of stone that lay in front of her.

"Why do you think he is lying?"

"Because no one else is talking about it, no one else is doing anything. He thinks I'm so stupid, that I'll just believe anything he tells me." Ilana pouted and stamped her feet.

"Well then maybe you should do something about it. If you think that there should be a revolution, go into the city and raise one." Bracha said comfortingly.

"You think I can do that?" Ilana asked with curiosity.

"Why not? You are smart and strong, more than capable of leading a revolution." Jephthah's wife said with a smile.

"I'll go into the city tonight then and raise revolution. Then Helez and Asahel will stop treating me like a child." Ilana was resolute in her conviction. She jumped to her feet and disappeared through the men and women leaving the Gibborim hall.

Bracha smiled to herself and rose to her feet. She hated living in the sewers. She had never wanted Jephthah to remain as Hermia's shield when they had married. She had begged him to resign from the position, but he had refused. When they came to live in the tunnels below Grashindorph, Bracha had wept for days.

She had left her family and friends behind to come and live in this foul place and her husband had never asked what she wanted, never once considered her feelings. His only concern had been for Hermia.

Since he had been dismissed from her service he had been drunk and brooding. He refused to stir from their home because of the shame. He sent his daughters to stay with Asahel and his parents because he didn't want them to be tarred with the same brush of disgrace.

His dismissal had been the answer to Bracha prayers. She had spent the days since trying to persuade the man mountain to leave the Gibborim, to return to the surface world and begin a new life, whether in the city of Grashindorph or beyond.

Jephthah had refused, hoping that the woman he loved more dearly than his wife would come back and take him back into her service; would allow him to give his life to protect hers.

With each passing day his grief grew less and his anger towards the Lady of the Gibborim grew greater. As his anger grew, Bracha began to plant ideas in his mind, ideas of revenge and betrayal, ideas that culminated in Jephthah wanting to leave the Gibborim.

Bracha had left Jephthah to pack what they needed in their home whilst she went to the market to buy supplies when she had come across Ilana. The stupid girl was the perfect sacrifice to prove that the Gibborim threat was real. It had taken very little convincing to send Ilana off on a fool's errand. She would be caught very easily; tortured for information and that would be the end of Hermia's treason.

When they reached the surface, Bracha would talk her husband to see the Baron of Fintry and seek a pardon in exchange for their freedom. She returned to find Jephthah waiting for her, two bundles of clothing packed, the rest of their possessions left behind.

Bracha had insisted that your daughters be left behind with Asahel until they were safe and then they could send for them. Her daughters were loyal to the Gibborim; they wanted to fight for the freedom of the people that they had grown up with. Bracha was certain that her daughters would hate her for handing over those that they thought of as family.

Bracha was happy as she and Jephthah left their home to return to the surface, she felt free for the first time in fifteen years and her husband was finally listening to what she wanted over the former queen.

Jephthah leaving the sewers was not an uncommon sight, so no one questioned it when they spied him and his wife using the entrance to the lower tunnels that led into the city.

The giant man led the way through the passageways, not needing a map or any landmarks to guide his way, he strode with confidence. Bracha followed behind, her feet slipping as she tried to navigate through the stagnant water.

"I will be glad when we no longer live amongst this filth." She said as she slipped and landed face first in the dirty water.

"It will not be long now." Jephthah grunted as he forged ahead.

"To feel the grass under my feet again." She sighed with a wistful smile.

"Where are we going to?" Jephthah asked as he paused at a junction where the tunnel split into three.

"To the south market. He is meeting us there." Bracha said as she slipped again. Jephthah grunted and turned down the left arm of the tunnels.

"Who is he?" He asked as the darkness around the two grew deeper as the torch Bracha carried spluttered.

"A man that can help us start a new life and leave all this behind us." She replied with excitement and hope.

"I see." Jephthah sighed. "For what price?" He grunted.

"What does it matter?" Bracha asked as she dropped the torch into the water, plunging the tunnel into darkness.

"I would say that price is always an important consideration." A female voice called out in the black. Bracha screeched as she recognised the voice as Layla's.

"You witch!" She howled. "You couldn't just leave us alone."

"Leave you alone? I couldn't do that, Bracha. You know how seriously we take desertion down here." Layla teased her, the shadow's voice bouncing off the walls of the tunnel.

"Stay where you are." Asahel warned as he approached Bracha. Behind him Helez carried a torch that cast long shadows. Bracha was collapsed on her knees in the water, her face a fright to look upon. Veins of rage bulged across her face and neck; her eyes were wide and bloodshot. At the far end of the tunnel, Jephthah was stood beside Layla looking down on the figure of his wife.

"How could you!" Bracha cried as she looked up at her husband.

"I was ordered to find the mole, no matter who it was and no matter how much it hurt me." Jephthah replied clearing his throat.

"Mole? MOLE!" Bracha bellowed.

"You sent letters to the Baron of Fintry, you were taking me to meet him, to hand over all those we have lived and fought beside. You were the mole and you broke my heart." Jephthah growled as he walked towards his wife.

"Your heart? Do you have any idea what it is like to be married to a man that loves another woman more than he loves you? To watch every day as he pledges himself to die for her without giving you a second thought? My whole adult like I have done exactly what you have wanted and received nothing in return except you running off to be with Hermia. To serve her. You broke my heart every day until there was nothing left to break. I wanted my husband back and my freedom from this terrible life. Are you that shocked that I would give up everything just to have you back?" Bracha demanded as she punched the water.

"It is my duty to die for Hermia, to put her first. You married me when I was already her shield. You pledged to follow me. I am sorry that this is where it led to, but my duty was always to her first and you knew that. You cannot make your treachery noble by blaming an inattentive husband." Jephthah spat as he looked down at the woman he had once married and realised he didn't know her any more.

"You should know, Bracha, when we discovered there was a mole, we knew it was you." Layla said brightly as she moved to stand behind Jephthah. "We just needed to find a way for you to let us catch you attempting to pass information."

"The fight in the hall?" Bracha looked at Layla with loathing.

"Staged so that Jephthah would be dismissed and so you would do what we anticipated." Layla was smug as she crowed over Bracha. She had never liked the woman, never trusted her, for what now looked to be good reason.

"On your feet, you're being taken back so all can see you for what you are." Helez said as he grabbed Bracha by the arm to pull her to her feet.

"Take your hands off me." Bracha wrenched her arm out of Helez's grasp and started to laugh hysterically. Layla stepped forward and slapped her hard across the face. "You are all so superior, so clever."

"Silence, woman." Jephthah barked but Bracha ignored him.

"So high and mighty, so sure your little rebellion will succeed, yet you don't even tell those closest to you what is happening." She cackled as she rose from the floor. She turned to Helez with a grimacing smile. "You should have talked more to your sister, not filled her head with such silly dreams."

Helez lunged forward and grabbed Bracha round the throat.

"What did you do?" His voice was barely above a whisper and shaking with rage.

"I told her what she wanted to hear. Such a pity you'll not see her again. She was such a pretty thing." Bracha crowed. Layla slapped her again as Asahel separated his friend from the traitor.

"I'll take her back." Layla assured them. "Go, find Ilana."

Asahel nodded and steered Helez away from Bracha back down the tunnel. Jephthah looked at Layla and his wife.

"Are you sure?" He asked gruffly.

"I'll be fine, and she will reach Hermia alive. Go, help your protégés." Layla smiled as she took out a cloth and placed it over Bracha's mouth. The traitor struggled for a moment, but the fumes on the cloth flowed into her lungs with each breath and soon she was unconscious. Jephthah watched as Layla hoisted his wife onto her shoulders and disappeared.

*****

Renta had bought some time for the escaping travellers by holding off Kelmar's forces, but the time she had bought had not been enough. For a few hours there was hope that they might be able to outrun the Delmarian forces but Kia's horse became lame.

The princess refused to put the creature through unnecessary pain, so the group had stopped to set it loose and have Kia share Kasna's mount. By the time this had been accomplished, Kelmar was visible not half the horizon away.

Instead of trying to catch up with the party he sent a messenger to ask for a parlay so the two groups made camp, half the horizon apart.

"**We won't make it to Kasnata at this rate, the horses won't survive and Kelmar will catch up to us. Renta barely managed to hold him off for a few hours and we are no warrior generals.**" Mathias observed in a quiet voice to his cousin as the three girls were setting their tent and building the fire.

"**What do you suggest then?**" Tola asked distractedly. His attention was focused on Kelmar's camp, trying to make out the figures, searching for any sign of Renta.

"**We should head for Tulna. We'll be safe there and it's a much shorter journey than it would be to Kasnata's camp.**" Mathias suggested as he kept his eye on the women.

"**Three days ride to the north? The horses should be able to make it and in good time. I can lead Kelmar's forces away and give you time to reach safety.**" Joab agreed "**We can find some way of getting the three girls to Kasnata's camp once we are protected by Kania and Nodarto.**"

"**Then let us take this parlay. Tola and I will go, Joab can you explain to the girls what is happening? This shouldn't take long so you should be ready to move once the parlay is complete.**" Mathias instructed with a grim smile and patted his cousin on the back. "**Let's go.**"

The cousins trudged forward to where the parlay flag had been planted by the messenger. It was a good distance from both camps meaning that no help would be able to arrive in time should violence break out. As they approached the flag the two men could see Kelmar was stood beside a figure forced to their knees, hands and feet bound.

"Renta!" Tola cried out and made to run to the Anaguran woman. Mathias caught his cousin and tried to calm him down.

"I'm okay." She called out and was struck across the head by Kelmar.

"Touch her again and I swear I will tear your arms from your shoulders." Tola was shaking with rage. Mathias had never seen his cousin so angry before, so moved by emotion that he threatened terrible violence.

"I doubt you would be able to perform such a feat." Kelmar said idly. "Now hand over the princesses and you can have your lover back. It's not her life I want but I am more than prepared to take it, should you refuse to be reasonable." The Regent of Delma sounded as though he was haggling over the price of cattle at market, not the lives of women that were beloved by the Queen of Nosfa and the Order.

"I am prepared to lay down my life to see them safe." Renta spat at the feet of Kelmar, who struck her again. Tola made to lunge past his cousin, but Mathias held him tightly.

"We won't give them up." Mathias said flatly.

"Very well then, there is little point to this exercise. Ah well." Kelmar shrugged and drew his sword.

"Stop!" Tola cried out as Mathias dragged him backwards.

"It's okay, my love." Renta smiled sadly at Tola. The hero of the east struggled violently against the strength of his cousin, but he could not free himself.

"No, please, Renta, you can't." Tola begged her as tears began to fall from both of their eyes.

"This is war. We die for those we love. Take them home to her." Renta soothed him as Kelmar severed her left arm from her body. The Condor General screamed in pain as the blade bit into her shoulder.

"No!"

"Tola, go. I love you, but go!" Renta urged as blood poured from her body, draining the colour from her skin. Kelmar stepped round to her other side and cleaved her other arm clean away.

Mathias was struggling to keep his hold on Tola but kept pulling him slowly back with every step.

"**Joab!**" He yelled and the shadow rode forward with the horses of the two Roencians in tow.

"**By the Goddess**..." Joab's eyes were wide as he watched

Kelmar swing his blade again, this time he trust it through Renta's side. The general screamed in pain and fell forwards to the floor. The sand and dirt of the plain already stained with her blood.

"Kelmar! I swear by all that I am and all that I love, you shall know pain beyond reckoning at my hand before you die." Tola swore his revenge as Mathias forced him onto his horse and Joab led the beast away, Mathias mounting his own horse and following not far behind.

"Run then little rabbits, I'll soon catch you again." Kelmar laughed to himself and listened to Renta's dying breaths. "You silly woman, you should have stayed with your precious queen."

Chapter 19

Ilana wept bitterly and tried to pull her clothes around her body to keep out the cold. She was sat on the floor in the corner, as far back from the door as she could be.

When she had emerged in the upper city she had no idea of how she should go about starting a revolution. She had not been told by her brother how these things worked, how people were stirred to passion, but she knew she had to find some way of talking to the people.

She had gone into the taverns and listened to people's conversation. She had spent hours in the market trying to find those who would rebel but all that she discovered was that she was in a world that was alien to her, a world she had no way of understanding and she had no money to help her survive.

Her mind began to turn to returning to the Gibborim, of going back to her brother and her friends beneath Grashindorph. She was tired, cold and hungry. Her feet hurt from walking about the city and her eyes hurt from the light from the sun. It began to rain as the morning became afternoon, the water stealing what little heat she still had in her body.

Since she had been asking questions in the market she had felt like she was being followed. No matter where she had gone or tried to hide, she could not shake the feeling.

Ilana had continued to walk around the city, instead of asking about rebellion, she had begun to ask for food, water and shelter. People had spat at her, pushed her into the mud and kicked her for her trouble. She wished more than anything else that she could be back amongst the Gibborim and began to look for a sewer entrance that would let her go home.

She snaked her way through the streets, the number of people growing less and less as she wound her way into narrower streets.

The feeling of being watched had not gone away, if anything it had intensified. Ilana kept expecting to turn the corner and find a group of thugs and ruffians waiting to rob her. Instead, when she turned the corner she found her way blocked by men in uniform. She turned to run from them, but found that there were more uniformed men behind her.

She was beaten and thrown into a prison cell by the men and left to starve in the cold, dank room until a man came down to see her. He was a slight man with a hook nose and long fingers that looked more like icicles.

"Who are you, girl?" He asked in a high-pitched voice that sounded closer to screeching than speech.

"My name is Ilana." She replied, her voice shaking as much as her body was.

"Your name means very little, you could say any name and it would mean just as much to me as that." The man sneered. "You have been asking questions, unsettling questions. So I ask again, who are you?" He spoke calmly as he drummed his fingers together

"My name is Ilana, I was born here." She said, still shaking. Ilana was terrified; she didn't know what was going on. The man that was stood opposite her was demanding something that she didn't understand. She was cold and missing her brother.

"My dear girl, I don't think you quite grasp the gravity of the situation that you find yourself in. You have been asking people about rebellion and revolution against the king. That is treason. I have been given free rein by the king himself to do whatever I need to do in order to find out what you were planning and who else is involved. The sooner you tell me, the less pain you will have to endure." He said lightly as he reached over and stroked her face with his freakish fingers.

Ilana shuddered and started to cry.

*****

Asahel ran through the tunnels, he was desperately searching for Helez amongst the crowds of people. He spotted his friend saying goodnight to four of the eligible women of the Gibborim.

"Helez!" He bellowed as he skidded to a halt beside his best friend.

"What is it?" Helez laughed as he caught Asahel before he fell.

"It's Ilana. She has been arrested and sentenced to death for treason." Asahel gasped.

The colour drained from Helez's face.

"When?" He croaked.

"Two days, it's going to be held in the market." Asahel reported sadly.

"We have to stop it, have to do something." Helez had begun to shake uncontrollably.

"We'll talk to Hermia, but you need to sit down right now." Asahel's tone was kind as he took the weight of his friend round his shoulders and half led, half carried him home.

*****

The walls of the city of Delma could be seen on the horizon when the snow was not falling and the wind was not screaming across the open plain.

Benaiah was roaring at his apprentices as they ran about constructing the new design he had devised to allow the army to camp in the northern wilderness during the winter.

The forge master had gone ahead with the scouting party to start making camp. He had begun by making windbreaks for the tents from lines of logs that rose to a height of two feet clear of the top of any tent in the camp. It was a long curling line that braced against the north wind that buffeted the apprentices as they struggled to hold the logs in place whilst they were secured.

The drifts of snow were being cleared to form banks around the edge of the camp, compacted, to form a natural barrier and reduce the cold on the ground. The apprentices and foragers had been sent out to gather leaves and smaller, finer twigs on the journey north until there were two wagons packed with them.

The tent design itself was not to be changed, it was erected s normal, save for the roof and ground. The twigs and small pieces of wood were lashed together and used to create a sloping roof that was held over the tent by a four post wooden frame. The leaves were scattered on the floor of the tent to provide a barrier between the frozen ground and those that were to sleep in the tents.

It was not a pretty sight to behold, in fact it could be considered ugly, but the forge master was certain it would be functional. When Kasnata had arrived she had approved of the Benaiah's ideas and ordered the camp was to be erected according to his design.

The men and women grumbled as they were forced to work harder than before in freezing conditions for longer than any of them wanted to, but when the camp was set, the wind could barely reach the tents and the snow was caught by the break, the banks and the wooden roofs. Their fires were safe from being extinguished by the elements and when each of the warriors and soldiers crawled into their beds that night they felt warmer than they had since Sagma/Sumar.

*****

Tulna was an oasis in the Shango Desert that lay just to the north of the Marsden forest. The buildings were flat-roofed and made of sandstone that made them seem as though they appeared out of nowhere.

In the centre of the approach to the largest building in the village there was a huge fountain that water flowed down over to a large pool below.

Men and women were holding buckets and skins into the flow to catch the water to drink from. In the pool, children were playing and washing off the sand. Sand was something that the princesses and Mia had not been expecting to be so invasive. It had permeated through their clothing and now sat, rubbing their soft skin raw as they rode.

As they entered the village, people poured from their houses and lined the streets. Flowers were thrown in the path of the horses, the people cheering and waving at the weary travellers. Mia looked at Joab with a questioning look as he and Mathias waved back.

Girls blew kisses to the men; Mathias returned them, Joab tried to ignore them, Tola was oblivious to them. He was lost in his grief, the image of Renta being dismembered and bleeding to death was burnt on the back of his eyes. He had known that here would always be a possibility that one or both of them would die in battle, but he had never dreamed that he would have to watch Renta die, hear her voice telling him to go, to leave her.

He couldn't forgive himself for letting her die, for not going to her rescue. He was the hero of the war of the east and he couldn't even protect the woman he loved from a spoilt Regent that had heartlessly hacked her apart before his eyes.

Mia, Kasna and Kia all had all avoided the grieving Roencian since Renta had been killed. He didn't offer conversation to Joab or Mathias, but instead grunted and growled responses.

Behind the fountain in Tulna there were steps that led up to the largest building in the village and four figures stood waiting on those steps for the travellers to reach them.

"You!" Kasna shrieked as she spotted the Abbott was one of the four. "You promised help!" The princess leapt from the back of her horse and charged headlong at the Abbott. She was about to hit the man when she found herself lifted off the ground by a single arm around her waist.

"Peace, little one." Cassandra said half-laughing as she carried the struggling child away from her brother. "There is no call for violence."

"She died because of him!" Kasna yelled as she was set down by the Guardian of the Wilds.

"Who died?" Cassandra asked as she knelt in front of the princess and looked her directly in the eyes. Kasna felt herself tremble under the gaze of the woman who could carry her so easily.

"Mother's friend, Renta. Kelmar killed her because he did not help as he promised he would." Kasna shouted waving her hand in the Abbott's direction in an accusatory manner.

"He did send help, Kasna." Mathias said sighing. "He sent me."

Kia and Kasna both looked blankly at the assassin.

"You?" Kia asked in disbelief.

"Yes, Mathias is an excellent bodyguard in normal circumstances, but it would seem that things were more complicated than we first thought." The Abbott said as he chewed his lower lip in thought. "Sister, do you think he will have been discouraged by their arrival here?" He asked turning to Cassandra as she stood and stepped away from the princess.

"No, he is stupid beyond reckoning. There is something I wish to know, but it can wait until you have been fed, watered and rested." She sighed as she thought. "Joab, you need to tell her." Cassandra said abruptly as she looked up at the shadow and frowned.

Joab open and closed his mouth several times before he nodded slowly.

"Who are you people?" Mia asked in confusion at all that was happening around her.

"My Lady Mia, please do not be worried." The older woman that had stood observing on the steps beside a man that looked to be her husband, descended to offer a hand to Mia to help her dismount.

"You are in the safety of the oasis of Tulna." Her husband smiled as he followed her down the steps.

"I am Kania, and this is my husband Nodarto, we are the leaders of this place. This is our daughter, Cassandra, Guardian of the Wilds and our son, the Abbott, Guardian of the Spire. We are friends of the Order and enemies of tyranny and war. Joab was raised her and trained for the task he now does; protecting you. Mathias and Tola are friends and allies from the village of Roenca. We have all been working for quite some time to change the terrible state that our world is in." Kania smiled as she helped the lady dismount.

"You are all working together?" Mia stuttered as Joab dismounted and came to stand beside her.

"Yes, alongside Queen Kasnata. There is much that you do not know that I must tell you, but you need to sleep first and eat." Joab said gently, soothing the panic that was rising in the chest of the young lady.

"He is quite right." Nodarto agreed. "Come, all of you, we shall see to all that is needed. The Abbott is good with horses and even found a lame mare wandering around the eastern plain that he has been nursing back to health. Your steeds will be safe with him and Cassandra is more than capable of holding off any attack that might be made against us." The older man smiled warmly as he ushered the travellers inside.

As Tola passed her, Kania reached out her hand and gently squeezed his forearm.

"I am sorry." She whispered. Tola nodded in response, but Kania was not sure he had even listened to her.

Nodarto had seen to feeding their guests and Kania had shown them to their own rooms within the larger building that seemed to be there to host guests. Kasna and Kia had fallen asleep quickly; Mia had been given a room apart from the princesses and asked Joab to stay with her until she fell asleep.

Mathias sat and wept for Renta and for his cousin. He had known that the two had been lovers for many years, only together when the country was at war. He had known that both of them had decided not to take the relationship too seriously, but it seemed to Mathias that neither of them had managed to stop themselves from falling in love with the other.

Cassandra walked to the edge of Tulna and sat down on the ground. She sat and waited for Kelmar to appear and was not waiting long.

"Woman, what is this place?" He demanded as he reined in his horse beside where Cassandra sat.

"A place you are not welcome." Cassandra sat shortly as she drew patterns in the sand with her finger.

"Woman, I would have more respect when you speak to your betters." He sneered as he forced his horse closer to where Cassandra sat.

"Turn your men around, take them back to Delma, if you can pass Kasnata's army. You will go no further here." Cassandra said calmly as she ignored the horse kicking sand over the patterns she had drawn.

"No woman talks to me like that." Kelmar scowled as he raised his sword to strike at Cassandra.

"You should rethink your current path." Cassandra advised. Kelmar laughed and ignored the warning.

The men that travelled with Kelmar jeered the woman, but none of them saw her move. Kelmar cried out as his blade was held across his throat, his arm pinned against his back.

"For the life of Renta, payment is due." Cassandra hissed in his ear, "but that is not mine to demand."

"You have no idea what is happening, what Mercia is going to do. The princesses have to die!" Kelmar argued as he struggled against Cassandra's grasp.

"I know exactly what he intends to do." Cassandra growled as resisted the temptation to snap Kelmar's wrist. "And I will find a way to stop him. Run home to Delma, little Regent." She cautioned as she released him and broke his blade over her knee.

"I will not see my homeland destroyed by Mercia's greed." Kelmar's bravado was returning now he was free of Cassandra's grasp.

"You will leave or you shall die." Cassandra said flatly.

Kelmar glanced at his men and hurriedly mounted his horse. With a backward glance at the Guardian of the Wilds, Kelmar spurred his horse back into the forest, his men following behind, none of them understanding how a single woman had defeated their leader.

"I'm sorry, Renta." Cassandra whispered as she turned back to the village.

Chapter 20

Ilana cried as she was led to the market by armed guards. People lined the streets and jeered at her. She was pelted with rotten fruit and vegetables and insults were hurled at her that she didn't understand but knew were meant to be hurtful.

The stage for her execution had been built in the market. There had been deliberation as to how to execute Ilana, whether she should be beheaded or hanged. It had been decided that hanging would teach a better lesson to any within the city that sympathised with the young girl.

The market was full of people all straining to see the stage; there was excitement and bloodlust hanging in the air. Amongst the rabble Helez and Asahel were trying to force their way forward.

"This is not a good idea." Asahel hissed to his friend as they were jostled by the crowd.

"We can't let them kill her." Helez responded with fear in his eyes.

When Hermia had been told about Ilana's arrest and the setting of an execution date, she had brought Bracha before her and ordered her shadow and shields to leave her alone with the traitor.

They had all waited the other side of the door and listened to Bracha screaming as Hermia discovered all she wanted to know. Jephthah had stood with a passive expression, flinching slightly every time the screaming started.

After the torture, a stony faced Hermia had given permission for Helez and Asahel to go into the city. She had to make sure that it was not a trap with Ilana as the bait to capture more of the Gibborim.

Helez had not needed telling twice, he had bolted for the surface, Asahel following behind, desperate to keep his friend out of trouble. It had been early morning when the two men had emerged on the outside of the city. Asahel had insisted that they exit beyond the walls to avoid attracting more unwanted attention.

They had to wait outside the gates until they had opened and headed for the market as quickly as they could. The market had been full of people when the two shields had arrived. Anger had swelled in Helez's chest that so many would desire to witness his fourteen year old sister being hanged.

Ilana was being held a half an hour walk away from the market in the prison, dungeons built away from the palace and castle to protect the crown from criminals when they escaped. She stumbled several times as she was pushed along by the guards. Her legs were shaking violently so that she could barely put one foot in front of the other.

The guards seemed deaf to her tears as they forced her through the city and they did nothing to protect her from the insults and the rotting food that was thrown at her.

As they reached the crowd in the market, the noise from jeering and the pelting with rancid produce intensified. The guards barely held back the mob as Ilana was dragged up on the stage.

She looked out over the sea of people and wept more. She could feel the hatred of the people directed at her, she begged the gods that she would be saved, that she would be able to go home, go back to the safety of the Gibborim, but the gods did not seem to be listening.

She was pulled over to the noose that was fitted around her neck, her feet on a pedestal that was unstable beneath her feet. Helez was still too far from the stage to help her; the crowd had surged forward but had become harder to move through. Asahel had grabbed hold of his friend and now held him across the chest as the executioner stepped forward.

"ILANA!" Helez roared, his voice was lost amongst the crowd

screaming for her blood.

"Don't look." Asahel begged his friend as the executioner kicked the pedestal from beneath the feet of Ilana. But Helez could not take his eyes from the form of his sister as her body jerked and danced at the end of the rope, her pale clothes stained by excrement and urine as she lost control of her body. There was an eerie silence wrapped around the marketplace as she thrashed at the end of the rope. Then all was still and the crowd cheered whilst Helez and Asahel wept.

*****

Joab awoke with a start. It was dark in the room, still early in the morning. There was nothing out of place in the guest quarters of Tulna, Cassandra had returned to present Tola with the broken blade of Kelmar with the instruction that he should return it to its owner.

Whilst the Guardian of the Wilds was in the village there was no need to worry. He looked down to see Mia lying next to him and the shadow realised that he had fallen asleep whilst waiting for Mia to drift off.

She was breathing softly and curled up next to his body. He smiled down at his ward and began to slowly rise from the bed.

"Please don't go." Mia begged him in a sleepy voice. Joab looked down to see the lady was not asleep but looking up at him with pleading eyes.

"You need to rest, my lady." Joab soothed her.

"Stay." Mia repeated as she sat up and threw her arms around his neck. Joab tried to pull back but found Mia was far more insistent than he could resist.

"My lady, you are tired, you have been searching for a protector, but that does not mean that you should, that we should…"Joab tried to remove her arms from his neck as he tried to reason with her.

Mia raised her eyebrow and kissed him. Joab was surprised by the passion there was in the fragile, frightened creature as she pressed herself against him, forcing him to lie down again.

"Stay." She said as she lay on top of him.

"Please, my lady." He begged her with little conviction.

"You have slept in my room every night for months and yet you have never done anything to take advantage of me, made no advances towards me. I want to know why." Mia said as she slowly began to remove her clothing whilst she straddled Joab's chest.

"Because it is my duty to protect you, to keep you from harm. If I could have stopped what the king did to you, I would have." He said earnestly as he took hold of Mia's hands and stopped her undressing herself.

"Then stay and protect me." Mia gave a wry half-smile to the shadow as he rolled the lady onto her back.

"Goodnight, my lady." Joab said as he rose, bowed and quickly left Mia's room before she could try to seduce him again.

Outside her room, Joab leant against the wall and let out a long breath of relief. He knew he was feeling more than he should for Lady Bird, that if he had stayed any longer then he would have succumb to her insistent charms. He shook his head and laughed to himself at how strange the situation was; when Layla and the Abbott had trained him neither of them had mentioned that this could happen.

He waited until he heard Mia climb back into her bed before he moved from beside the door.

Mia watched Joab leave her chamber and felt the twinge of disappointment at his rejection of her. She had never been treated like a woman or an equal by a man before and it intrigued her. Mia didn't know what he wanted from her, so she offered the only thing that she felt she had to give, but he had refused her.

She pouted as she wondered what on it was that made Joab so loyal, so eager to protect her and climbed back into her bed.

"What a precious little child you are." A female voice cooed from the window. Mia squeaked as she turned and saw a woman with chestnut hair and golden eyes sat in the frame of her window.

She had a slender figure that she wore tight fitting travelling clothes over. Her hair was plaited from the crown of her head and trailed down over her shoulder.

"I can understand what he sees in you." She said with approval as she looked the girl up and down.

"Who?" Mia croaked.

"Mercia, of course. He was most unhappy to learn that you had not gone to Fintry like a good girl. It seems you have made him quite cross. He wants to see you immediately, so I have been called on to fetch you back to him." She smiled cruelly at the young woman as she grabbed hold of her and proceeded to bind Mia's hands and feet and gag her. "Don't worry; he won't damage your pretty face."

The door to her room opened as the woman picked Mia up and made for the window.

"Neesa!" Joab shouted with hatred.

"I don't have time to deal with you now, traitor." Neesa said turning her golden gaze on the shadow. "I have a woman to return to my lord, master and king." She smiled as she dropped out of the window holding Mia.

Joab scowled and punched the wall, he ran from the room down to the hallway below and straight into the Abbott who stood with three women that Joab didn't recognise.

"My, my, what a hurry!" The Abbott exclaimed as he picked himself up from the floor.

"I'm sorry, Lady Mia, she's been taken." Joab explained as he regained his feet and continued to run out of the building into the cool desert night. The three women exchanged meaningful glances as the Abbott tutted.

"Tsk, tsk, Cassandra." The Abbott said with a wry smile as he shook his head.

"You called?" Cassandra asked as she entered the hallway from a side room on the ground floor.

"It seems your talents as protector are slipping." The Abbott said lightly as Cassandra's eyes narrowed. She paused for a moment before stamping her foot.

"Neesa." She scolded herself as she darted out into the night after Joab.

Cassandra scanned the darkness as she ran for any signs of Neesa; the shadow was a few steps ahead of her. In his head he cursed himself for leaving Mia alone, for not having the strength to resist her whilst remaining beside her.

"I'm sorry." Cassandra apologised as she caught up to the shadow. "I didn't think she would attack Mia."

"Neither did I." Joab admitted. The two searched around the village looking for any signs of Neesa and the direction she had taken. "She said she was taking her to the king." Joab said when no trail could be found.

"To Grashindorph, Fintry or elsewhere?" Cassandra asked and received a blank stare in response. "Come, we'll fetch the horses and search further afield. No matter how good an assassin she is, she cannot fly, there will be signs of her somewhere."

"What is all this commotion?" Mathias shouted as he descended the stairs. The noise of Joab and Cassandra had roused all but Tola from their beds.

"Lady Mia has been kidnapped by the assassin Neesa. Joab and Cassandra have gone after her." The Abbott said without concern.

"And who are they?" Mathias yawned as he pointed at the three women with the Abbott.

"We, sir, are the Guardian Lavinia, the Guardian Lacenta and the Guardian Muse." The older of the women said with a waspish tone.

"And they are here because?" Mathias spoke to the Abbott again, still ignoring the guardians.

"How is that any of your concern?" The Guardian Lavinia spoke again, fixing Mathias with an icy stare.

"Peace, peace." Kania stepped forward to mediate between Lavinia and Mathias. "They are here to see me and Nodarto. Do not fear they are no threat to you or your charges." The leader of Tulna soothed the Roencian.

"You should all return to bed, there is nothing that you can do to help Joab and there is much to discuss in the morning." Nodarto said kindly as he ushered Mathias, Kasna and Kia back to their rooms.

The two princesses kept their eyes on the guardians as they were hurried back down the corridor.

"Do you remember them?" Kasna asked Kia as the door to their room was shut.

"The Guardians? They look familiar but I don't know from where." Kia shrugged.

"I think they have helped mother before." Kasna mused and sat down on her bed.

"Do you think we should be trying to get to mother?" Kia asked as she walked over to look out of the window.

"Why? Because the Regent of Delma is trying to kill us?" Kasna replied smugly.

"No, because we are not warriors; we have not been trained. If we go to mother then we put her in danger. She has to protect us as well as fight the enemy." Kia said with frustration. She disliked it when Kasna spoke to her like she was stupid.

"What do you suggest then?" Kasna was curious as to what her sister was thinking.

"What if we stayed here? Asked if Mathias and Cassandra could train us?" Kia suggested as turned back to look at her sister.

"Then we go to mother when we can fight?" Kasna followed her sister's unspoken train of thought through to its conclusion.

"Yes."

"I think that we should sleep and ask Mathias in the morning." Kasna said with a smile as she climbed into bed.

Kia stood by the window and looked out at the distant lights of Grashindorph that could be made out on the horizon. She prayed to Arala that Mia would be rescued and returned safely to Tulna. She laid her head on her hands as she gazed at the lights and slowly drifted off to sleep.

*****

The new structures that Benaiah designed proved to be much warmer than Kasnata had expected. The forge master had out done himself in his creation of the camp that Kasnata had asked for.

The queen had felt the cold more than she normally did in the last few weeks. She hadn't realised why until she found her armour had begun to feel tighter than before. She woke up feeling nauseous and found she was experiencing phantom pains.

Rathe's quarters were now positioned next to the queen's, allowing their affair to continue without raising the suspicions of the men of Nosfa, or more importantly, the colonels and commanders of Nosfa.

Since the Abbott had brought news of Kasnata and Kia's freedom, the queen had been happier and with Renta and Tola having gone to escort them back to her, she felt her worries were over.

Despite this new freedom she could not shake the feeling that something was amiss. Rathe rolled over in the furs next to her and kissed her shoulder.

"You couldn't sleep?" He asked with concern.

"No, there is something I think I should tell you, but I am not certain of it yet." Kasnata said as she chewed her bottom lip.

"I see, well unless you want to end this and run back to your husband's bed. I am sure I can handle it." He yawned and pulled the queen into his chest.

"I'm pregnant." She said quickly.

"Say that again?" Rathe said, unsure he had heard her properly.

"I'm pregnant." The queen repeated.

"Well, that is not what I was expecting." Rathe sighed as he tried to recover from the shock of the statement.

"I don't know for certain." Kasnata continued, fear rising in her chest that Rathe would not want to have children.

"I'm going to be a father? I assume I'm the father. Am I the father?" He rambled as nerves and shock took over his system. Kasnata resisted the urge to slap him to snap him out of his mild fit of hysteria and kissed him instead.

"You are." She said gently stoking his face.

"I'm going to be a father." Rathe said with joy. Kasnata giggled with relief and relaxed in the general's arms.

Printed in Great Britain
by Amazon.co.uk, Ltd.,
Marston Gate.